No_ Calm

Hend Hegazi

ISBN: 978-1-7340921-0-3

Cover Design by Elizabeth King

Interior Design by Scribe Freelance
www.scribefreelance.com

To Baba, for always wanting me to be better
and
To Mama, for being the foundation of everything good in me

Chapter 1

SHE WAS OBVIOUSLY VERY nervous about the speech. Not only had she not been able to find her note-cards, but she was having issues getting ready. The blouse she had been planning to wear under her yellow sun dress had a huge hole in it thanks to her professional ironing, so she decided instead to wear her more formal white pants suit. It was slightly heavier than she'd like in that weather, but at this point she had no choice. She combed back her thick auburn hair and tied it in a bun near the nape of her neck. She wrapped her head scarf so that it covered all her hair as well as her neck. She'd started covering during her freshmen year in high school, despite some of her "friends'" disapproval. She was, of course, the only *muhajaba* at her high school, and even though there were plenty of students sporting Mohawks or pink hair or shaved heads, everyone, including Amina, knew that she stuck out the most.

At first, a lot of the students she was meeting for the first time in high school were hesitant to get to know her. They figured she belonged to some cult, or was some kind of religious fanatic. Even some of the classmates she'd known since kindergarten seemed standoffish when they first saw her covered. But as the weeks went by, most of them realized she was just a normal teenager. She was into music, movies, going to the mall, and driving around aimlessly, just like everyone else. They still wondered why she covered, but even if they didn't understand, they accepted her as a regular teen. On a few occasions some of her peers, and even a couple of teachers, asked about her *hijab*. She got to explain to them that covering was a subtle but firm way of respecting herself as well as demanding respect from those around her. She liked being given the opportunity to explain why she did it; what she didn't like was when the students visiting for freshman orientation yelled to one another, "That girl's wearing a sheet on her head!" Usually these comments weren't at times appropriate for her to stop and enlighten them. "Dumbass!" was the word she chose to mumble under her breath at them.

But she was always very careful never to curse at anyone out loud.

Not so much because she didn't want to offend, but because she knew that covering made her a walking representative of Islam and all Muslims, even if she refused this position... she had no choice. Anyone who saw her, especially who'd never met a Muslim before, would automatically think of her as a model of Islam and her actions would be seen as some form of her devotion to her religion. It was a heavy load for her to bear, but she accepted the responsibility, everyday asking God for patience and guidance.

She was running low on patience that morning, trying to find her speech and get ready. Kayla walked in just as Amina threw her disobedient shoe across the room. Kayla had never seen her friend's room in such a state; there were clothes all over the place, evidence that it had taken her quite some time to decide what to wear. Her bed hadn't been made and all the drawers were wide open.

"I like what you've done here. It's very... bohemian," Kayla mocked as she made room for herself on the bed. "I thought I'd come over a little early in case you wanted to go over your speech once more."

"That would be great... if I could find it!! Sometime between last night and this morning I've managed to make my note cards disappear. I looked around all morning with no luck. I'm pretty sure the speech is lost forever, and of course that means we're all dressed up for no reason, because I'm just not going." Amina threw herself backwards on the bed, defeated.

"Well, I'm sure it hasn't disappeared. You're talented... but not quite that talented." Kayla got up and slowly started searching— under clothes, in the waste basket, under the bed. "That is, of course, unless the tornado that blew threw here earlier took it as a souvenir. In that case, you're screwed."

"I've been working on that speech for two months. I will not get up on that podium today, appear unprepared, and make a complete jackass out of myself."

"You're absolutely right. You should definitely not get on that podium and make a jackass out of yourself. But you should get on that podium and give this speech." Kayla held up the note cards she'd just found under Amina's keyboard.

Amina gave her best friend a big hug. She had started to lose hope of ever finding the speech and was having waking nightmares of how ridiculous she would look trying to recall the entire thing from memory.

She was valedictorian and would be giving the speech in front of her entire graduating class, their friends and family and the entire high school faculty. There would be somewhere between 1500 and 2000 people.

And although she knew the vast majority of these would be attending out of a sense of duty and would be eagerly anticipating the end of the ceremony, she wanted to try to affect them even if it were only for a moment, in a tiny way.

"*Bism Allah Alrahman Alraheem.* In the name of God, Most Gracious, Most Merciful. On behalf of the class of 1995, I would like to thank you all for being here today to join us in celebrating our graduation. But more importantly, I would like to thank you for the love and support you've given us all throughout the past 18 years. For waking us each morning, for the bag lunches, for the rides to the mall and to the movies, for taking time out of your schedules to watch our tennis matches and football games.

"It must not have been easy— telling us to walk on the straight path, then holding your breath as you watched us. Sometimes you were successful in convincing us, and we walked along safely. But sometimes we didn't agree with your reasoning, so we strayed from the path. And we fell. And even though we had disappointed you, you always caught us. And we thank you for that.

"You've given us the foundation we'll need to move forward. You've started us on the path and taught us how to tell right from wrong. Now we need to walk along that path alone, without our safety nets.

"Some of us will be going to college, some will be joining the work force, and some will be serving our country. But all of us will give up some degree of dependency on you. All of us will try to make it on our own.

"And when we fall—and **eventually**, we all will—your advice will be gently appreciated. And when we succeed—and eventually, we **all will**—well, that success is dedicated to you, for laying our foundation, and for having the strength and wisdom to set us free.

"And that success, although it will come in many forms, will not be measured by how large our house is, nor how expensive our car is, nor how much money we make. It will not be measured by how famous we are, nor how many children we have. It WILL be measured by how much we make this world a better, safer, more loving place. It will be measured by how positive our influence was on society.

"Class of '95, I pray that our successes come from righteousness and honesty. I pray that we never forget our foundation and we never forget to always put love and goodness first. Dedicate your work and energy to goodness and love, and they will multiply. Thank you."

After the diplomas had been distributed and the caps tossed, Amina and her family drove home. "So, what did you guys think of my speech?" Amina asked.

Ruwayda answered first, "It was good that you dedicated it to the parents of the graduates, but don't you think you should have focused more on your class?"

"In my opinion," Osman began, "the whole ceremony is too much for such a minor event."

Why did I ask? Like I didn't know they wouldn't have anything positive to say. Why don't I ever learn? Amina thought. But despite herself, she was disappointed by their reactions.

Kayla hadn't given her opinion yet, but now she couldn't, not vocally anyway. She squeezed her friend's hand and mouthed to her, "It was great! Very positive!"

Amina smiled at Kayla, but her friend's efforts were not enough to remove her from the mood her parents had inflicted on her.

"Are you still upset by your parents' reaction?" They'd been home for a few hours now, and the girls sat in Amina's kitchen. Kayla fidgeted with her straight, shoulder length, dirty-blond hair. Her rosy skin framed a thin, tall body, with hazel eyes. Sitting next to her friend, she seemed to be her exact opposite; Amina's soft, pale brown skin suited an average build that made her appear slightly shorter than she actually was, and her eyes were so dark brown, they could almost be mistaken for black. Her wavy auburn hair, now uncovered, was tied in a loose pony tail.

"I think I'm upset at my reaction to their reaction. I've seen this from them so much in the past; I don't know why I thought this would be any different. I guess I sort of got lost in how everyone else's parents were reacting."

"Well," Kayla comforted, "don't feel badly. At least they attended. I'm sure you remember that at my graduation two years ago, my dad didn't even bother to show up. I don't mean to sound unsympathetic, but you **are** the one who always says we need to be grateful for what we have because so many people have so much less."

"You're right, I know. I know, I'm being spoiled. That's it, I'm done sulking."

But words simply have to be released from the lips; emotions have to be pried from the heart. Kayla wanted to get her friend's mind on something else... and only one thing would work.

"Lady, you are officially a high school graduate. We need to celebrate. Let me take you to my favorite bar."

Amina's face betrayed her confusion. Kayla knew Amina didn't drink and she would never offer to take Amina to a bar; she respected her friend's beliefs more than that. And one second later, the light bulb went off.

"I think a chocolate soft-serve dipped in chocolate is exactly what I need!"

Kayla laughed that Amina had understood her so quickly. "I think the people at Dairy Queen are starting to get sick of me. The girl said to me the other day, 'you know, we **do** have flavors other than chocolate.' Like any sane person would ever choose something other than chocolate!" And their giggles started lifting the mood.

Amina's summer passed pretty uneventfully. She spent most of her time reading and hanging out with Kayla and some of her other friends. A week before she was to leave for school, her mother called her into the study.

"Amina," Ruwayda began, "I just want to talk to you about some things before you go off to school. It'll be the first time you've been away from us, and we just want to make sure you're prepared for what might be waiting for you.

"You're going to meet lots of new people, some good and some not good. But you can't give your trust to ANYONE, not even your roommate. When you leave your room, make sure your money is locked in your closet. And when you leave the room and your roommate isn't there, lock the door, too. You have to be very careful.

"And not just with your money. Never walk through the campus at night alone. We read in the handbook that the school has a service of providing escorts for people who do not want to walk alone at night; take advantage of that.

"And I know that eventually you're going to make friends, maybe even good friends with some of the boys at the school. Make sure you're NEVER, EVER in a room alone with any of them... no matter how close you think they are."

Amina couldn't hold in her laugh, "Mama, I've heard this all from you a thousand times, starting when I was six! I know all this stuff. And I'm not careless enough to let any guys into my room. And before you go on, I know to make sure I lock the door at night and not to talk to strangers."

Ruwayda's face was starting to turn red from frustration. "Amina, I'm being serious. You need to take care of yourself and always be safe."

"I know, mama. I will. Do you have any other warnings for me?"

Ruwayda was sure there were more; there were too many evils lurking in the world for those few pieces of advice to be all the protection she could arm her daughter with. But they were sly enough to elude her now. Hesitantly, she shook her head. "No, that's all. Just know that if there's any kind of emergency or you need anything, we're only a four hour drive away."

Amina stood up and kissed her mom on the head. "Thanks, mama. I love you, too."

Chapter 2

COLLEGE ORIENTATION WAS three days of adjustment and excitement for Amina. Most of the people in her dorm seemed nice enough; but she knew that only time would uncover which of those people she would eventually consider her friends. Her roommate was polite, very soft spoken and reticent. She barely smiled when anyone tried to make a joke. Amina felt a bit awkward around her and she knew that they would not be very close. Instead, she ate her meals with a group of girls who were more sociable... *maybe too sociable,* Amina thought as she saw how they gawked and flirted with the guys at the other table. But she remained friendly, hoping that soon she would find her niche.

The dinner picnic held the day before classes began was one of those college traditions Amina felt like she would carry with her forever. Seeing her peers kick around the soccer balls or dance in the middle of the field to the Dj's music made her feel like a kid again. She stood up to join the group playing ball, but before she made it to them, she heard an unfamiliar voice.

"*As salaamu alaikum.*" Amina turned to the smile of a blond haired, blue eyed girl. Standing next to her was a darker girl with brown hair and brown eyes.

"*Wa alaikum as salaam,*" Amina replied as she shook each girl's hand.

"My name's Layal. And this is my roommate Sahar. We're freshmen here."

"I'm Amina. I'm a freshman, too. It's nice to meet you, Layal and Sahar."

"Really, you're a freshman? I thought for sure you were a sophomore or junior; you look like you know what you're doing... like you've done all this before. I feel overwhelmed, and I'm afraid it shows on my face."

"Trust me, I'm just as overwhelmed as you are. But, just so you know, you don't look overwhelmed." And with those first few giggles of embarrassment, and that brief introduction, came Amina's niche.

Amina soon learned that Sahar was a Pakistani American from

Chicago. She was very close to her family and being away from them was both sad and stressful for her.

"It's my first time away from home, too," Amina comforted. "And most of the kids here are probably going through the same kind of emotions, on one level or another. But eventually this will be the norm for us and being home will feel strange. Until we get to that place, we have to try to enjoy ourselves."

"I don't think I'm ever going to get to that place. Don't get me wrong, my parents drive me crazy just as much as the next girl, but something about being home makes me feel safe."

"Are you the first one to go to college? I mean, you said you have two brothers, are they older or younger?" Layal was also trying to pull Sahar away from her homesickness.

"They're both older. But you know how guys are... you can never really know what they're feeling. Plus, they both go to school much closer to home. The only piece of advice my oldest brother gave me before I came to school was 'make sure you get there early so you can pick the good side of the room.'"

"So, did you get the good side of the room, or should we have your brother come here and beat Layal into surrendering her side?"

Sahar smiled, "No, I think we're good."

Layal faked haughtiness, "I don't know... I think my side is pretty darn good. I think you're just saying that out of fear. I mean, your brother's only... what, probably about twice or three times my size... I could take him! You just don't want to call your brother here to get beaten by a girl. I can understand that."

Their attempts to lighten her mood were a bit pathetic, but Sahar appreciated it. "So Layal, how come you have an Egyptian name, when... you're clearly not?"

The girls laughed at Sahar's comment. "My American parents, whose ancestors came from Europe, spent their honeymoon in Egypt. They heard the name, and it stuck with them until I was born."

Amina was curious. "So... are you a convert?"

Layal explained that her parents were both converts. Amina thought that was so inspiring. "Did they convert together? I mean, did they know each other before they converted, or did they meet after?"

Layal replied, "No, they met after. My mom was introduced to Islam by a good friend. Then, when she thought that perhaps the religion did hold the Truth, she took it upon herself to read and learn more.

"My dad was doing some kind of research on world cultures or something, and he found Islam and was convinced by it that way.

"A year or so later they met through some mutual friends, and that was that." Layal smiled to her friends.

Amina was uplifted. "That's great. Hey, do you think it would be okay for me to introduce my friend Kayla to your parents? She's still searching."

Layal became very sad. "My parents passed away a few years ago in a car accident."

"Oh my God, Layal. I'm so sorry. God have mercy on them and give you patience."

"God have mercy on them," Sahar whispered.

The three friends were quiet for some time. Layal was the one to break the silence, "Sorry I bummed you guys out. It's been three years, but it still seems like yesterday. Anyway... so which cafeteria are we eating at tonight? Or... why don't we go downtown and check out what kind of restaurants they have there?"

"I don't know..." Sahar was hesitant. "My parents warned me about going off campus for any 'non-emergency.' Maybe we shouldn't."

"Come on Sahar. We need to check it out. If we don't feel comfortable, we won't stay, and we'll catch the next bus right back. And tomorrow's Sunday so you can't make the excuse that you need to study or that you have to be up early in the morning.

"Let's do it this once, and if you don't like it, then, we won't do it again. Come on. What do you say?" Amina was excited to experience everything about being away at school... and that included checking out the town they were living in.

And, to a big extent, Sahar felt the same way. She was just nervous about being in a new place without the comfort of family near by. "Fine. Let's go."

Soon the girls found that family was closer than they thought; they became like sisters, despite the fact that Amina didn't live in the same dorm with Layal and Sahar, nor did they share any classes. Amina was science oriented, Layal was a business major and Sahar was focused on education. They got into the routine of eating dinner together and meeting, at least once a week, simply to hang out.

As the weeks went by they made friends with people from their dorms and classes and through the Muslim Students Association. At one of the MSA's pot luck dinners, Amina saw a face she'd been seeing in her classes.

"Hey, aren't you in my physics class?"

"Yes, I am. I'm Tariq and this is my roommate, Rami."

Tariq was a tall, very well built black man. His grandparents had first been members of the Nation of Islam before they became aware of the real peace and human harmony of Islam. His parents were devout Muslims who had managed to raise a son who was both successful in his worldly practices as he was devoted to his religious and spiritual worship. Tariq graduated high school with the highest GPA in his state and was attending college on a full academic scholarship.

Rami was an Egyptian American whose parents lived across the country in California. He always wore khakis and a button-down shirt, but something about the gleam of his eyes told Amina that he preferred partying to studying.

As the weeks went by, the girls saw more and more of Tariq and Rami at the different MSA events. Then they started to get together for brunch on Sunday mornings, or to watch a movie Friday nights, or to study together at one of their dorm rooms during the week.

When spring arrived, it brought with it the Muslim holiday. It fell on a Monday in late April, and Rami reluctantly accepted Tariq's invitation to spend it with his family. "I don't want to be a burden on your family. Especially not now... I mean, I'm sure they don't want some stranger staying with them during a time that's all about families being together."

"You'll be no burden, trust me, Rami." Tariq said sincerely. "*Eid* is a time for family, and I can't leave you here to celebrate alone. What kind of *Eid* would that be for you? And what kind of brother would that make me? You are my brother in Islam, which makes you family. We're leaving in the morning, we'll spend Saturday, Sunday, and Monday with them, then we'll head back Tuesday before it gets dark. That's the plan, so pack your bag."

Likewise, Amina convinced Sahar and Layal that spending *Eid* alone at school made no sense when they could spend it with her family. "Believe me, you'll have fun. We go to the *Eid* prayer at the mosque in the morning, then if the weather's nice, we have a picnic in the park with some hundred or so other Muslim families, and at night we usually go out for dinner."

"It's not going to bother your parents... to have us over?" Sahar didn't want to put any one out, and at the same time it was killing her to think she might have to spend the day alone at school.

"My parents will be happy to meet you guys, and it'll make them feel good that they're rescuing you from a lonely *Eid.*"

Amina was only partly fibbing; her parents were strict and would definitely like to meet Amina's friends, but the reaction she'd gotten when she first told her parents about Sahar and Layal was less than enthusiastic; they were very weary that Amina had befriended girls that seemed to be totally on their own.

"They have no family. You know a person by knowing their family and there is no way you can really know these girls," Amina's mom told her.

"Mama, I DO know them because I'm practically living with them. They're good Muslim girls, mama. And they **do** have family; they just don't live close enough to visit them every month. You have to get over this idea that girls living away from home are promiscuous drug addicts. Plus, I'm living away from home… is that what you think about me?"

"You're different, Amina," her mother defended, "your family asks about you. You call everyday. We see you at least once a month. Not like girls who only contact their family during winter and summer vacation."

Amina knew that Sahar and Layal were conservative girls who never did anything Amina's parents would disapprove of. She just hoped that her parents wouldn't embarrass her by telling the girls how they feel about them going to school so far from their families.

But, of course, they did. On the night before *Eid,* as they all sat eating dinner, Osman asked, "So girls, why did you decide to go to college so far away from your families? It seems to me that girls your age shouldn't be so far away from the people who love them and provide for them. It's not really healthy."

Oh my God. Did he really just say that? This is too much!

But Layal's confidence diminished Amina's embarrassment. "All my life my parents taught me to strive to be the best. And to strive for knowledge, no matter how far or how difficult the journey. When I got my acceptance letter to one of the best colleges in America, I told my sister that it was too far away, and I would choose a local school. But she wouldn't have it; she said our parents would be very disappointed in me if I let this opportunity slide, especially if I was doing it just to stay close to her. She said 'God is all you need. And He is always with you. So go on… begin your journey to success.'"

Then Sahar spoke. "My story is sort of similar. I was actually planning on going to the state university, but when my acceptance letter came, my parents were the ones pushing me to go. When I told them I was worried about being so far away, they said, 'you're going away for an honorable reason, so God will protect you.' And of course they call me almost everyday, so it's not so bad."

Amina hated that her dad had put her friends in that position, but she was also glad that they had replied with such confidence. Maybe now her parents would see that these were good Muslim girls who just wanted to get the best education available.

To a great extent, her parents did get it. They knew these were good Muslim girls who were only far away from their families due to specific circumstances. They were pleasant to the girls for the remainder of their stay. On *Eid* morning, when Ruwayda went into her daughter's room to hug her and wish her a happy *Eid*, she happily did the same to Layal and Sahar. She gave Amina an envelop containing her *Eid* present, and much to everyone's surprise, she handed one envelop each to Sahar and Layal, as well.

"Auntie, we can't take this… we appreciate you treating us with such kindness…"

But Ruwayda didn't let Sahar finish, "Today is *Eid*, and this is how our family celebrates *Eid*. And you are part of our family." The girls hugged her and were so touched that Sahar's eyes began to swell with tears. She hid it well until Ruwayda left the room.

The weather was beautiful that morning; the sun was shining and it was neither too cool nor too hot. After they attended the *Eid* prayer at the mosque, they drove to a park that was buzzing with people. Little kids were flying kites, or attempting to, anyway. Teenagers were playing volleyball and soccer in the different fields. The older people were just sitting around and talking. Amina introduced Layal and Sahar to all the friends who came over and greeted her. Everyone was in the holiday spirit, and although Layal and Sahar were strangers to the crowd, they felt like they fit in perfectly.

That evening Osman took them to their favorite Italian restaurant. When the waitress came to take their orders, he began with the usual speech.

"Before any of us order, we need you to know that we can't have anything containing alcohol or pork products. At this whole table. No alcohol, nothing cooked in alcohol, no pork."

"Okay," the waitress said.

But, of course, Osman didn't think she fully understood.

"So if anyone orders anything containing alcohol or pork, please let us know so we can change the order."

"No problem," the waitress again confirmed.

And, as usual, Osman himself was the only one who chose a meal that was cooked with alcohol. "Could you ask the chef if it would be possible to cook it without the alcohol?"

"Sure, I'll go check."

A few short minutes later the waitress came back and apologized, "I'm sorry, we can't make that dish without the alcohol. Would you like to choose something else?"

And he did. And as soon as she had taken their menus and left, the suppressed bitterness erupted. "What's so hard about making a stupid dish... and just leaving out the alcohol? Why is that so difficult?"

Amina and Ruwayda knew enough to just keep quiet, but no one had warned Layal or Sahar.

"I think they make the sauces before hand, in one big batch. So the alcohol has already been put into the meal before you even order."

Poor Layal wouldn't have said anything if she'd known what her words would spark.

"But so what? What, it's so difficult to make some more sauce, enough just for one person, and make it without the alcohol?"

And from there he went on to explain how that was the problem with the big chain restaurants, that they easily lose the personal touch. Somehow that led him to how corporate America is so evil, and by comparison, the whole corporate world. By the time the food arrived, Osman had somehow managed to connect the fact that the restaurant refused to make him an alcohol-free dish with the demise of the universe.

And the whole while, all the women sat around pretending to be interested, and praying for the arrival of their meals.

Once they started eating, Ruwayda managed to successfully maneuver the conversation away from anything her husband could bore them about again. They finished their meals with laughter filling their ears and their hearts.

When the check came, Sahar looked at Layal with nervousness.

"Uncle, please let us pay…"

But Osman's laughter cut her off. "When I come to visit you, then you can pay. Here, you're my family. And the head of the family pays."

The girls felt badly that their visit kept costing Amina's parents, but all they could do was thank them for their generosity and graciousness.

The night passed by quickly, and before they knew it, Tuesday had come and Osman and Ruwayda had dropped the girls back off at school. They met Tariq and Rami for a late dinner and the friends discussed how they'd spent the holiday. The guys had also prayed *Eid* at the mosque, but then instead of going out, they went back to Tariq's parents home where they enjoyed the company of his three siblings, nine cousins, and 20 or so other relatives. Tariq's mother single handedly cooked a feast for her guests, and everyone, especially Rami, thought the food was more than delicious.

That weekend set a precedent for the following few years. The guys would spend each *Eid* with Tariq's family, and the girls with Amina's. Then, once they were all back at school, they would get together for their own, albeit minor, *Eid* celebration. The time they all spent together at school and at each other's homes strengthened their relationship and truly made them family.

Their junior year arrived and progressed quickly. Before they knew it the snow had all melted and the weather was starting to look like spring. On one exceptionally warm March day, the group had decided that a drive-in movie would be the best way to enjoy the weather. So the five of them got into the car and Tariq drove them to a small, almost hidden, drive-in theater. When they arrived at the movie, they each paid for their own ticket and shared two jumbo sized buckets of popcorn.

"That was pretty good. Now was that Matthew Broderick or John Cusak?" Sahar asked.

Amina and Tariq both said "Matthew" while Rami blurted out "John".

"You guys are ridiculous," laughed Layal. "How can you not see the difference between Matthew Broderick and John Cusak? They look nothing alike. Cusak did 'Say Anything'; Broderick, on the other hand was Ferris Bueler."

"Oh, well. That clears it ALL up for me now. Thank you so much, Layal, for your marvelous insight," Tariq mocked, getting into the car.

Their drive back to campus was filled with jokes and laughter. Once Tariq had parked his car, the five friends made their way towards Amina's apartment. Although she had wanted to room with Sahar and Layal, her parents were still weary that the girls' lack of parental guidance would have a negative effect on Amina, so they encouraged her to rent an on-campus apartment instead. She had no roommates.

"You guys want to come in for some coffee or something?" Amina invited.

"Yeah, that would be great. Let's go, guys." Rami insisted.

"No, I can't. I have a long day tomorrow. I need to get some sleep," Sahar said, yawning.

"And I have a test I still need to study for," Layal said.

Tariq just shrugged his shoulders.

"Well, you go and walk the girls home, Tariq. I'll just have one cup of coffee with Amina, then I'll meet you back at the apartment."

Amina was torn; on the one hand, she trusted Rami completely... he was like a brother to her. But on the other hand, she knew it was inappropriate for her to have a guy friend over while she was all alone. She was hoping one of the girls or Tariq would say something to Rami and save her from embarrassment, but they just said their good nights and walked away. Hesitantly, Amina opened the door and let Rami inside.

"Wow, you've done a lot of re-arranging since we moved you in here." Rami looked around, then sat on the couch.

"Yeah. How much sugar do you take with your coffee?" She was already in the kitchen. She figured the sooner they could drink the coffee, the sooner Amina could claim that she had some studying she needed to get done.

"Two spoonfuls, please."

A few moments later, Amina joined Rami in the living room with two cups of coffee. "Thanks," Rami said as he took his cup from Amina. He sat there mustering up the courage to tell her what he needed to say. Finally, he spoke. "Amina... we've known each other for a while now, and I feel really close to you. I enjoy spending time with you."

"Thanks, Rami. I enjoy spending time with you, too." Amina smiled.

"Really?" Rami got up and sat next to her on the couch. Uncomfortably, Amina told Rami that she enjoyed spending time with all of her friends.

"But you're special to me," Rami explained. "What I mean is, I think I'm falling in love with you."

And before he could give her a chance to respond, he had moved closer, attempting to kiss her. Amina pushed him away and got up, but Rami went after her.

"Rami... I'm sorry, but I never thought about you like that."

"But you can always start. I want you to think about me in that way." He grabbed her waist and pulled her towards him, but she managed to back away. He traced every move she made.

"I think you should go, Rami. You're scaring me."

"No, I don't want to scare you. I just feel like we're meant to be together... I need you."

He had her cornered. He pulled her to him firmly and wouldn't let go. Despite her telling him to stop, he kept kissing her face and then her neck.

"Don't do this!" Amina screamed as she tried to wriggle out of his grip.

"I can't stop," he whispered.

She kept struggling, but he was too strong. Nothing she said or did was having any affect on him. He had managed to bring her to the floor and quickly he had torn off her clothes. She had been trying to fight him off for several minutes, but her body was getting weaker. She began to cry. A few minutes went by, and then it was all over. Rami got up off of her, adjusted his clothes, and walked out of her apartment, leaving her cold, alone and crying on the floor.

Chapter 3

WHAT SHE DIDN'T KNOW was that Rami was also crying. He hadn't planned that... that wasn't why he went up to Amina's apartment. He had just wanted to talk to her, to tell her how he felt. *"So why did I do that?"* he thought, sitting on the steps of Amina's apartment building. *"How could I do that to her? What am I, an animal? Oh, Amina... you shouldn't have let me in. I'm so sorry."*

He tried to think of what to do, where to go. For a split second he thought he should go back and apologize, then he realized that seeing him right now was not what Amina needed. He went back to his apartment and began packing some of his things. When Tariq walked in on him, he couldn't understand what was going on. "What happened, Rami? Is everything okay? Are you going to visit your family?"

"I'm leaving, Tariq. I'll send for anything else I need, and the rest you can have. Tell her I'm sorry... I wasn't planning on... Just tell her I'm sorry."

"What are you talking about, Rami? Tell who you're sorry?"

But Rami didn't answer. He closed the suitcase and ran off. Tariq was left wondering at Rami's strange behavior. What could have happened to make him pack up and leave so abruptly? He called Amina, thinking that since she was the last person to see Rami, she might have some answers.

Amina heard the phone, but she didn't answer. After lying on the floor, cold and hurt, for several minutes, she forced herself into the shower. She tried to wash away his smell, his grip, his breath. But she couldn't; her body remembered what had just happened too vividly, and all she could do was hope her tears would be able to cleanse her mind from the horror she had just experienced. She needed not to be alone. She called Kayla, and just from the sound of her voice, Kayla knew something was wrong. "I'll be there in exactly three hours," she told her friend as soon as she heard her crying.

Kayla hung up, grabbed her keys and left. She was so frantic and so distracted that she didn't even realize she'd left in her slippers.

What could possibly have happened? Amina never sounded like that before. Did she have a fight with someone at school? No, this is something much more. Was she hurt maybe? Oh, no... that must be it. She must have been in an accident. Oh, poor Amina. Kayla couldn't stop her mind from imagining all sorts of devastating situations that her best friend may have endured. She just kept hoping it was nothing fatal. These thoughts kept her company on her three hour trip.

When she finally arrived, she parked her car and sprinted to her friend's front door. She tried the knob first, not wanting to waste time knocking, but it was locked.

She rang the doorbell and knocked impatiently on the door, "Amina? Amina, it's me, Kayla."

Amina let her friend in, then locked the door right behind her. She was still crying. "I'm sorry I made you drive so late like this."

"Don't be ridiculous."

They went over and sat on the couch. Amina, realizing that only extreme circumstances would bring Kayla so far from her apartment, her work, her life, and at this time of night, couldn't help feeling even more sorry for herself. The tears flowed harder.

Kayla held her friend as she cried. She was both relieved to see that her friend appeared physically unharmed, and at the same time bursting to find out what was wrong. More than a few moments went by before Amina began to tell Kayla what happened.

Amina detailed the whole experience to her friend. Although she cried the entire time, Kayla did not; she kept getting angrier and angrier with each word. When she had finished, Amina was exhausted and all cried out. Kayla was a ball of fire. She wished Rami were standing in front of her so that she could castrate him. *"If you don't know how to use it properly, then you don't deserve it,"* she would say.

She was seething. "What a shit! What a fucking little piece of shit!! I'm gonna find him and cut off his balls! I am."

Kayla's very volatile reaction was somewhat therapeutic for Amina. Maybe this meant she hadn't somehow provoked Rami to rape her. Maybe this meant she hadn't deserved it. Maybe her friend's anger over what happened proved her innocence.

After a few minutes of Kayla imagining, partly to herself and partly out loud, all the ways she could make Rami pay for what he did, she suddenly realized that she hadn't comforted her friend... not properly, anyhow.

She sat down next to Amina and pulled her chin up with the palm of her hand, forcing her friend to look her in the eyes.

"You didn't do anything to deserve that! You didn't act inappropriately and you didn't 'ask for it'! This was an evil act that he committed... and you were the victim. You didn't deserve that."

Amina didn't reply, but her eyes asked a question.

"Yes, I'm sure," Kayla answered. "I'm so sorry you had to go through that." She held her friend tightly and hoped that her love could help heal Amina's wounded spirit.

Kayla stayed with her friend for the next few days. They stayed in and didn't answer any phone calls. Amina knew her friends were probably worried about her, but she wasn't capable of recounting the whole experience all over again. She didn't want to see or talk to anyone besides Kayla.

But knowing she had to leave soon and not wanting to leave Amina alone, Kayla finally answered the phone. She told Sahar they should all come over as soon as possible.

When they arrived, they were startled to find Kayla greeting them at the door. They knew something must be wrong. Amina asked them to sit down, then she compelled herself to tell them. Her friends cried tears of sympathy and told her they would stick beside her for whatever she needed.

"What am I supposed to do now?" Amina wondered out loud. "He's ruined my future, the way everyone sees me... He's ruined my life." The tears that had been gradually dwindling over the past couple of days began again. Her friends held her tight and tried to reassure her that this was not the end of her life and that her future was just as bright as it had been a week before. Their words didn't really soothe her, but knowing she had friends she could lean on was a comfort.

"What do you guys think I should do now? I mean, do I press charges, or what?"

Tariq had been waiting for the right moment. He figured this must be it. "He came home that night crying. He went straight to his room, packed a suitcase, and left. But before he did, he said to me, 'tell her I'm sorry.' I didn't know who he was talking about till now."

"So he's gone?" Amina asked, hopeful.

"Yeah, he's gone."

Chapter 4

ABOUT TWO WEEKS LATER Amina pulled into her parents' driveway. She had borrowed Tariq's car for the weekend but she hadn't told her parents she was coming; she hadn't felt like hearing their predictable speech about how she needed to concentrate on school and if coming home would distract her, she shouldn't do it. She had just needed to be home, she needed to feel safe the way she did around her parents. But now, as she sat in the car in their driveway, she couldn't manage to get out. Telling her parents was not going to be easy, so she put off facing them for a few more minutes as she listened to the end of the song that played on the radio. Once it ended, she forced herself to turn off the ignition and get out of the car.

As she stood at the front step, fumbling for the keys in her purse, the door opened suddenly. Her father stood for a moment in disbelief.

"Amina? Amina what are you doing home?" he asked, giving her a big hug. She struggled to hold back the tears. "I just felt like I needed to be home."

"What a wonderful surprise. You're mother's going to be shocked, she's down in the study."

Amina walked silently down the stairs and knocked on the door, but didn't wait for permission before turning the knob. Her mother was flipping through a magazine and stopped short when she saw who had walked in on her.

"Amina? Amina, I didn't know you were planning on coming home today," she said hugging her daughter.

"I wanted to surprise you."

"And you've done just that. I just hope that being here this weekend won't interfere with your studies."

"Don't worry, mama. I've got it covered."

She felt safe being home. For the first time since her childhood, Amina appreciated her parents' overprotective nature and their concern for her wellbeing. She slept peacefully for the first night since her rape.

The next morning, after the family had eaten breakfast, just as Amina's mother was clearing the table and preparing their tea, Amina began:

She reminded her parents of the group of Arab students who had become her family away from home. She explained how they'd all gone to see a movie, and how after the movie she had invited them in, but only one person accepted that invitation. Amina told her parents that she'd hesitated to let him in, but since she did think of him as a brother, she ignored her instincts. Then she continued with all the details from when Rami first confronted her with his feelings, to the actual rape. And although the tears streamed down her face as she played with the ring on her finger so she would not have to meet her parents' eyes, her voice was clear and steady.

Amina's parents listened in disbelief. Amina could not possibly be saying what they were hearing. But the whistling of the tea pot soon became ear piercing, confirming that this was not a dream.

Amina's mother was the first one to speak once Amina had finished. "Have you seen a doctor? Are you okay physically?"

"I have some bruises that might take a week or so to clear up, but besides that I'm fine."

"FINE?! Who's fine?" Amina's father's voice felt like thunder. "You did this to yourself! How could you let a strange man into your apartment? Haven't we warned you about this over and over?! You did this to yourself! You know, of course, that now no respectable Arab man will want to marry you! You were careless and you disobeyed us, now you're paying the price!"

Amina knew from experience that now was not the time to respond to her father's accusations. She sat quietly in her chair, listening to the ranting and raving, and waiting for there to be peace again.

When he had said all he needed to say, Osman went downstairs and locked himself in the study.

"Did you tell any of your friends?" Amina's mom asked.

"I called Kayla right away. She drove over in the middle of the night and stayed with me for a few days. Sahar, Layal, and Tariq all came over to check on me a couple of days after the rape. They were worried about me because I hadn't been around. I told them then."

"And how're you feeling... emotionally?"

Having this conversation with her mother was having a calming affect on Amina, but she didn't know how to answer that question.

"Well.... I've been in touch with a rape victim's support group, and that really helps me. I think that with their help, and with my focusing on finishing this year with a decent GPA, I'll be alright."

"Have you met many girls in this support group? I mean, are most of them around your age, so you can connect with them easier, or are most of them older?"

It took a minute for Amina to respond. "You know mama... I never really thought about that before. They're all women who've been through similar experiences... their ages don't matter. I mean, I connect to all of them the same way. I haven't really made any friends there, if that's what you mean."

"But you're still close with Layal and Sahar?"

"I guess so."

"No, Amina, you don't 'guess so.' You either are or you're not."

"They're still great friends, but things are difficult now. They've offered to help, to listen, to do whatever they can to make this whole experience less painful, but I find it hard to really talk to them. I think I don't want to burden them. I definitely don't want to depress them."

"Amina, do you know why friendships dwindle? Why people grow apart? Even why some marriages fail? It's because people stop communicating. For whatever reason, they stop talking... I don't mean they never speak to each other, but they never talk about anything important.

"You've been telling me for the past few years that these girls are like your sisters. If that's true, and if you don't want to lose them, don't hide from them. Include them in your joy and in your sadness. Real friends don't feel burdened by hearing their friends' troubles; they feel burdened when they know you're hurting and you keep pushing them away."

Amina would have never guessed that would be her mother's reaction. She was sure her mom disapproved of how Sahar and Layal lived, and she was positive that her mom would've taken advantage of the situation to widen the gap between her and the girls. But she didn't. She stood beside her daughter and told her not to shut out her friends.

Amina got up, kissed her mom on the forehead, and said, "Thanks, mama." Then she went to her room and made a couple of phone calls. Ruwayda, all alone in the kitchen, cried silently for all the horrible things from which she could not protect her daughter.

Chapter 5

FINALS CAME AND WENT. Amina had been so focused on her studies that when the school year ended in May, she didn't know what to do with herself. She didn't feel motivated enough to get a summer job, but at the same time, she felt suffocated being at home. Her dad had calmed down— it had been almost 2 months since Amina had told them about her rape— but still, things at home were not the same.

None of her friends were available during the summer either. Layal was spending the summer working and living with her sister. Sahar had gone home to Chicago to spend the summer with her family.

After a few days of sleeping till one in the afternoon and staying up watching meaningless television shows until 3 a.m., it finally dawned on her that this was the last summer of freedom she had. Next year, the summer after her senior year, she'd be looking for a real job, so this might be her last chance to travel. She quickly got on the phone with a couple of travel agents, got some rates, and booked her tickets. Now came the hard part— convincing her parents to let her travel alone. But she felt confident that they wouldn't resist once they heard her destination.

She decided to wait until after dinner to bring it up. That evening, as she was washing the dishes and her parents were having dessert, she explained to them that she'd always wanted to travel and her chances to do so were beginning to dwindle, "So I got on the phone and got a pretty good rate to travel the Middle East. If it's okay with you guys, I'll be leaving the day after tomorrow."

"Wow, Amina. You must have some kind of a sixth sense; your father and I were just discussing that you should use this summer to see another part of the world."

"Really... So I can go?" The excitement in Amina's voice was unmistakable.

"We think it would be a beneficial experience for you to visit your family in Egypt. You haven't been there in almost ten years. Where else in the Middle East did you want to go?" Her dad's question was, surprisingly, not rhetorical.

"Well, I was thinking of taking a tour that would include Lebanon,

Dubai, and Bahrain." She dried her hands on the kitchen towel, and sat back down at the table with her parents. "It would be a two week tour."

"Well, what if instead of coming home after your tour, you fly to Egypt to see your family. Your cousins are all starting their summer vacation and they would be more than happy to show you all the sights. What do you think?"

"A whole month? You'd really let me go for a whole month?" This was very uncharacteristic of Amina's over-protective parents. There had to be a catch.

"You're not a little girl anymore, Amina. And we're not going to live forever— sooner or later you'll have to learn to be on your own. Plus, this will be a great opportunity for you to meet some good Arab men. Maybe you'll be lucky enough to find a husband."

"A what?! You think that during one month in the Middle East I'll meet someone I want to marry?!" Amina couldn't believe the absurdity of what she was hearing.

"Well, stranger things have happened. At any rate, you'd better get back on the phone with the travel agent to revise your itinerary. Then you'd better pack." Amina's mom took her cup of tea, gave Amina a kiss on the forehead, and walked down to the study. Her father picked up the newspaper and was instantly engrossed. She ran up to her room, called the travel agent, and began packing her bags.

Chapter 6

BEING HER FIRST TIME traveling abroad alone, Amina felt anxious every time she had to board a plane. She was even more nervous navigating through the foreign airports to catch her next flight. But she had gone through the whole process so many times during her trip that when she finally got to customs in Egypt, she was completely at ease. Part of the reason for that was that although she had a great time during her two week tour, and she saw places and things she probably would never again get the chance to see, she had started to get lonely. Being on her own was at once freeing and isolating; she looked forward to being with people who, although she didn't know well, were still family.

The warm, stiff air almost choked her as she stepped out of the airport. Her eyes searched the crowd for any familiar faces, but with no luck. Then a man in his fifties asked her, "Is this the flight from Bahrain?" He didn't recognize her— he was simply asking any passerby about the arrival of that flight. But her answer surprised him, "Yes, Uncle Hassan, that flight arrived. It's me... Amina."

"Amina?! Wow, you've gotten so big... I didn't recognize you."

He greeted her with a hug and a kiss, and pushed the cart carrying her luggage in front of them.

"*Hamdila 'al salaama.* I hope you had a good trip. We were all very excited when your dad told us you were coming. *In sha' Allah*, you'll have a great time here. All your cousins have finished their exams so they can take you sight seeing wherever you want to go.

"Come this way. The car's just up ahead. Then it'll be about a half-hour till we're home. Your aunt's been cooking for the past two days, so I hope you're hungry."

It took them about forty minutes to get to Uncle Hassan's house. Along the way Amina imagined how it would be to see all her cousins and aunts and uncles. She reminded herself not to get her hopes up... life in Egypt and the Egyptian culture was different in so many ways from the American culture she was raised in. She felt certain that there would be a barrier between her cousins and herself... that they wouldn't really understand her. *But it'll be good to see them again after all these years*, she thought.

Amina's uncle parked the car on the side of the street and took her luggage from the trunk. Amina remembered that the apartment was four stories up, with no elevator, so she went to take one of the bags from him.

"No, no Amina. Lifting heavy objects is the man's job. Or in this case, the doorman's job." He handed the two suitcases to the man who had just run up and greeted her uncle. He was fairly young, in his early thirties, Amina thought, and he was wearing a sparkling white *jalabaya*. He carried the suitcases with great ease and muttered, "*Hamdila 'al salaama*, miss." and ran to take the luggage up to the apartment.

When Amina and her uncle were only about six steps away from the apartment, Amina looked up and saw a familiar site: a woman in yellow standing at the doorway, and two heads peering out from behind her.

Why is this so familiar? Where have I seen this before? After a few seconds, Amina remembered that she had dreamed this exact scene a few weeks ago. She took it as a good omen.

Inside there were about thirty people waiting to greet her. They each gave her a kiss on each cheek and a giant bear hug. Even though she hadn't seen her extended family in ten years, her aunts and uncles were somewhat familiar, but she figured it would take a few days to get straight which cousins belonged to which aunt.

They all talked with Amina for a while, asking about her trip and about the health of her parents. They inquired about her studies, and even though she knew they probably couldn't care less about her college, they all listened attentively as she described her campus and the friends she'd made there. About an hour went by, and then Amina's aunt came in from the dining room and announced that dinner was ready.

Amina almost gasped when she walked into the dinning room; she had never seen so much food set at one table. *Maybe at a wedding catered for one hundred and fifty people, but not for a family dinner of thirty.*

"Tant Fatma, you shouldn't have gone to so much trouble. This is too much."

"No, no. This is nothing. It's how we eat whenever we all get together."

Yeah, right. But there was nothing she could do but take the plate that was being forced into her hands. Before she could blink it had already been filled with all sorts of foods, some she knew, others that were completely foreign. And when she started to object, to explain this was much more than she could eat, no one seemed to hear, leaving her no choice but to find a chair and begin devouring the mountain that sat before her. As she ate, she hoped that each meal wouldn't go like this one had. She knew this was their way of being hospitable, of welcoming guests, but it made her uncomfortable. Knowing that her aunt had spent a majority of the past couple of days in the kitchen just for Amina made her feel guilty, not more welcome.

It only took her family a couple of days to accept the fact that Amina preferred to serve herself and only in the portions she chose. Of course, they continued to comment, "That's not enough, Amina. Take some more of this, or try that," but they knew she would politely ignore their suggestions.

Although she was enjoying the time with her cousins, she still felt like an outsider. They told jokes that she didn't understand, they talked about things that had happened in the past that she hadn't been around to witness, they talked about friends Amina had never met. And although they tried to include Amina, she never felt like she fit in.

But they *were* generous with their time and took her everywhere she wanted to go. She saw the Sphinx and the Great Pyramids. She swam in the crystal clear water of the North Coast, enjoyed scuba diving in the Red Sea, and shopping in Khan el Khalili. Although she had hoped this trip would be more than just sight seeing and shopping—she had wanted to form a bond with her cousins, to give her some reason to want to visit regularly—she eventually came to accept that bond would not be formed during this trip, and allowed herself to enjoy being a tourist.

And sooner than she had imagined, the two weeks were over, and she was back in the car with Uncle Hassan on her way to the airport. As he was bidding her farewell, Uncle Hassan said, "We really enjoyed having you here, Amina. I know you're used to a different lifestyle, but we hope you enjoyed being here. We hope it won't be another ten years before your next visit."

"Thanks for everything, Uncle Hassan. I had a great time. I plan on coming more often."

They kissed goodbye and she was on her way, walking through the airport, headed towards her gate.

Sorry, mama. My trip's over...and no prospective husbands.

She only waited a few minutes before hearing her boarding call. When she arrived at her seat, she found a young man, about twenty five or twenty six years old, in her seat. She double checked her ticket to make sure she wasn't mistaken, and when she was sure that he was indeed in her seat, she said, "Uh... I think you're in my seat."

He didn't even bother to look at the ticket in his hand before getting up.

"Sorry, I was hoping they had given me a window seat, so I just sat here. I'm in this seat, right beside you."

He let her pass to her seat, and then he settled down in the seat beside her.

"Are you leaving home or returning home," he asked, once the plane became airborne.

"Ah... I'm going back to my parents, back home. What about you?"

"I've been working in the states for the past four years, but I still consider Egypt my home. It's still hard for me to say good-bye; all my family's in Egypt, I don't really have anyone in the States. I've made some good friends— don't get me wrong— but it's not the same." His eyes and hair were a fair brown, but his most attractive characteristic was his warm accent.

Amina nodded. When she was certain he'd stopped talking and didn't want to chit-chat anymore, she began flipping through the magazine on her lap. It was the airline magazine that had been on her seat. Skimming through it she noticed that the movie was scheduled to play in about forty five minutes. It was one she had wanted to see in the cinema, but didn't get a chance to.

"I'm Sherif, by the way," the young man's voice startled her back to reality.

"Amina," she almost whispered, shaking his extended hand.

"Nice to meet you, Amina. So tell me, what were you doing in Egypt?"

She explained that this was the summer before her senior year of college, and she used the time to travel the Middle East. Since her extended family was almost entirely in Egypt, she'd spent the past two weeks there, both site seeing as well as visiting her family.

The two talked about Egypt and compared the differences in culture that were so apparent between their two home countries.

"So were you just visiting your family, too, or were you there for another reason?"

Sherif let out a quiet laugh, "My grandmother called me on the phone about three weeks ago and said, 'there's a girl here I want you to meet, I think she'd make you a good wife.' And before I could object, she said the plane ticket was already in the mail."

Amina joined in on Sherif's laughter. *So Egyptian grandmothers and mothers are all the same.*

"They couldn't understand why I would refuse the girl. I'm twenty six years old, I've finished college, and I'm settled in my job. She was only eighteen years old and still had three years of school left. I think my parents are feeling a bit desperate; they refuse to believe I can find a good Muslim girl in the States, and they're convinced the longer I'm a bachelor, the harder it'll be for me to marry."

A few minutes of quiet passed before Amina asked him about his job and where in the states he lived. She learned that he was an architect working and living in Chicago. He rented his own apartment and he lived walking distance from a mosque, which made him feel just a bit less homesick.

Sherif asked about Amina's schooling. He was surprised to learn that she lived away from home during the school year.

"Your parents didn't try to make you go to a college closer to them?"

"They wanted me to, but the university I'm enrolled in has a much better reputation than any of the schools near my parents. When they realized this, they didn't say or do anything to change my mind; they figured a degree from this school would help me in the future.

"And I know you probably won't understand this, but I'm glad being away from home. I mean, I miss my parents, of course, but I like feeling like I can be independent... that when I have to, I can find my own way."

"But on your own like that," Sherif wondered gently, "you never lose your way?"

Amina's face became sad, "Sometimes I do." She was quiet for a few seconds, then she smiled, "That's why I'm only a four hour car ride away, and not a fourteen hour plane ride." They both laughed.

They continued to talk about their respective relationships with their parents, comparing childhood stories and stories about how they spent *Eid.* They talked about events that had occurred recently in the news. There didn't seem to be any issue they couldn't— or wouldn't— discuss.

Sherif was mid sentence when he stopped short and exclaimed, "Oh, Amina, I'm sorry. The movie's already begun... did you want to watch it?"

"No, I can watch it later. I'm enjoying our conversation."

"Me, too," Sherif gave her a warm smile, then picked up right where he'd left off.

After the meal had been served, the flight attendants turned off the lights, and Amina and Sherif both decided they should get some sleep. Amina placed her head against the window, using the small pillow that was provided as a cushion. Sherif rested his head against his seat and reclined it slightly.

A little while later Amina's eyes slowly opened. After a couple of seconds she realized that her head was no longer cushioned against the pillow, but was resting on Sherif's shoulder... and she had been drooling! She quickly adjusted herself, wiping her mouth. She was mortified to see Sherif was watching her.

"Good morning, Amina. I guess you really were tired. Three hours you slept."

"Really? Wow. Sorry I ended up leaning on you."

"I'm not." His smile was genuine.

Before the flight landed, Sherif handed his card to Amina and he took her full name and phone number. "I know that once school starts again, you'll be busy studying, but do try to stay in touch."

"I will," Amina lied, "you, too." She knew that unless he made an attempt to call her, this would be the last they would ever see of each other.

They walked through the airport and made it through customs. When Sherif had helped her load her luggage onto a cart, he told her he had to go catch his next flight.

"Take care." His wink was for everything they had shared together, from stories and memories, to that feeling of "maybe... this might be it."

Chapter 7

AMINA TOOK ADVANTAGE of the remainder of her summer catching up on some light reading, connecting with her friends, and enjoying the sun. She called Layal and Sahar to fill them in on her trip and share with them all the sights she'd enjoyed overseas. What she did not relay to them, however, was her meeting Sherif. She figured nothing would come of their chance meeting, so there was no need to tell her friends about it.

But even though she was certain she would never see Sherif again, she kept his card. *A girl can hope, can't she?*

Her hope continued to dwindle as the days passed. September began and she would be going back to school in just a few days. Her mother helped her pack— they started with her clothes, then made their way to her books and notebooks. Amina gathered her journal and some papers off her desk, and she didn't notice when a small card fell to the floor.

"Be careful. You dropped something, Amina," Ruwayda told her, picking up the card. And before Amina could stop her, her mother was already reading the name on the card.

"Sherif Mahmoud? Who's Sherif Mahmoud?"

"Oh, just some guy I met on the plane. I forgot I still had that."

"So you want me to throw it away, then?" Ruwayda teased, smiling slyly.

"No, no. I'll keep it with the rest of the business cards I have." Amina grabbed the card from her mother and placed it back in her journal.

She tried to think of anything to change the subject, not wanting to discuss Sherif with her mother, but she could think of nothing. Luckily, her mom simply went back to packing and didn't mention the card, or the name on it, again.

A few days later, Amina loaded up the car she'd rented, said goodbye to her parents, and drove back to school. Almost as soon as she got there, she was back into her routine of studying, going to the Arab Association meetings, and hanging out with the girls on the weekends. One day she sat on her bed studying when the phone rang.

"Hello?"

"Hi. Amina?" A man's voice came through the other end. The accent was one she'd heard before.

"Who's this?"

"It's Sherif."

Sherif? Really? Maybe it's a different Sherif. No it can't be a different Sherif, I don't know any other Sherif. All these thoughts raced through her mind in one instant.

"Sherif from the plane?" As though her asking that question meant she had not been hoping for his call since the day they met.

"Thank God you remember me. I was so worried you'd be like, 'I don't know any Sherif' and hang up on me. How are you?"

"I'm well. But how did you get my number here? I could have sworn I gave you my home phone."

"Yeah, I tried you there first. Your dad gave me this number."

"My dad?!" Amina almost shouted.

"Yeah."

But Amina's shock was not diminished in the least. "He just gave you my number? Just like that?!"

"Well, no. I'm an Arab man Amina, I know what's acceptable behavior in our culture. I told him that I had met you on the plane and I asked his permission to get to know you. I heard him double check with your mom, making sure you know someone named Sherif. Then he asked about my parents, my family, where they live in Egypt and what my brothers do for a living, my job, and where and how I live. Then he took my phone number and address and made me promise we'd see each other only in public places. Then, of course, he told me he would have my head if he found out I harmed you in any way."

"Really." Amina was amazed that her father had agreed to let them meet. The last part sounded more like her father. She remembered a day when one of her classmates in eighth grade called her to get some homework; instead of giving the phone to Amina, he told the boy if he ever called her home again he would call the police and have him arrested. She was so amazed by her father's reaction that she didn't realize Sherif had said they would be able to see each other.

"Yeah. Anyway," Sherif continued, "I'm in town for a few days, and I was hoping we could get together."

"That would be great," she made sure not to sound too excited.

"How's eight o'clock?"

"Oh, you mean tonight?"

"Yeah, are you busy?"

"Well... no. Not really, but..."

Sherif cut her off, "Great, then I'll see you at eight at that Japanese restaurant in town. My colleagues said it's pretty good."

"Um... ok. Eight then," she managed with a hesitation that Sherif pretended not to notice.

"See you then. *As salaamu alaikum.*"

Amina hung up and collapsed back on the bed. She had thought for sure that Sherif had forgotten her and would never call. Here he was, not just calling her, but insisting that they meet. Before she let herself get too excited, she called her parents to make sure they approved of her meeting him. Her mother told her to be very careful, only meet him in public places and never, under any circumstances, get into a car with him if he was driving. She expected those kinds of warnings from her parents, but the fact that they didn't object completely made her elated. Once she was off the phone, she realized it was already six, so she put away the books and notebooks she had been studying from and got up to get ready.

Two hours later she stood in front of the restaurant that Sherif had mentioned. Taking in a long breath, she walked in and told the hostess she was meeting a friend. The hostess said Sherif hadn't yet arrived and led her to an empty table.

Waiting for Sherif to arrive, she nibbled on a piece of bread, fidgeted nervously in her chair, and admired how colorful the tablecloths were, despite their cheap plastic material.

"You're absolutely right. The colors are beautiful, but they should have used a nicer material." Sherif's words made her do a double take. When she looked up and saw his face smiling at her, her stomach flipped.

"Was I talking out loud?" She smiled.

"No. But your eyes were," he flirted. "You look great. Even prettier than I remembered. I'm glad you agreed to meet me tonight."

"Me, too," was all she could manage from behind her flushed cheeks.

They ordered their meals and ate them in between sentences. They talked about all sorts of things, from what they'd been filling their time with lately, to their families. Amina learned that Sherif had one older and one younger brother, both still living in Egypt. She learned about how he moved to the states four years ago, and how he came to work at his present job. Sherif listened while Amina shared her career goals with him. He sympathized when Amina told him she didn't feel like her parents approved of what she'd decided to study.

After they had eaten desert and the check came, Amina took out her wallet from her purse and asked, "How much is my half?"

"What? No, no, Amina… It's on me."

"No. No way. Whenever I go out with my friends, we always split the bill. That's how we do it. Why should going out with you be any different? Just tell me how much I owe."

"Why should going out with me be any different? Maybe because I traveled all the way here just to see you. I don't have any business in town… in fact, I have a few days off. I just said that so you would feel more comfortable meeting me."

Amina couldn't decide if she should be flattered or freaked out. She flashed back to right after her rape, when she remembered that Rami had seemed normal for three years, then he'd just attacked her. *Please, God. Not again.* She started to get up, she wanted to run, then she realized that she was in a completely public place, and was perfectly safe. Settling back in her chair, she looked up to see Sherif give his credit card to the waiter. Putting away her wallet, she let out a barely audible, "Thank you."

Seeing that her face had changed, Sherif said, "If it bothers you that badly, I'll let you pay your share next time. Fair enough?"

Amina snapped back to the present, putting all her thoughts about Rami away. "Fair enough," she said, smiling.

"So do you think we can meet again tomorrow?" he asked. But as soon as he had spoken the words, he thought, *Oh my God… I can't believe I just asked that. She's going to shoot me down, and now she's going to have to do it to my face.* He held his breath waiting for Amina's reply.

But Amina had no intension of turning him down. "We can meet, but let's make it lunch instead of dinner. I have an exam the next day and I'll need the evening to study."

Sherif let out a silent sigh of relief. He admired her discipline and determination, even in spite of the fact that she was living independently of her family. Most of the people he had grown up with were dependent on their parents to guide them— to tell them when to study, what to study, how to live their lives. Amina was different; the fact that she had been raised in the States meant she was raised differently. That difference attracted Sherif… that, and the fact that she retained the essence of a proper Arab upbringing.

They planned to meet at twelve thirty at the Italian place they'd both spotted down the street. When it was time to part, Amina became a bit uneasy; would they hug good-bye? Of course not, that was inappropriate. But a handshake was too formal. She was at once confused and relieved when Sherif held out his hand. But when she placed her hand in his, instead of shaking it, he brought it to his lips and kissed it ever so gently. She was glad it was dark out so that Sherif wouldn't see her blush.

"How'd you get here? Do you have a car, or did you take a cab?" Sherif wanted to be sure that she returned to her dorm room safely, but he knew it was inappropriate to take her there himself.

"Yeah, I took a cab."

Almost as soon as the words had escaped her lips, Sherif had hailed a cab, paid him in advance through the window, and held the door open for her.

"I'll call you in twenty minutes to make sure you've arrived safely."

Amina got in the car and waved goodbye to him.

Their lunch date the next day was just as full of conversation as their previous evening. They talked and joked and laughed. It was obvious that they enjoyed each other's company. And when it was time to go, they both hesitated, making it obvious that they didn't want to leave.

When Sherif kissed her hand this time, he took his time, letting his lips linger. After reminding her that he'd be going back the next day, he asked if it would be okay for him to visit again in a few weeks. Even though he knew the answer, he felt relieved upon hearing her approval. As she got into the cab, they said their goodbyes and he told her he'd call her.

And he kept his promise— he called her everyday, sometimes twice a day, for the next three weeks. They got to know each other pretty well during that time. Sherif looked forward to hearing her voice, and she continued to get butterflies in her stomach every time she heard his voice on the other end say, "Hey beautiful. It's me."

He brought her flowers when they met again. It was the most beautiful arrangement of roses Amina had ever seen. It was also the first time a guy had given her flowers. She was even more blown away by the fact that Sherif was acting unlike any Egyptian man she'd ever met; in Amina's experience, men from Egypt didn't seem to think that paying money for something that would last only a few hours, was really worth it.

Sherif sensed her surprise, "This is the first time I've given flowers to anyone. I see it all the time on TV, but to be honest I never really understood it. But seeing your face light up like that... now I get it. I'm glad you like them."

They wanted to make the most of the weekend, so they decided to spend the entire day Saturday together. They started out eating breakfast at the local pancake house.

"I'm not so sure about this Amina. Pancakes? What are pancakes? And what's wrong with foul and falafel sandwiches?"

"I can't believe you've been in this country for four years and you've never been to a pancake house! Just wait till you try them."

Once the waitress had brought their plates, Sherif watched Amina drench her pancakes in one of the four different types of syrup that sat on the table. He was a bit hesitant to take that first bite, but when he finally did, he was not sorry. Three platefuls later, he put down his fork, sat back in his seat, and let out a sigh.

"That was the most delicious breakfast. I wasn't even that hungry, but I couldn't resist."

"I'm glad you enjoyed it," Amina giggled at Sherif's change of heart.

After breakfast they went to the aquarium where they sat front row to watch the show.

"Sherif... listen to me. These are definitely NOT the best seats in the house! Let's sit back up there."

"What are you talking about? We have front row seats. Why in the world would we give up front row seats?"

Amina didn't want to ruin it for him, but at the same time, she knew what they were in for. Deciding to keep quiet, she slouched back in her chair with a sigh, and watched the performance.

The inevitable occurred about 20 minutes into the show. The dolphins swam the length of the pool, gained incredible speed, and jumped up high into the air. The sound they made crashing back into the water was nowhere near as awesome as the splash they created. The first two rows became drenched, then the whole place burst into laughter. Everyone was enjoying the show... everyone except for Sherif. Amina looked over to see him cursing under his breath as he wrung out his shirt. A few minutes later, he leaned over and announced that they were leaving. Amina followed him out to the main section of the aquarium.

"They should warn people if they plan on soaking them like that! It's very inconsiderate. I think I want to complain to the manager."

"Sherif, it's a routine they've been doing for years," Amina tried to calm him. "Most of the people enjoy it... it makes them feel like they're part of the show."

"You don't seem surprised," Sherif accused. "Did you know about that?"

"I tried to warn you," Amina shrugged. She sat there for a few minutes, watching Sherif wring out his clothes and try to air dry. Then she started to giggle. Slowly her giggle turned to a laugh, and her laugh became hysterical. Sherif couldn't understand what she was laughing at, but her laughter cooled his temper and brought a smile to his lips.

When she had calmed down a bit, she tried to explain, between one bought of laughter and the next, "You should have seen yourself." Then she opened her mouth to form a giant O, and widened her eyes as much as possible, imitating Sherif's surprise as the tidal wave emerged from the pool and headed towards him. Her face made Sherif laugh out loud. "I'm glad you find humor in my misfortune," he joked.

Once they had composed themselves and Sherif was almost completely dry, they left the aquarium with him holding a little stuffed dolphin that Amina had bought for him as a souvenir. They came across a Friendly's Restaurant and Amina suggested they get some ice cream.

"Ice cream? Amina, it's October."

"So? What's that got to do with anything? Ice cream is a food for all seasons, Sherif. Obviously, you still have a lot to learn about the States."

"I guess so," Sherif chuckled. "I hope you can teach me."

She smiled back at him and led him into the restaurant. Once they had been seated, Amina asked him what flavors he liked. "Well, strawberry and vanilla. Maybe I'll just get a scoop of each."

"What other flavors do you like?" Amina asked casually as she flipped through the menu.

"None."

"What do you mean, 'none'?" But Sherif didn't understand

Amina's look of confusion. He just shrugged.

"There are over thirty flavors here, and you only like strawberry and vanilla?"

"Well, to be honest, I haven't tried all of them. But I know I like strawberry and vanilla, so that's what I'll get."

"Why don't you try something new? Try pistachio or maple walnut. They have so many flavors that are in some way related to chocolate— chocolate chip, raspberry chocolate chip, oreo, fudge. Try one of those."

"No, I don't like chocolate. I'm going to stick with strawberry and vanilla."

Amina gasped at what she'd just heard. "You don't like chocolate?! What kind of person doesn't like chocolate?" She was in shock.

Sherif laughed. "Me. I'm the kind of person who doesn't like chocolate. Why's that so hard to believe?"

"I just didn't know it was possible to not like chocolate. Are you sure you don't like it... I mean, have you tried it, or are you just dismissing it along with the other 28 flavors you're prejudiced against?"

Sherif's laugh grew louder, "Yes, I have tried chocolate and I really don't like it."

A few minutes later they sat enjoying their ice cream and discussing how to spend the remainder of the day. Amina thought they should try hiking, but Sherif claimed it would be too exhausting. When he suggested they see a movie, Amina pointed out the fact that that would mean 2 hours of sitting silently, staring at a movie screen.

"So you don't like going to the theatre, then?" Sherif asked.

"No, no. I do. It's just that... um... I was hoping we could use our time to get to know each other better, and we can't very well do that if we can't talk."

When Amina shared with Sherif her idea of spending some time at the park, Sherif agreed immediately. They finished their ice-cream and headed toward the park. Just before they arrived, they came across a convenience store. Sherif asked Amina to wait for him while he ran in to grab something. A few minutes later he emerged carrying a medium sized pink plastic ball in his hands.

Amina laughed, "What's that for?"

"Well, so I can beat you at a game of football, of course. Why else would we go to the park?"

"Football?" Amina didn't understand. He wasn't holding a football in his hands.

"Yes, football. Ah, no... here you don't call it football. You call it... soccer. So we can play soccer."

"Oh. Soccer. I can do that. Let's go."

The park was filled with people— families enjoying picnics, mother's pushing their babies in strollers, kids playing on the swings. Amina and Sherif managed to find a field that wasn't overflowing with people, and then they began their game. They chased the ball around for a few minutes, then Amina kicked it with all her might. Instead of passing between the two trees Sherif was using as goal posts, it hit one of the trees, bounced off and knocked Sherif on the head. The two burst out laughing.

The game ended in a tie, with neither of them scoring any goals. But Sherif promised her that he'd beat her at least 2-0 at their rematch. They lay on the grass for a while, and Sherif had been silent for so long that Amina thought he'd fallen asleep. But when she looked over at him, his eyes were looking straight up and they seemed somber. Amina was just about to ask him what he was thinking when he began.

"My mom used to take us to the sports club when we were young. They had fields like these that my brothers and I used to spend hours playing in. When she passed away none of us felt like going again."

"Were you very young when she died?"

"Ah... maybe 12 or 13. The doctors didn't discover her cancer until it had spread all over her body. It was too late for them to do anything. She passed away about a month later."

"I'm sorry."

They were quiet for a while; he didn't move until the quacking of a family of ducks jolted him back to the present. He propped himself on his forearms, looked over at Amina and asked, "What about you? What's the worst experience you've been through?"

Suddenly Amina's face grew very hot, her eyes showed anger, and her mind was racing. *Should I tell him? But rape is an intense issue... I don't know how he'll take it.*

Amina's thoughts were interrupted by Sherif's voice, "If you don't want to tell me, that's fine. I understand."

"No, it's not that... I just don't know if I'm ready to tell that story."

"That's fine. We should probably just enjoy the present anyway. I'm really enjoying my time with you; I hope you feel the same way. I'd like to... would it be okay if during Thanksgiving break, when I come back, I can meet your parents? I mean, if I can pay them a visit?"

Amina blushed and looked down at her hands. "I think that would be okay... just don't book your ticket until I confirm— I just want to make sure they don't have any travel plans for that weekend."

She knew that this was it— he wanted to ask for her hand in marriage... an Arab man doesn't ask to meet a girl's parents for any other reason. But she hadn't yet discussed Sherif with her parents. She knew they would scrutinize every aspect about him, but she was confident he would meet their approval.

Amina went to see her parents the following weekend, and just as she'd predicted, it took them a few minutes to warm up to the idea that she had met someone she felt would make a good husband.

She answered all of their questions about Sherif, about the time they had spent together and how he treated her. Then they told her that after Sherif had called a few weeks earlier, they had immediately got on the phone with their relatives in Egypt. They gave Uncle Hassan Sherif's full name, his brothers' names and careers and the cities they lived in. They asked Uncle Hassan to investigate Sherif and his family; make sure the information he provided them with was correct and ask his neighbors about the type of person he is. Amina was amazed to learn they had gone to all that trouble; she knew that checking up on the potential groom was common practice in Egypt, but she figured since they were so far away, they would focus more on meeting and knowing Sherif than doing a background check on him.

"And... what did Uncle Hassan find out?"

"Sherif seems like a nice young man, Amina. His brothers are both successful in their work and all their neighbors only have good things to say about the entire family." Ruwayda's voice eased Amina's anxiety. "It will be nice to meet him over the Thanksgiving break and *in sha' Allah*, God will do what's best for you."

Amina called Sherif that night and told him to go ahead and book his ticket.

Chapter 8

THE FOLLOWING FEW WEEKS passed by surprisingly quickly for Amina. She had midterms to study for and a couple of reports to finish, so she didn't really have any time to dwell on the countdown for Sherif's arrival. He continued to call her everyday, but they both knew she had a lot of work to accomplish, so their phone calls were not excessively long.

Before she realized it, mid-terms were over, she was back at home, and she was helping her mother prepare the house for Sherif's arrival. He had rented a car from the airport, but Amina was nervous he might get lost using the directions he'd acquired off the internet. He had told Amina that he would arrive at 4 o'clock. His car pulled into the driveway at 3:58. Amina watched him through the bay window. He got out of the car, adjusted his suit, locked the car and began walking in a very dignified fashion towards the front door. When he was about three steps away, he stopped, looked down at his hands, patted his front pocket, took out his keys then put them back. He patted his back pocket, making sure he had his wallet. When everything was accounted for, he stood there for a minute. It looked to Amina like he was talking to himself.

"What did I forget?" he whispered. "I have my keys, my wallet... so what is it?" Then it dawned on him.

Amina laughed as she watched Sherif run back to the car, take out a wrapped gift and one large bouquet of flowers. He locked the car doors again and tried to re-compose himself. A few minutes later, he rang the doorbell.

Amina's mom put the final pin in her headscarf and opened the door.

"*As salaamu alaikum*, Tant. I'm Sherif."

"Sherif? Sherif who?" Amina's mom looked very confused, and Sherif's face lit up he was so embarrassed.

"I'm just kidding, Sherif." Ruwayda giggled. He let out a sigh of relief. "Come on in."

"Thank you," Sherif said as he stepped inside. "This is a small gift for you." He handed her the present. "And these flowers..." he pulled them apart to reveal two separate bouquets. Handing the larger bouquet to Amina's mother, he continued, "...are also for you."

"Thank you very much, Sherif. You didn't have to do that. You know, I've been married for 30 years, and this is the first time a man has given me flowers." Sherif just smiled. "Please, come downstairs. Your uncle's waiting for you."

Sherif followed her down to the living room. When they entered, Osman stood up to greet Sherif.

"*As salaamu alaikum,* Sherif. Welcome. It's nice to meet you."

The two men shook hands then sat down across from each other. They made small talk for a few minutes, until Amina made her entrance.

"*As salaamu alaikum.*"

"*Wa alaikum as salaam,*" both men replied. Sherif stood up and handed the flowers to her.

"Thank you," Amina blushed.

"Excuse me, I'm going to go help mama get dinner ready."

After Amina left, there was an awkward silence for a few moments. Then Sherif began, "Uncle Osman, I hope you'll excuse me for coming alone. I know that in these matters, it is customary for the elders to sit together, but all my relatives are back in Egypt.

"As you've probably figured out, I've gotten to know Amina pretty well over the past few weeks, and I've come to ask for her hand in marriage." Sherif continued, telling Amina's father all about himself and his family. He concluded by saying it would be a great honor to be welcomed into their family.

"Well, we've asked about you and your family, and it would be an honor to accept you into our family, Sherif. But before we can take any steps or make any kind of announcements, we first have to come to an agreement regarding the *shabka, mahr*... you know, all this formal business."

"Of course, Uncle... of course. Please excuse me; I don't really know how these matters are supposed to go. Shall you tell me what your expectations are?"

"Why don't you tell us what you're capable of offering our daughter?"

"Yes, of course. Well, with regards to the *shabka*, I think we'll be able to find a suitable diamond ring that Amina will like in the range of $2,500. And at this time I can afford to offer her a *mahr* of $15,000. Of course, I have my apartment in the city... it's fully furnished, but if Amina wants to change anything, I think it'll be fair to sell whatever she doesn't like and with that money, she can choose what she likes."

"How large is your apartment?"

"I'm not sure what the measurements are, but I have two large bedrooms, one bathroom, a dining room, living room, and family room. Of course, I don't plan on living there forever. When we decide to start a family, I'd like to look for a house."

"Good, good. That's all very good," said Amina's father. Sherif was just about to let out a sigh of relief, when Amina's father stated, "That just leaves the wedding."

Sherif knew this was his cue, to offer what he could, but he had no idea what to say. All the other marriage expenses would make a significant dent in his savings; he didn't know how much more he could afford to offer. But to his surprise, Amina's father began, "Recently, many of the families have started splitting the cost of the wedding. I think that would be fair."

Sherif smiled, "That would be great." He waited for a minute, then he asked, "Is there anything else we need to come to terms with?"

"No... I think that covers everything. Let's say the *Fathōa*, as a promise of marriage between you and my daughter."

The two men recited the *Fatha* silently and when they were finished, Amina's father welcomed Sherif into the family with a hug and kiss on each cheek. Then he called out, "Amina! Bring the *sharbat* for your fiancé!"

At this announcement, Amina's mother let out a trill and the two women entered with Amina carrying a tray holding 4 wine glasses filled with *sharbat*. The four of them celebrated the new engagement with the feast Amina's mother had prepared. During dinner Ruwayda dominated the conversation about preparations for an engagement party that would take place during Amina's winter break.

Two weeks later, Sherif and Amina were having dinner at one of their favorite restaurants. Amina noticed that Sherif had been acting strange ever since they sat down. He kept fidgeting with the silverware and squirming in his chair. She could tell he was preoccupied with something, but she had no idea what.

"Sherif... you don't seem yourself tonight. Is everything alright?"

"Yeah, everything's fine." He patted his chest pocket, drank some water and continued fidgeting.

Amina, trying to ignore his strange behavior, started discussing the engagement party, but he changed the subject almost as soon as she brought it up. When she mentioned it a second time, he did the same thing. She tried one last time, "My mom and I are going shopping for my engagement dress in a few days."

"That's nice. Did I tell you I have a new coworker? She's actually Egyptian, from Alexandria, and turns out our families are friends. Isn't that so weird? It's such a small world."

This last topic set off a light bulb in Amina's head. Was this what his strange behavior was all about? Was it possible? *No way. He wouldn't bring me here to break up with me... would he? No, no. He's already made plans with my family and calls my parents every few days just to say hi...* But still, doubt had gotten the better part of her... doubt and jealousy.

"Really? What department is she in?"

"Mine, actually. We work very close together. Her name is Yasmine and she hasn't been here for very long, so she doesn't really know her way around. She asked if I could show her where the malls and cinemas and restaurants are."

"And of course you agreed?" Amina tested.

"Of course. She's a stranger from our country and she asked me to help her out... I can't very well refuse."

"I see," Amina thought she said, but the words didn't actually come out. *So this is it... He really brought me here to break up with me.* The devil's advocate within her tried to convince her otherwise; *maybe Yasmine is just a colleague and nothing more.* But, deciding that if Yasmine was just a co-worker Sherif would have invited the stranger to meet his fiancée, Amina gave in to the doubt. She took a sip of water, trying to distract herself from crying. She didn't notice when Sherif took the small box from his pocket and hid it in his hand.

"Amina, I think we need to talk."

She was barely breathing, hating what she knew was about to happen. Sherif continued, "I've been thinking about this a lot lately and I think it's really important that I tell you something."

With that he stood up, adjusted his jacket, opened the small box he held in his hand, got down on one knee, and held it out towards Amina. "I never thought I would love anyone the way I love you. I thought I would marry a girl my parents pick for me, and I'd go through life just like everyone does... content, but normal... calm. You make me happy and you bring out all the passion I have inside. I don't think I can go through this life without you by my side. Will you marry me?"

Amina was stunned. That's not what she had expected at all... it surprised her so much that she began to suspect that she hadn't heard him correctly.

"What... What... What did you say?" she finally managed.

"Will you marry me?" Sherif was smiling. This was the exact reaction he'd been hoping for.

Amina nodded her head as she wiped away the tears. She pulled him towards her for a hug, then they both began to giggle. Sherif took the ring from the box, placed in on her finger, and gave her hand a soft kiss. The entire restaurant was clapping for them, and the applause didn't die down until they had sat back down.

Sherif could tell that Amina's head was still spinning, partly out of happiness, and partly out of confusion. "There is no Yasmine. I made her up so that the proposal would take you off guard."

"But why? I mean, we're already... what made you... I mean..." It was too soon for her to formulate any coherent sentence.

Sherif laughed, "When I told the guys at work that I was getting married, they asked how I proposed; when I said I went and asked for your hand from your father, they made fun of me for about an hour, then they told me that the formalities were all fine and good, but no woman doesn't want to be swept off her feet with a romantic proposal. Only now do I get what they were saying."

He was obviously very proud of himself for making Amina so happy, but he had every right to be. In the Egyptian culture, women don't expect romantic, get down on one knee, 'proclaim my-love-to-you' proposals. For them, having a suitor ask her father to marry her was as romantic as any woman could expect. But in the States, all those romantic notions are built up so much that women who don't get those proposals feel cheated and disappointed. Sherif was glad that Amina would have a great story to tell whenever anyone asked, "so how did he propose?"

Chapter 9

AMINA'S MOTHER HAD STARTED preparing for the engagement party the same day Sherif had met with them. Amina begged her to wait, just a little while, but her mother saw no reason to procrastinate. She forced Amina to go shopping for an engagement dress, and after a couple of days of searching, Amina finally found the perfect dress. One of her mother's friends added the finishing touches to it to make it fashionable for a *muhajaba*. It took a few fittings, but Amina loved the result of her entire outfit, including her headscarf.

"The caterers need us to decide on the appetizers, then they're going to need a down payment," her mother filled her in.

"Isn't it kind of soon for all that, mama? We still have about 5 weeks left."

"Why should we put it off, Amina? I made an appointment with them for Monday. That way you can discuss any changes with Sherif when you see him this weekend. Besides that, we'll just need to order some flower arrangements as centerpieces and to decorate the house. I can take care of that tomorrow after work."

"No, mama... please. I want to pick the flowers out myself. But after the weekend."

Ruwayda let out a heavy sigh, "Fine. But if you don't take care of it Monday, then I will."

Amina's mother couldn't understand why she wanted to postpone the preparations, but there was a nagging, nervous feeling Amina felt whenever anyone discussed anything about the party. There was something major she had to tell Sherif, and the weight of it was so heavy, sometimes she thought it would suffocate her.

Why are you letting your mom do all this, she said to herself. *You're letting her make all these plans and you don't even know if he's still going to want you once he knows... once he knows you're not a virgin.*

But of course he's still going to want you, she convinced herself. *He loves you and once he hears your story, he'll hate that you experienced something so horrible, but he'll continue to want you.*

But the final thought in this conversation with herself was always,

But he's Egyptian... he won't get it... and he'll blame you, just like dad did.

The next day, Ruwayda knocked on her daughter's bedroom door. "Are you ready, Amina?" she said as she walked in. Without waiting for an answer, she continued, "Come on... I don't want to be late." Then just as quickly as she'd come in, she walked back out, leaving Amina anxious and confused.

"Are we going somewhere? Did I know that we're going somewhere?" Amina asked, following her mother. But her mom didn't answer; she grabbed her keys and purse, checked her headscarf in the mirror and just said, "Come on. I'll wait in the car while you put on your scarf and shoes." She had one foot out the door and one hand still on the door knob when Amina insisted, "Mama, why are you in such a rush? What's going on?" Her mom's behavior was too suspicious for her to just ignore.

"I'll tell you in the car," Ruwayda said, standing outside now, but still holding the door open. This just intensified Amina's suspicion.

"If you don't tell me now, I won't come." She stood just inside the doorway, arms crossed.

"I have a doctor's appointment and I want you to keep me company."

Bullshit. Her mom was used to running all her errands, including doctor's appointments, all by herself. She actually preferred it that way, so that she could go at her own pace, and no one else's dillydallying or rushing would get to her. Amina just raised her eyebrows, making a visual proclamation of what was going on inside her head.

Amina's mother let out a sigh and hung her head for a minute in defeat. She stepped back inside and let the door swing half shut. But when she spoke, her voice wasn't softer or unsteady; she knew this was her only chance to get her daughter to do what needed to be done, so she continued to speak with authority.

"The doctor's appointment is for you. We have exactly half an hour, so be quick and go get ready."

"But I'm not sick, mama. And I just had my physical a couple of months ago."

Ruwayda didn't say anything. Amina racked her brain, trying to figure out what was going on, but for the life of her, she just couldn't.

"I don't understand, mama. A doctor's appointment for what?"

Her mother's face was stern, and she looked her directly in the eyes. "To fix what happened."

"To fix what happened?" Amina repeated to herself. "To fix what happened?" She hoped if she said it enough times she would be able to resolve the ambiguity. She was right. Now instead of confusion, she was astonished.

"You want to restore my virginity!" The sentence started off as a whisper, but the final word came out as a scream. "Why would you do that?"

"Amina, you don't know how Egyptian men think. This is important… if Sherif finds out on your wedding night that you're not a virgin, he'll divorce you. It's that simple. Is that what you want?"

"He won't divorce me, mama. He loves me… he's going to understand, and anyway…"

But Ruwayda cut her off, "It doesn't matter if he loves you. It's a matter of honor, and he won't be able to get passed this. He will divorce you."

"He won't divorce me because I'm not going to wait till we're married to tell him. I had already planned on telling him this weekend."

Now it was her mother's turn to be stunned. Gasping she said, "Amina, you can't do that. He won't want you. Don't do it, Amina."

"Oh, you think it's better for me to trick him?"

"He won't want you, Amina." Ruwayda repeated.

"Please stop saying that. He WILL want me, he'll understand. And if he doesn't, then it'll be a good thing I told him before the wedding."

"But if you just get this procedure done, he won't ever have to know."

"I can't trick him. And I don't want for there to be anything I can't tell him."

"Amina," her mother paused, searching for the right words. "He won't want you."

"Well, mama, I guess if he doesn't want me, then he doesn't deserve me." She held back the tears long enough to turn around and walk away from her mother. *Please, God, let her be wrong.*

Chapter 10

"WHAT'S WRONG? You seem preoccupied. Listen, Amina, I know that party planning can be really tiresome and time consuming. If it's paying too much of a toll on you, we can just have an intimate family dinner. I'd actually really like that."

"Oh, no, no," Amina protested, trying to smile and force her face to look at ease. Deciding that any further procrastination would be pointless and just intensify her anxiety, Amina took the box from her purse, opened it to make sure the ring was still secure inside and placed it on the table. "Sherif, I have something to tell you, and I want you to hold onto this until I'm finished."

He opened the box; discovering Amina's engagement ring inside, his face went pale. "What's going on? Are you... are you leaving me?"

"No, no. I mean, not really. I just want you to hold on to it until you hear what I have to say. If, when I'm done, you still want me to have it, I promise I won't ever take it off again. Okay, here goes..."

Then Amina began. She reminded him of the group of friends she had at school that had been like a family to her. She explained how close she was to Sahar and Layal, and how she'd considered Tariq and Rami her brothers. Then she told him about the night of the rape, leaving out no details. A few tears rolled down her face as she spoke, but her voice never faltered. She looked down at her hands the whole time.

When she was finished, she wiped the tears from her face, wishing Sherif would cross the table and take her in his arms. She wanted to hear him say, "I'm so sorry. I wish that had never happened to you." She just sat in silence, waiting for his reaction. A few minutes later he finally spoke, making her wish he never had.

"When did you say this happened?"

"The spring before we met."

"And it only happened one time?"

The accusation infuriated her, giving her the courage to look Sherif straight in the eyes. "Excuse me? You make it sound like I just told you I had casual sex with a guy I met... and I can't tell you how offended I am. I was raped."

He was quiet for a while, until Amina gently asked him what he was thinking.

"Well, for one thing, why didn't you tell me about this earlier?"

"Sherif, it's not the kind of thing I go around announcing to everyone. I told you when I felt you should know." All of his questions, his mannerisms, his overall reaction could mean only one thing: Amina's mother was right.

"Tell me," Amina snapped, figuring Sherif had already made up his mind anyway. "Why is it so important that you be the first one to enter me?"

Sherif was shocked by her brashness.

"Oh, please. That's what this is all about, right? Your bride has to be a virgin, even if you've slept with hundreds of girls before. Right? I mean, if I were divorced, or widowed, you wouldn't have given me a second glance."

"No, Amina, that's not right. In those cases there would have been a legitimate reason for you not to be a virgin, but this…"

Amina cut him off with a tone that startled even herself, "But rape isn't a legitimate reason?!"

"It's not that Amina, it's just that…."

"That what?" she urged.

Her insistence and tone made him answer without thinking, "That I have no way of knowing how many other men you've been with," and even before the words had completely been spoken, Sherif wished he could take them back.

"I'm not going to sit here and defend myself to you when I've done nothing wrong. You have your ring… if I hear from you in the next couple of days… fine. Otherwise, I'm sorry we've wasted so much of each other's time."

Amina grabbed her purse and left. The days turned to weeks, and the weeks to months, until finally Amina stopped jumping every time she heard the phone ring. She tried to make herself forget him, forget all the moments they'd spent together. But no matter how hard she tried, she could not block his image from her mind.

Her experience with Sherif had made her much more jaded and apathetic to the world. She was convinced that happiness was a mirage people believed in just to keep from feeling miserable. She went about her days, studied for finals and ran her errands, simply because that was what was expected of her. She forgot how to laugh, how to smile;

she was broken.

At school she refused to participate in any of the graduation events that Sahar and Layal suggested. They tried to get her to open up about what had happened, to vent, but she was not interested. She simply said she had a bad experience with a guy who turned out to be cruel and heartless. Then she swore to herself that she would never mention it again.

Unfortunately, thoughts of him didn't leave her as quickly as she'd hoped. Often she saw him in her dreams. One night she dreamt that she was walking on a long pier, her feet getting wet from the water below as it splashed against the boards. When she came to the end, there was Sherif, standing beside a large empty basket.

"I've caught so many fish," he told her.

"But your basket is empty, Sherif." she replied.

"No, it's not here. I caught a lot; I'll bring them to you."

But she did not wait for him to return. She kept walking and met a man whose basket was overflowing with fish. He invited her to join him, and with a feeling of contentment, she sat down and stared off into the ocean. Her dream was so vivid that she would have recognized the man if she'd seen him in real life.

One day before graduation, Sahar and Layal finally managed to convince Amina to go out to dinner with them. Sahar said she had something important to share with them, and she'd be extremely offended if Amina wouldn't go. So, with a heavy hesitation, she agreed.

When they had been seated at the restaurant and were deciding what to order, Sahar made her announcement.

"So, I have some news… my engagement party is in a couple of months."

"What?!" Amina and Layal were both shocked. Sahar had never mentioned any suitors before, so they didn't understand where this was coming from.

"His name is Yasin. His dad's worked with my father forever. He's not Pakistani; his mother's Lebanese and his father's American, which sort of shocked me…"

"What do you mean it 'shocked' you?" Layal asked, confused.

"It shocked me that my parents approved of me marrying a non-Pakistani. I know they've always had dreams that I would marry a traditional Pakistani man. And my dad always talks about interracial marriages in a negative way: 'The children get confused, they don't know which culture is theirs. They don't know where they belong.' And now he's encouraging his only daughter to marry interracially— it's weird.

"But anyway... I think part of the reason that my parents aren't having issues with this is because our families have known each other since I was a kid. Yasin graduated last week, and the very next day he went and asked my father for my hand. I guess he's been interested in me for a while."

She was speaking in a very matter-of-fact tone. Neither Layal nor Amina could figure out how Sahar felt about her upcoming engagement.

"Wow, Sahar," Layal said, "Are you happy about this? I mean, are your parents forcing you into this?"

Sahar didn't let her finish. "No, no. Not at all. I mean, they definitely like Yasin, but they told me it was completely up to me, and that in making my decision, I shouldn't even consider the fact that he's a family friend; I should judge him like I would judge any stranger. And that's what I did. There's nothing major wrong with him. I mean, he comes from a good, Muslim family. He's been offered a respectable job working as an accountant for some company in Chicago. He's polite with his parents and treats them kindly. And he seems to care about me."

"But Sahar," Amina was always weary of sudden engagements or marriages. She believed any couple needed some time to get to know each other before they could make a binding commitment. "You can find a million guys out there with the same characteristics you've just described. To make a marriage work, there has to be... well, more. An attraction. A spark. Even the promise of a spark. I don't know, something. But it has to be there."

"Oh... well, he's cute enough, I guess," Sahar answered. "I mean, I'm not in love with him. I think that may come later, after we're married."

"Sahar, you don't seem too excited." Layal asserted.

"'Excited' isn't the right word," Sahar replied. "I mean, it would be great to marry someone I'm madly in love with, who sweeps me off my feet. But how often does that actually happen? And how often does it last when it does happen? I think entering a relationship using your head, leads to a more successful marriage than entering it using your heart."

The girls were silent for a while, pretending to read the menus they had open in front of them.

But Amina couldn't get over the news. "But how happy would you be, stuck in a loveless marriage for the rest of your life?"

"I told you, real love comes after marriage. And if it isn't passionate love, that's fine. I think the passion runs out after a few years of marriage anyway. I'll be content."

It wasn't her place to do so, but Amina disapproved. It always made her melancholy when she heard that someone was settling for less than what she deserved, and in Amina's eyes, that's what Sahar was doing. She could have so much more— where does it say that passionate relationships don't work out?

But despite herself, she knew that was the truth; it surely hadn't worked out for her, why should she think it was possible at all? The fact that somebody else in her life was resigned to contentment instead of bliss made her even more depressed.

She noticed, though, that Sahar didn't appear upset about it. It seemed she was accepting her fate with a reservation to have no regrets. In her heart, she envied Sahar's self-discipline. And on the spot, she made a resolution to let go of the past. Well, to try harder to until, she hoped, time would cast a haze over her memories, and the whole experience would simply become a forgettable dream.

Chapter 11

EVENTUALLY HER PARENTS stopped blaming her for driving away a perfectly suitable husband... at least they stopped blaming her to her face. Amina was sure they'd had countless conversations about the matter and had apparently surrendered to the idea that Amina would never be married due to her "condition." That didn't bother her, though; now that they had finally accepted that the Sherif chapter in her life was over, she could move on. She made a conscious decision not to look for love and finally conceded to her parents' way of thinking— that no respectable Arab man would want her now. So her only choice was to focus her energy into her career. Four years at one of America's top universities would not be put to waste.

She immediately started researching jobs in her field and sent out what seemed like hundreds of resumes. So as not to waste any time, she took on a part time position at a local department store while waiting to hear back from her applications. As the weeks went by, Amina began feeling discouraged, until she received what appeared to be a promising phone call.

"Hello?"

"Hello. May I please speak with Amina?"

"This is she."

"Hi. This is Suzan from United Pharmaceuticals. We've just looked over your resume and we'd like to schedule an interview with you if you're still interested in working in the lab here."

Amina was elated, "Yes, of course. That would be great."

"How does Tuesday at eleven work for you?"

"That's perfect," Amina lied. She knew she was scheduled to work that day, but that was not going to hold her back.

She had four days to prepare for the interview, which involved picking out her most professional looking outfit, driving to the company to see how long it would take, and preparing answers to all the interview questions she could think of. She was nervous and excited; it was only a few days before she would be employed at her first professional position.

On the morning of the interview she gave herself fifteen extra minutes to reach the company. Along the way she listened to the Qur'an and prayed for God to do whatever was best for her and her future. Just before entering the building, she recited the last two chapters of the Qur'an and asked God for guidance.

"Hello," Amina said as she entered the HR department. "My name is Amina Abdul Mu'min. I have an appointment for an interview today."

The woman looked somewhat bewildered as she stared at Amina blankly. When she didn't say anything, Amina asked, "This is United Pharmaceuticals, isn't it?"

"Ah… yes, of course." The woman snapped out of it. "Please have a seat while I let Suzan know you've arrived."

After a few minutes Amina started feeling as though she was being watched. Looking over her shoulder she saw men and women staring out from behind their cubicles. They were staring at her.

Oh, no, she thought, *do I have a huge stain on my suit that I didn't notice?* But upon close inspection, she discovered her clothes were fine. *Oh, please, God, tell me I don't have anything sticking out of my nose.* But a look in the mirror put that anxiety to rest. *So what is everyone staring at?* Then as she unconsciously started fidgeting with her headscarf, it dawned on her. *Oh, great. Is this the way it's going to be? Wonderful.*

She'd been covering since high school… it was just a part of her wardrobe and she often forgot that it made her stand out. But now everyone's stares made it clear; getting this job at this point would have less to do with her qualifications than with her physical appearance. She was not going to go down easily. She turned back around and made eye contact with everyone staring at her, making sure to give them her best smile.

The receptionist peeked her head out of the HR office. "Please come in, Amina. Suzan is ready for you."

Suzan seemed like a pleasant enough woman, who managed not to lose a beat on Amina's scarf. After about 20 minutes, Suzan called for Brian, the head of the lab she'd be working in, to meet and interview Amina. Brian asked her a little about her qualifications and skills, then he showed her around the lab, giving her a chance to ask the questions she had prepared. He seemed like a respectable guy, only about 7 or 8 years older than Amina, but she noticed he constantly kept looking up at her scarf. She had answered all their questions with eloquence and a smile, but she knew they would not be offering her that position.

Despite her confidence in their lack of interest, she followed up her interview with two thank you notes—one addressed to Suzan and the other to Brian. A few days later, she placed a call to the company.

"United Pharmaceuticals?"

"Hello, may I speak with Suzan from HR?"

"Who shall I say is calling?"

"My name is Amina Abdul Mu'min."

"One moment please."

Amina was put on hold, but only for a few seconds.

"Hello, this is Suzan?"

"Hello Suzan. This is Amina Abdul Mu'min; I interviewed with you and Brian a few days ago. I hope you've had time to review my application."

"Yes, Amina, we have. We appreciate your interest but we've decided to go with someone with more experience. I'm sorry."

"Really? Brian said he didn't have a problem hiring new graduates… and actually he preferred it because he could train them properly before they got into bad lab habits."

"Well, he changed his mind."

"Of course he did. Thanks."

Amina hung up before she heard Suzan's response. She was furious. They couldn't discriminate against her because of her appearance. *I'm going to sue them! This is America, where you can sue the coffee shop for making their coffee too hot and become a millionaire doing it. I'm going to sue their asses!*

But she knew she wouldn't be suing anyone. They would stick to their claim that they wanted someone with more experience.

She was extremely discouraged and remained in a foul mood for the rest of the day. But she felt like she needed to vent, to get things off her chest, so she called the only person she knew would be there for her and tell her the honest truth: Kayla.

Kayla had been Amina's closest friend since elementary school. She knew Amina better than anyone else; she could tell what she was thinking simply by looking into her eyes. They were connected in a way that didn't really exist any more between friends— they hardly ever fought because each of the girls always spoke with her friend's best interest in mind. And even if that honesty was sometimes harsh, it was never hurtful because the girls understood that it was spoken out of love.

Kayla arrived at Amina's house a half-hour later. They grabbed some snacks and went to Amina's room to talk.

"Alright, lady... what's wrong?"

Amina recounted the entire pharmaceutical company incident, starting from the stares she got at her interview all the way to her feeling of suing the company. When Amina had finished, Kayla just sat there, quietly munching on the pretzels. Her silence annoyed Amina.

"So?!" she yelled.

"So, what?" Kayla responded.

"Don't you think I have to do something about those prejudiced assholes?"

"I definitely think you should do something about those prejudiced assholes. But you and I both know you're not going to sue them. I'm not a lawyer, but I'm pretty sure that 'not getting offered a job' is insufficient grounds for filing a law suit."

"So what do you think I should do?"

"I think the best way for you to feel like you got revenge on them is to get a job! So you sent out a bunch of resumes and had no luck... so send out a hundred more. You can't give up just 'cause you had one bad experience. For some people it can take a year or more before they get a job. You've been trying for what, like, two months, and you're already discouraged? Welcome to the real world, stop being a wimp, and suck it up!"

"But they discriminated against me. I didn't get the job, not because I'm under qualified or because I messed up the interview, but because they didn't like the way I looked." Amina knew Kayla was right, but these feelings just wouldn't go away.

"Amina, can you prove it?" she paused long enough for her friend to shake her head. "Then it's your word against theirs, and being a big company, I'm pretty sure they'll be able to hire a lawyer who'll make any lawyer **you** can hire look like a high school debater." She went over and sat near her friend. "I'm not saying you're wrong. I think they probably did discriminate against you. But there's nothing you can do to change it, so you have to shake it off and keep going. You've never been a quitter before."

"No, I'm not a quitter... I'm just pissed. And I hate that there's nothing I can do about it."

Amina and Kayla just laid on the bed for a few moments. They both calmed down and were silently contemplating the reality of yet another injustice.

"I know what would cheer you up... bowling!"

Kayla sat up with a new found energy.

"Bowling?" Amina said. "What do you mean, bowling?"

"You know, ten pins at the end of a lane, you try to knock 'em down using a heavy ball." Kayla replied sarcastically.

"Punk! I know what bowling is! I mean, where in the world did that come from? We've never been bowling before."

"All the more reason to go. We'll have a blast making fools out of ourselves. Come on."

Kayla pulled her friend up from the bed and managed to convince her to go. Once they started playing, it only took them about five minutes before they caught themselves laughing uncontrollably at their utter lack of skill. Almost all their balls went straight to the gutter—despite the fact that they were rolling the balls using two hands, swinging them between their knees. They figured if the five year old in the next lane could roll strikes that way, they surely could... but they were wrong. Nobody in the entire alley was doing quite as badly as they, but nobody was having as much fun, either.

Walking out of the alley, Amina remembered her interview. This time, instead of becoming red faced and clenching her jaw, she smiled and let out a sigh, determined not to get knocked down again. *Oh God, give me patience and strength. Let me face all my hardships with dignity, and help me to overcome them.* She would take whatever came her way with head held high and eyes on success. As soon as she got home, she printed up twenty more resumes and mailed them off.

Chapter 12

THE FOLLOWING SATURDAY was Sahar's engagement party. Amina's parents wouldn't let her travel and spend the night in a strange hotel room all alone, so her mother agreed to join her for the event. They arrived in Chicago on Friday night and checked into a hotel near where the engagement party would be held.

Amina was so excited about seeing Sahar and Layal, but her feelings of doubt about the engagement hadn't changed. Nevertheless, she promised herself that she would be supportive of Sahar and not show any signs of apprehension. Ruwayda had made her daughter buy a new dress for the occasion. It was much fancier than Amina cared for, but in the end she decided that since it was decent looking, she would buy it to make her mother happy.

Ruwayda had a way of over dressing for occasions like engagement parties and weddings. Actually, Amina thought her mother over dressed for everything; even if she was just going to the mall to window shop, she always wore a nice dress and high heeled shoes. Over the years Ruwayda had accumulated more gold than many jewelry stores have in stock, and she always made sure her rings, bracelets and necklaces were elegantly on display.

While Amina thought her mother went too far with her appearance, Ruwayda thought her daughter lacked that pizzazz.

"Amina, did you want to wear your grandmother's tennis bracelet?" They were both getting dressed for the party.

"No thanks, Mama. I'm going to stick to this one you bought me a few years ago."

"So wear them both."

Amina had anticipated this response from her mother. "I think that'll be too much."

"Don't be silly, Amina. Look at me: I'm wearing three bracelets on one wrist, one on the other and six rings in all."

"Yeah, Mama. And that's too much!" Amina laughed.

Ruwayda rolled her eyes at her daughter's lack of style. "When you own pretty things you should show them off at the right opportunity. We don't get to attend engagements or weddings everyday, so we should look special."

Amina had learned a long time ago not to try to change her mother's style or her attitude towards dressing up. Ruwayda always looked classy, never gaudy, so Amina accepted her high maintenance style because it worked for her. Plus, many of the Arab women Amina knew tended to overdo their wardrobe or their jewelry in one way or another, so at an event like this engagement party, Ruwayda would fit right in.

The hall where the engagement party was being held was simple but elegant. There were between 50 and 75 people in attendance, and those who were not family could be counted on one hand.

Sahar spotted Amina as soon as she walked into the hall and she waved her over. The girls hugged and shared how much the other had been missed. Amina complemented Sahar's beautifully embroidered yellow dress and told her how wonderful everything looked.

"My parents wanted a more simple engagement party; closer to what they're used to in Pakistan. But Yasin's mother insisted it be done in a hall because neither of our houses could support this many people. She also warned me about how Arab women like to dress; otherwise, my dress would be more simple, too."

"Everything looks wonderful... and you're beautiful."

"Thank you, Amina."

Sahar was laughing and smiling. It seemed to Amina that she was genuinely happy. Amina just hoped it was because of where she was in her life, not where she was in the room.

Sahar introduced her friend to her fiancé and Amina gave a quick hello. Then she stepped back from the bridal stage and went over to where her mother was sitting. She scanned the room many times looking for Layal, but she didn't see her anywhere.

Amina was wondering what could possibly be keeping her friend away, when her mother's voice interrupted her thoughts.

"Amina, this is Tant Farah," she said. Amina hadn't even noticed that her mom had been speaking with the woman sitting next to her. She smiled and shook Tant Farah's hand, then she sat uncomfortably while her mother proceeded to relate to this stranger Amina's life story. Then, when her mother had embarrassed her more than she thought was possible, Tant Farah started speaking of her son, Mohsen. Only to Amina's surprise, the speech wasn't directed towards her mother; this woman was telling Amina all about her son! And Amina knew right away that no matter how hard she tried to get out of it, she would be forced to meet this Mohsen character, who, of course, couldn't make her life easier by just being at the party so she could get this blind date over with.

Amina had lost faith in Egyptian men and she had promised herself to put out of her mind the idea of ever finding someone who would understand her, love her and accept her as she was. And she didn't let this meeting with Tant Farah shake her conviction, but it did make her wish she had never sat down at this table.

She waited until Tant Farah had finished, then she politely excused herself to go speak with the bride, whose groom seemed to have disappeared.

"Where did your man go?" Amina asked.

"Oh… he's making the rounds," she pointed out at the sea of guests, spotting her fiancé mingling with the crowd. "He told me I should go with him, but there's no way I'm gonna spend an hour standing in these shoes, carrying around this dress.

"Hey," Sahar's tone changed from chipper to serious. "Do you know where Layal is? I spoke with her a few days ago and she confirmed that she'd be coming, but I haven't seen her."

"I've been looking for her, too. I hope everything's okay with her. I can't imagine what would keep her away, especially after she told you she was coming."

A few minutes later Layal walked through the door, slightly out of breath but looking perfect, with a new addition to her wardrobe. She knew she was late so she immediately walked up to congratulate her friend. Sahar was elated to see her. "Layal! I'm so happy you're here," she said, giving her friend a big hug. "I was worried you'd changed your mind about coming."

"Never! I just had some issues to deal with that made me a little late.

"You look gorgeous! And you look so happy. May God bless your relationship and always choose what's best for you."

"Ameen. And May He bless you with an appropriate groom soon, too." The two friends laughed. Then Sahar continued, "And congratulations on wearing the *hijab*, that's awesome. Your face is glowing, *ma sha' Allah*."

"Thank you," Layal said as her cheeks turned pink. "It took me a little while to decide to start covering, but now I see how empowering it is. May God always let us choose the path of righteousness."

Then, after having been introduced to Sahar's groom, Layal stepped back and started to look for Amina. Amina spotted her first, and half-ran across the room to greet her friend. After staying in the hall for about half an hour, and congratulating Sahar's parents, Layal led Amina out to the lobby of the building so they could catch up.

"So, how've you been? What's new?" Layal inquired.

Amina racked her brain to find anything of importance to tell her friend.

"I've been good, *alhamdu lillah*. The same really... nothing new. Still looking for a job. The whole process is frustrating and discouraging. I nailed an interview last week and I'm pretty sure they didn't give me the job because of this." She tugged gently on her head scarf. "But I'm trying to keep at it and *in sha' Allah*, He'll send something my way soon. What about you? What's up with you? Congratulations on wearing the *hijab*, by the way. You look like an angel. Really."

"Thank you," and again she couldn't stop her cheeks from turning color. "It took me a while to decide. I was so afraid of how much I'd stand out, how people would look at me differently, how my friends would react. And to be honest, I felt like I couldn't give up that part of me that wants to be pretty. Finally, I made myself choose: people's acceptance of me, or God's pleasure. *Alhamdu lillah*, He guided me.

"It's funny, when you tried to convince me to start covering, I never really understood what you meant when you said that it was empowering. But now, I get it. It really puts you in a state of self-confidence. And you gain respect from people so much easier. The other day, I was walking behind this woman, she was about our age, to the door of the department store. A man on the inside took a good three or four steps out of his way to open the door for me. And he hadn't even noticed the woman who walked in just two seconds before me."

"Maybe he just thought you were hot," Amina joked.

Layal's laugh was sincere. "Yeah, I'm sure my ankle length dress and turtle neck really turned him on."

After the girls had regained their composure, Layal continued, "Anyway, the reason I'm late is that I got a phone call from Tariq just as I was walking out the door. I was already late and I knew that if I answered the phone I'd miss my plane for sure, but it was like someone kept whispering to me, pushing me to answer. And once I picked up, he told me to apologize to Sahar for him; he'd been planning on attending the party but his mother had become ill and he felt like he should stay with her. I said I hope she feels better soon, but that I had to run. But that didn't stop him, he kept going, as though he hadn't heard what I'd said."

When her friend's pause was longer than her curiosity could handle, Amina urged, "Well, go on! What was so important that he needed to talk to you on the spot?"

Layal went on. "He said that he had been planning on sharing all this with me at the party, but since he wasn't going, he didn't want to put it off any longer. Then he said that he was at a good job and a good place in his life, and he was starting to think about settling down. And when he'd made that decision, my face was the one he saw. He said starting a marriage with a friend is the best because you already know all about the other person. And he'd always thought I was smart and kind, and I'd make a good wife and mother. So basically he was calling to ask me when a good time would be for him and his parents to visit my sister and her husband... so he could ask for my hand in marriage."

Recounting the conversation renewed its surprise factor. Even as the words came out of her mouth, Layal found herself amazed at the story. She could see by Amina's expression that she, too, was shocked. As she sat there wondering at all that Layal had said, she realized that there was an essential piece of the story missing.

"Well, what did you say?" Amina almost shouted.

"I'm not sure," Layal answered, trying hard to remember how she'd verbalized her reaction to Tariq. "I think I told him that I would think about it. I think I said that it was a lot to take in and I needed to think about it and discuss it with my sister first. I think." She paused for a while. "God, I hope that's what I said," she sighed.

"That's all so... so..." Amina searched for the most appropriate word. "Weird. I mean, good, but definitely strange. He never let on that he was interested in you. I mean, did you know?"

"No, not at all. But I think that he wasn't interested in me."

Amina guessed what her friend meant, but she wanted to be sure. "What do you mean?"

"I mean, I don't think he loves me. Not romantically anyway. I think he made it pretty clear that this was a decision he made with his head. Settling down is the next step, and he thinks I'll make a good wife."

They were quiet for a few minutes.

"And how do you feel about that?"

"Well, I'm not sure. You know how focused I am at work. I don't want my personal life to get in the way of my success. But can I say that I don't want to be swept off my feet? No, of course not. Every girl wants that, but is that real? And let's say that it is real, does that love supersede everything? Is it enough to make a marriage work? I don't know." She paused for a few seconds, "But on the flip side, what kind of a life do you live if you're stuck in a marriage with no love? I mean, let's assume someone who's really career oriented finds herself in that kind of a marriage... is that so bad?"

"If it helps at all, I do believe in what they say about love coming after marriage. I definitely think that spending time together helps people become closer." Amina wasn't sure if what she said helped the matter or made it more confusing.

"You know, I actually believe that, too. But is it the same kind of love? Is it passionate love?"

Amina's voice became softer, sadder. "Passion wears off."

Layal, on the other hand, was more anxious, "See! I definitely believe that, too!"

"Well, then, it kind of seems like you've got your mind made up."

Layal shook her head, "That's what's making this more confusing. My real dilemma is this: am I willing to live the rest of my life with a good man, who I know will treat me well, but will never give me butterflies in my stomach? Am I willing to accept that I will never know that feeling?"

Only Layal could answer for herself, but Amina suggested she discuss it with her sister and also pray to God for guidance.

The girls sat in silence for a few moments, then Layal pointed out that they'd left Ruwayda at the party with no one she knew. The two began walking back towards the hall. "Don't worry," Amina said, "My mom's in a room full of Pakistani and Arab women... I'm sure she's made ten new friends already."

And sure enough, they returned to the table to find her mother engrossed in conversation with three women Amina had never seen in her life.

After the meal had been served, Amina and Ruwayda started to say goodbye to their friends.

"Please stay a little longer, Tant," Layal pleaded with Ruwayda.

"Who knows when I'll get to see Amina again."

Ruwayda gave her daughter's girlfriend a hug and kiss, "*In sha' Allah*, God will unite you again soon. Take care, Layal."

Amina kissed Sahar goodbye, told her it had been a beautifully successful party and prayed again that God would bless her coming union with her groom. As she stepped off the bridal stage, she bumped into someone.

"Oh, I'm sor…" but as soon as she saw who it was, she froze.

Chapter 13

WHAT WERE THEY SUPPOSED to say to each other? Amina had been relieved that he lived so far away; she thought that meant she'd never bump into him. But now here he was, standing in front of her, and she was not prepared.

"Amina. Hi," Sherif was just as shocked as she was. "How are you? You look..."

But she didn't wait to hear what he had to say. She quickly walked back to her mother, said an abrupt goodbye to everyone standing there, and walked out of the room.

"I'm so sorry. She's very tired, it's been a long day." Ruwayda apologized for her daughter's rudeness. "It was nice meeting you all, please keep in touch." The women said their goodbyes and Ruwayda went out to meet her daughter.

"What are you doing Amina? Why were you so rude?"

"Sherif was in there, mama." Amina's tone was angry. Ruwayda wasn't expecting that answer, so her ears didn't hear what her daughter had said.

"Sherif was in there."

"Oh." Ruwayda understood now. She wanted to blame her daughter; she wanted to tell her that if she'd just listened to her mother and gone to the doctor that day, that this wouldn't have happened, that she wouldn't have had her heart broken. She wanted to, but she restrained herself. That chapter in their lives was over, and it had taken time, but her daughter's wounds had healed. And they were not going to let a tiny set back like seeing that man again open it back up. Ruwayda took her daughter by the arm. "Come on, let's go back to the hotel. It's still early, maybe we can get some dessert on the way."

Amina looked at her mother with tears in her eyes and thanked her silently for being her rock. Amina was too emotional. She had done such a good job of forgetting Sherif— she convinced herself of that anyway— but in either case, she had managed to move forward. Seeing him again awakened in her a loneliness and anger that she had put to rest.

"Well, that sucks," Kayla tried comforting her a few days after

Amina had returned from Chicago. "I guess it really is a small world."

"It's not a small world," Amina said softly. Kayla looked at her friend, confused. "It's a test. God is testing my patience and my faith."

Kayla nodded her head slowly, taking in what her friend had just said. After a moment she asked, "And how're you gonna do on this test?"

Amina was emotionally drained. She sighed, "I'm going to do just fine. I don't regret having told Sherif the truth. And I don't regret that I didn't take my mom's advice and trick him into believing I'm a virgin. I'm not sure if I regret having met him... I'm not so sure that saying about 'better to have loved and lost than never to have loved at all' is true. But it doesn't matter. I had my few days of anger and sadness, and I know everything happens for a reason. And all I can do now is pray that God heals my broken heart and gives me the strength to forgive Sherif for having broken it. I think that's what God was trying to tell me, throwing him back in my face again. I think I need to forgive him. And I pray that happens soon."

"You want to forgive him? I want to kick his ass." Kayla's voice was calm yet sincere.

Amina laughed, "Believe me... I've kicked his ass a hundred times in my mind. But the only way I'm really going to mend is to forgive him. That's the only way I'm going to be able to see him and not lose it. I have to do it for me." She paused for a few seconds. "and for God, too, of course."

"OK," Kayla said, "I was with you all the way up until you said you have to forgive him for God. What?"

Amina knew that Kayla was still in search of something to believe in, so she prayed that the words would come out in a language her friend would understand, not in one that would frighten her.

"Well, we, as humans, are very imperfect. We make mistakes all the time. Sometimes without knowing or without evil intent, but other times we know full well that a given act is hurtful or immoral, and that doesn't stop us. And God knows and sees all that we do. As long as we ask for forgiveness, though, he graces us with it, almost always. He can forgive all sorts of sins; lying, stealing, even killing. So we should have enough compassion to forgive these far less evil wrongs done to us. God is so generous in his forgiveness, and for that reason we, too, should strive to be forgiving."

Kayla thought about what her friend had said. "But if God forgives people when they ask for it, doesn't that mean you should wait for Sherif— or whoever's done you wrong— to ask you for forgiveness?"

Amina thought for a minute. "Well," she began, "if I were forgiving him for his sake, then I wouldn't do it until he asked for it. But I'm not. I'm forgiving him for God, so God can be pleased with me."

Kayla sighed, "I'm not gonna lie to you and say that I get what you just said. But okay."

"Kayla, do you know why we're here? Why we're on this earth?"

"I have a feeling you're about to tell me."

"People spend so much time searching for the answer to that question: why was I born? But you won't find any Muslims wasting their time in that search because we already know that we are here to worship God. That's it. That's the secret so many people pretend not to know. Even though it's obvious... most people who are close to God don't have these doubts. And by close to God I don't just mean monks and nuns and clergymen who devote their lives to worship... but also your average, ordinary Joe, who asks himself before every action, 'What does God want me to do?' And even if that question doesn't pose itself to him on a conscious level, he chooses— always— to act according to the appropriate answer. And in that way, he worships God, even in his everyday interactions with other people."

Kayla sat up straighter, "Let me just make sure I get what you just said. First, God created man for the sole purpose of worshipping Him. And second, our daily interactions with people can be a form of worship. Is that right?"

Amina nodded her head, pondering her friend's recap. "Just about."

"Well, doesn't that make God selfish? I mean, creating a whole people just to worship him?"

"God is the Creator. He can do anything He wants and for whatever reasons. It's not for us to judge. But, just so you know, God created everything else in this world for us, for man's benefit. So there's no way He's selfish. It's like a parent who buys his son a kingdom, and all he asks for in return is a simple 'thank you.'"

"Really? Is that really how you see it?" Kayla didn't.

"Yes, I do," Amina said.

They both sat quietly thinking about this conversation. Then Kayla said, "How do you even know that God exists?"

"There are too many perfections in this world to have happened randomly. The birth of a child, the complexity of worlds living in the ocean, the enormousness of mountain ranges reaching up to the clouds, the beauty of-"

Her friend cut her off. "But what about all the imperfections? What about diseases? Wars? Parents who outlive their children? Even things that are not as dramatic as all that, like broken hearts? What about all that? If God existed, and if He were a benevolent God, all that evil wouldn't exist. I mean, a benevolent creator wouldn't create so much evil."

"But it's not evil," Amina replied. "Like I said before, it's a test. All those things you mentioned are sent our way to test our patience and our faith."

Amina could see that her friend was still skeptical. All she could do was say to her, "I pray you find what you're looking for. I pray you find the Truth."

"I hope I do, too," Kayla agreed. "And I hope you do whatever you need to in order to move on. If that means forgiving Sherif, then I hope you find the strength to do that."

They were quiet for a little while. Amina needed to get her mind off the subject.

"Oh, you know... something great happened at the party, though. You know Layal?" Amina paused just long enough for her friend to nod. "She's covering now. That made me so happy for her."

"Why?" Kayla's question was inquisitive, not rude.

"I really wish you could see it from my point of view, Kayla. I know that most people in this society look at women who cover as being oppressed or controlled. But really, covering is so freeing. You're free from people disrespecting your body, you're free to speak your mind and the *hijab* commands people to listen. When your male classmates or colleagues seek your attention, you know they're doing that because of who you are and not what you look like."

"But don't you think you can get that same respect from just dressing modestly?"

"'Modestly' is a relative term. In the States if you wear a skirt that barely covers your knees and a t-shirt, that might be considered modest. There are some cultures in the world where going top-less is the norm. So who decides what's modest? The One who decides must have dominion over all lands at all times. Only God has that."

"Okay. From a different perspective, though… don't you want men to look at you? I mean, don't you, on some level, want to feel like men want you?"

"I want a lot of things: I want a romantic, intimate relationship. But there are priorities— my want to submit to the will of God, my want to please Him, my want to live an eternity in heaven, all those outweigh any other desire. So, yes, I do want to be pleasing in the eyes of men, but what I want more is for God to be pleased with me. So if He tells me to cover, that's what I'm going to do."

"How did you get to be so religious?" Kayla wondered.

"I'm not," Amina protested, "I just recognize that God gave me many, many blessings, so the least I can do to thank Him is to follow His path."

Chapter 14

THE PROCESS OF FORGIVING Sherif was taking too much out of Amina. She hoped that maybe forgiveness would come naturally if she just got back to her normal routine.

She shifted her energy into finding a job. A few weeks later, she finally heard back from one of the companies to which she had sent her resume. She prepared for her interview, same as before, and she prayed that God would do what's best for her. Just two days after her interview, she received a call from the HR department offering her a position in the quality control lab. She was excited to finally have her foot in the door.

This was her first professional position, and every aspect of her new job excited her. She loved getting up early and getting ready for work. She loved having lunch with her colleagues in the cafeteria, and she loved the fact that she was doing something for the greater good. It gave her a sense of satisfaction to know that her job was essential in ensuring the quality of medications that thousands of people depend on. It was a tiny role, but she was doing something to make the world better.

Those are the feelings she kept with her when the newness of her position wore off. When she began to feel like the tests she was running were simple and repetitive, she reminded herself that they were necessary to maintain the integrity of the drugs.

The following month brought with it New Year. Kayla's friends were throwing a party, and like every year, Kayla invited Amina. Amina didn't usually like to go; New Year's parties meant lots of drunk people and the strong smell of fermentation infiltrating every molecule of air.

"I really don't like being around all that alcohol, Kayla. And with a bunch of people I don't know. Thanks, but no thanks."

"But it's Y2K, Amina! I want you to be there with me when the world stops turning!" The girls laughed. Then Kayla continued, "Seriously, I wanted to spend it with you."

"So spend it with me! Come over here. Bring a couple of your friends and we'll spend it in our sweats, eating chips and dip, and watching the Times Square Ball drop on television."

"But... your parents won't mind me being here so late? Especially if I bring a couple of friends?"

"No, of course not. It'll be fun."

The following Friday, Kayla pulled up to Amina's house at around eight in the evening.

"What happened? I thought you said you were bringing... Jane something from work?" Amina asked.

"I thought so, too. Turns out she likes the alcohol parties better." Kayla giggled.

Suddenly Amina became worried that Kayla was with her out of a sense of responsibility and that she, too, would rather be at the other party.

"Kayla... you know you don't have to be here. I mean, if you want to go, I totally get it."

"I know," was all she said, smiling, and taking the soda can from her friend.

They spent the evening talking, eating ice-cream and munching on an assortment of chips and veggies. At around 11:50, Amina's parents joined them, and they all reveled at the millions of people freezing in Times Square and shouting with excitement at the turn of a new year.

"Why is that fun? I don't understand. Wouldn't it be better for them to enjoy this same view from the warmth and comfort of their own living rooms?" No matter how many times he watched, Osman was always amazed by the seemingly illogical behavior of people on New Year's.

"Does anyone want anything from the kitchen? More drinks, more chips?" But all the women were too engrossed in the countdown to realize how out of character his questions were.

The people on television shouted, "10, 9, 8, 7, 6, 5, 4, 3, 2, 1,..." Then the lights went out. The women sat in complete darkness.

"Oh my God... I thought they were making too much out of this whole Y2K business, but I guess I was wrong!" the worry in Ruwayda's voice was unconcealed.

"Wow! I totally didn't expect this. This is so not good. This is worse than my worst nightmare come true." Kayla's anxiety only deepened Ruwayda's.

"Okay. It's okay. I'm sure.... um... I'm sure they'll take care of this confusion as soon as they can. I'll go get some candles from the kitchen." Amina said, trying to be calm.

"Be careful you don't bump into anything," her mother called out. Amina felt her way to the kitchen and made it to the drawer where they kept the candles and matches. Just as she was fumbling for them, something out of the corner of her eye caught her attention. A quick glance out the window revealed that no other houses had lost power.

"Hey, you guys, the rest of the neighborhood has electricity. It's just us."

Suddenly the lights came on, and with them came Osman's hysterical laughter.

"Oh! It was just too easy! I just wish I could have seen the looks on your faces, but even hearing your reactions was worth it." He couldn't contain himself.

At first Ruwayda was angry with her husband. "Only you would do something like this. Why is it fun for you to scare people? You're such a child."

But within seconds even she began to cool off. They laughed at themselves and how ridiculous they must have sounded. Between giggles Amina confessed, "I kept thinking we were going to have to return to living off of oil lamps and warming ourselves with fire from the fire place. For a second I pictured myself as one of the characters on Little House on the Prairie."

Kayla's laughter became louder, "Me, too! Only I had images of myself cooking soup over the fire while my laundry soaked in the tub."

For a few moments, their lives were only laughter, and Amina found herself wishing it could stay like that forever.

But life went right back to normal. Amina returned to her routine and found that she was becoming increasingly bored with her position at work. One day, a few weeks later, however, she was rewarded with a glimpse into the importance of those repetitive tests.

Up until then, all of her results had fallen within the normal range. But on that day, three out of the six units she tested from one particular batch had some abnormal results; they seemed to be too concentrated. She went over all the steps again, double checking that she hadn't made any mistakes in preparing the units. When she was sure she hadn't, she shared the problem with her supervisor.

Janice was a nice enough woman. She was in her mid thirties and Amina guessed she was about 4 or 5 months pregnant. "Well," said Janice. "it's strange that half the units were fine and half weren't. It's possible something just got messed up while you were preparing the units, but of course we want to be certain that there's no real problem with the batch. I'll order six more units; test them right away and let me know what you find. In the mean while, let me double check your beakers and test vials and your write up."

Amina handed the lab notebook to her boss and organized her lab station so that Janice could double check her work. It took production about 15 minutes to send the new units, and as soon as they arrived, Amina got to work.

"Well, Amina," there was a seriousness, a nervousness in Janice's voice. "I can't find any mistakes with your prep or your results write-up. Please take extra care with those units, but test them as quickly as possible." Janice didn't need to spell it out; Amina could tell by the wrinkles on her forehead and the stress in her voice that if the results came out as before, it would mean a serious problem for the company.

"I'm going to let Robert know what's going on," Janice told Amina hesitantly.

Amina wanted to ease Janice's concerns, but she knew it wasn't really in her power. "I've already started the prep and I'll keep you informed as the results come back— unit by unit." was all she could manage to say.

Amina was extra careful preparing the units. Results for the first two units came back normal. Amina was about to inform Janice of the results when Robert walked in the lab. He was the manager of the lab, and Amina didn't quite care for him. He never smiled and, unlike Janice who usually ate lunch with the rest of the lab personnel, he always sat with the administrative staff. And if no one from administration was in the cafeteria, he would sit alone. Amina didn't really know Robert, but he seemed very stuck on himself. She was pretty sure he didn't even know her name. But his hoarse, loud voice proved her wrong.

"Amina," his voice startled her, "how are those new units coming?"

"I was just on my way over to tell Janice. The first two units came back fine. I'm still waiting on the results for the others." She handed him the lab book so he could see for himself. After he'd looked over the results carefully, he made a close inspection of her lab station. He noticed a problem. "This beaker isn't labeled."

Amina turned the beaker slightly clockwise, showing Robert that the beaker was in fact labeled. Under normal circumstances, she would have said something like, "Next time make sure you look close enough before accusing someone of being careless and unorganized." but given the current situation, she figured there was enough stress in the air without making it worse.

"Good, good," he said. "Let me know how the rest of the units turn out. Good job, Amina."

She resumed her work as soon as she had informed Janice of the results. Robert's words had given her confidence a boost and she was feeling good about herself until the next two results came out. She informed Janice that they had failed, similarly to the three in the first group she'd tested. When Robert found out, he insisted that both he and Janice watch Amina for the final two units.

They were quiet, but their mere presence, sitting at her lab bench, watching her every move, made her nervous. She was used to working with one or two other chemists with her in the lab, but everyone kept to their own station. Now, Robert and Janice were sitting so close she could hear them breathe. And as if that weren't enough, they were 150% focused on her: how she opened the units, how she diluted them, how she injected the samples into the vials. Luckily, she made no mistakes. But the final results were, again, unsatisfactory. Of the six units, again three were over concentrated.

Robert immediately called production and ordered them to stop the lines pending further investigation. Of course this did not go over well with them. The production manager stormed into the lab only moments later.

"What the hell is going on? Why are we being told to stop production due to conspicuous lab results? Who ran those tests?"

"I did, Don. And I ran them twice. It seems that three of your lines are getting too much active ingredient." Amina was shaking inside, but her voice never faltered.

"Look, Amy-"

Amina cut him off. "My name is Amina, Don. Amina. A-M-I-N-A."

"Amina, I don't know what you did, but I'm sure you did something wrong. I've been production manager for 5 years and in that time not one of our batches has been bad. So look over your work and find your mistake."

"I've looked over my work four times, Don. Both Janice and Robert have also looked over my work, and if they had found 'my mistake' they wouldn't have called off production."

"This is bullshit!" Don stormed out of the lab.

"Don't worry about him," Robert sighed, "He's just mad that some one down there screwed up, he didn't catch it, and now it's going to cost the company." He paused for a few moments, and just as he was about to speak, Don walked back into the lab.

"You said three of the lines? Which three?"

Amina spoke while she double checked the lab book, "In both sets of units, lines A, B, and C were off. D, E, and F were within normal both times."

"And you said A, B, and C were higher than normal?"

"That's right."

"Well," Don was looking up at the ceiling. The words were coming out of his mouth, but he was clearly talking to himself. "A, B, and C are all fed by the same water source. If something's wrong with the pipe, that'll cause the units to be too concentrated even if they're actually getting the right amount of ingredient. OK."

Then he looked over at Robert and said, "In the meantime, lines D, E and F are fine, right? So we'll finish production with those lines. We'll salvage as much of this batch as possible."

Robert just nodded his head, and Don left.

"Amina," Janice still sounded concerned, "Have you been testing the batches all week?"

"There were two batches this week— the one on Monday and the one yesterday— that got tested on third shift."

"Can you please pull the lab books for the last two weeks and check them."

Her concern spread to Robert. "Why? What are you thinking, Janice?"

She forced a smile, "I just want to be sure that we haven't overlooked anything." As Janice turned away, Amina heard her mutter under her breath, "I have a sneaking suspicion that this wasn't the only bad batch this week."

Amina pulled the lab books and began checking. It was standard procedure that each write-up be checked by a peer and audited either by the senior chemist or Janice. The job of the checker and auditor was to make sure of a few things: that the results be reported in the proper format, that all materials used were still valid and not expired, and that the results fell within specifications. Both the checker and auditor had to stamp, sign and date each page. Amina flipped through the pages quickly, noticing that every batch, even the one from the night before, had been both checked and audited. This gave her hope that maybe Janice's instincts were wrong, but she went back and triple checked each page.

When she got to Monday's batch, she froze for a second; the 'checked by' and 'audited by' stamps were both empty. "Oh, crap."

Carefully she reviewed the page, line by line. Luckily, the results were fine and there were no other problems with the page. She signed and dated beside the 'checked by' stamp and placed a bookmark with a note for Janice to audit the page. She continued checking the lab book and was just about to let out a sigh of relief, when she noticed a problem with the results of the batch from the night before. The page had been both checked and audited, but despite that, the results did not fall within spec for three of the units. And as she expected, the units that were off came from lines A, B and C.

"Janice," Amina said, knocking on her supervisor's open office door. Janice put on her glasses and stood up as soon as Amina walked in.

"What's up, Amina? What did you find?" She took the notebook from Amina and scanned the results. "Oh, shit." She immediately sat back down at her desk and called Robert. Amina knew the situation was intense and meant big problems, but there was nothing more she could do, so she just went back to the lab quietly.

It was already an hour and a half past her usual leaving time, but Amina did not feel comfortable leaving just yet. She called her parents to let them know that she was still at work and that they shouldn't worry. Then she sat down at her lab bench finishing some overdue paperwork. About a half-hour went by, then the third shift chemists walked in.

"What's up, Amina? Janice called us all in… she said it was urgent."

Amina told them about her results, then about the results from the batch they had tested.

"Are you sure they were off? I audited that batch, I think." Kevin, the senior chemist seemed to be in disbelief. When Amina nodded her head, he sank into his chair and put both hands on top of his head.

Janice came out a few minutes later. "Thank you for staying a couple of extra hours today, Amina. Don't forget to fill in an overtime sheet and I'll sign it for you on Monday. Go home and enjoy your weekend.

"The three of you, meet me in Robert's office in ten minutes." Janice's voice was firm, making Amina want to get out of there as soon as possible.

Even though she knew this was a serious problem for the company that would probably cost them thousands, if not hundreds of thousands, of dollars, she went home with a sense of satisfaction that she had discovered the problem. That was the first time she truly felt like her job was important. If she hadn't noticed the out of spec results, hundreds of damaged units would have been delivered to hundreds of people, possibly making them even more sick. "*Alhamdu lillah*," she said over and over, all along her drive home.

The following week she learned that a leak in one of the water pipes was the cause of the over-concentrated units. Apparently the maintenance worker responsible for checking the pipes was absent from work that day, and his colleagues didn't bother to check his sites. They were reprimanded for their oversight.

Amina also learned that the company was suspending Kevin's senior chemist position. But, not believing that one mistake should cause him to be demoted, he gave his two weeks notice. The other third shift chemists were to be re-trained under Janice's supervision.

Things went back to normal at work once the leaky pipe was fixed. All the results fell back in the range of normal and the overpowering tension from the previous week was gone. But one thing wasn't the same, it was better; Amina felt a new found respect coming her way from both Janice and Robert. They both expressed their appreciation of her careful lab skills and her grace in handling the stressful situation. On that following Friday, Janice caught Amina right as she was about to leave. "Amina, can I see you for a couple of minutes before you go?"

"Sure," Amina said, completely unaware of why Janice wanted to speak with her.

"I know you're in a hurry to start your weekend so I'll get right to the point. You know that Kevin gave us his notice a few days ago. And although we don't usually offer senior chemist positions to people with less than a year's experience, both Robert and I feel that you're qualified for the job. You're the hardest worker here, and you're the most careful. You've proven you can be a strong team leader. We have faith that you'll quickly pick up on all the techniques and procedures that you may not already be familiar with. So, we would like to offer you the position of third shift senior chemist. You'll get a couple of weeks worth of training, and of course there'll be an increase in your salary. You'll be responsible for training all new chemists and you'll feel an increase in the amount of paperwork. You'll be in charge of any special testing and of basically making sure the lab is always running smoothly." Janice paused for a minute, seemingly waiting for a response from Amina. But Amina was in shock; she never expected this.

"I know it's a lot to take in, so take the weekend to think about it. But give a reply early Monday because if you decide not to take it, we'll have to start looking for somebody."

Amina thanked Janice for the offer and told her she'd get back to her on Monday.

Chapter 15

O N HER WAY HOME SHE was so excited that she almost missed her exit. She felt proud that Janice and Robert had seen her hard work and wanted to reward her. She knew that this was a one time offer; if she didn't accept it, she wouldn't be promoted to senior chemist for at least six months, probably more.

"Mama, baba. Where are you guys? I have great news!" she yelled as she burst in the front door. She found her parents snuggled on the couch in the living room watching television. They both smiled to see their daughter happy.

"What's up, Amina? What's your great news?" her father asked.

"Janice, my supervisor, offered me the position of senior chemist! Isn't that great?! She said normally they don't even consider candidates with less than one year's experience for the job, but they believe I'll be a good team leader."

"And why did they pick you?" Osman always had a way of draining the excitement from a moment.

"What do you mean, 'why did they pick me?' I just told you, they've seen that I'm a hard worker and a strong team leader."

Osman was about to say something else to kill Amina's spirit when his wife interjected. "So what does that mean, 'senior chemist?' What new responsibilities will you have?"

Amina described the position in as much detail as she could and didn't forget to mention the salary increase. Her parents were happy for her, but her father still had his doubts. "Amina," he tried to speak rationally, not condescendingly, but he was not successful. "Everything in this life comes at a price... what's the price of this position that you haven't earned? There has to be a down side."

"Well, I don't really consider it a down side, but the position is for third shift."

Osman smiled slyly and nodded his head. "Well, there you go. Third shift."

"Well," Amina began, "I know it's not ideal, and being awake when everyone else's asleep can be exhausting, but I think I'll manage fine."

Osman's face suddenly became very stern, "You're not serious, Amina? You can't work third shift, and I won't negotiate it."

"But, baba, if I don't take this offer, I won't be promoted for at least another six months, that's if a senior chemist position opens up. This is a good chance for me to get a head start."

"I said no, and that's final. No daughter of mine will be spending her nights away from home." Osman grabbed his book and glasses off the coffee table and left the room.

"Mama, do you think you can talk to him? Maybe he'll listen to you. This is a great opportunity for me and I don't want to pass it up."

Ruwayda was disappointed for her daughter, but she had to make her understand. "Amina, baba doesn't want to stand in the way of your success, but you know it's unacceptable for you to be out of the house so late at night. It's not safe for you to be alone at work so late…"

"But, mama," Amina interrupted, "I won't be alone. There will be other chemists working with me."

Her mother gave a little chuckle, "I think that's even worse. We're just worried for your safety, Amina. And, *in sha' Allah*, I'm confident that an even better opportunity will come your way."

Amina knew she was defeated. Her parents weren't going to change their minds and fighting it would just be a waste of her time and energy. She was disappointed and she was sure Janice would think she was crazy for passing up this opportunity. Not many Americans she met understood her relationship with her family. Kayla had suggested more than once that Amina move into her apartment and she couldn't really understand why a 22 year old employed college graduate would want to live with her parents.

"Kayla, it's not that I want to live with my parents, it's that it's unacceptable in our culture for me to move out."

"But Amina, I don't understand. You lived alone at school… I mean, they didn't force you to go to a community college. So how's that different from moving out completely on your own?"

"It's completely different. They let me go away to school because it was the best opportunity for me. I wouldn't have received the same education at a community college. But now, there's no need for me to be away. I mean, I'm working in the same field and in the same exact job that I'd be in, even if I moved out. So why should I? I don't really get why everyone makes such a big deal about living away from their parents."

"It's so they can retain their independence and take responsibility for their lives."

"I don't feel any less independent or responsible. I work, I help out with the housework, and sometimes I even do the grocery shopping. Yes, I tell my parents when I'm going out, who I'll be with and when I'm coming home, but they do the same with me. It's an act of courtesy. If I lived with a roommate, I would expect the same."

"Ah," Kayla thought for sure she had her. "But a roommate can't tell you not to go out… your parents can."

"Yeah, they can. But they don't. Even if I lived away from home, I wouldn't do anything or go anywhere they might disapprove of. Partly out of respect for them, but mostly because I know they make those judgments for my own good. I don't feel trapped living at home. I feel like I have people who love me, looking out for me. And to be honest, I like knowing that I'm close by in case **they** need **me** for anything. One of the girls I went to school with, her father had a massive heart attack and was all alone. That scares me… I don't want anything like that to happen to my parents while I'm living away from them for no good reason."

"OK. I mean, I don't get how you don't feel trapped… but okay." Kayla was not convinced, but she respected her best friend's beliefs.

Once she declined the senior chemist position, life at work went back to normal. She spent most of her days at work, ate dinner with her parents, and used her evenings to read, catch up on phone calls, or just veg in front of the TV. She rarely went out during the week. On the weekends she ran errands, spent time with Kayla, or just hung out with her parents. The routine worked for her; it helped her feel productive when she needed to and it allowed her to relax when she needed that, too.

One day in February after work, as Amina sat reading, the phone rang. Her mother answered and after a few short minutes, she called out to her daughter. "Amina, pick up the phone… It's for you."

"Hello?"

"*As salaamu alaikum* Amina." The man's voice was unfamiliar. She was confused.

"*Wa alaikum as salaam?*" She paused, waiting for the voice to identify itself. When it didn't she had no choice but to inquire, "Who is this?"

"Oh, I'm sorry. I thought maybe Tant Ruwayda explained to you.

I'm Mohsen. My mother, Farah, met you at Sahar's engagement party."

Amina was in shock. *Really? Really?? Mom's really trying to set me up with a guy she knows nothing about! I can't believe this!* She didn't know what to say. And although she didn't want to appear rude, she wanted to put an end to this before she got guilted into meeting this Mohsen.

"Oh… okay. Well, Mohsen, how can I help you?"

"Well, my mother was very impressed by you and insisted I meet you. I'm in the area for a few days so I was hoping to meet you for lunch tomorrow."

"I'm sorry, Mohsen, I'm working tomorrow. And please don't take this personally-"

He cut her off. "But I can meet you at your work. You still have to eat, right? Just tell me what time."

Amina sighed. She realized there was no way she was getting out of this.

"Fine. There's an Italian restaurant I sometimes go to for lunch. I'll be there at 12 tomorrow."

"See you then. *As salaamu alaikum.*"

Amina was glad he hadn't remembered to ask for directions or an address even. She was positive that meant he wouldn't show up, and she let out a long sigh of relief.

Even though she was confident Mohsen wouldn't show up, she went to the Italian restaurant anyway. A quick glance around the room showed no men sitting alone, anticipating any guests. But to be sure she asked the hostess, "I'm supposed to be meeting a Mr. Mohsen here. Has he arrived?"

"Yes, you're Ms. Amina?"

What! She was taken aback. "Ah… yes, I'm Amina."

"We've been expecting you. Please follow me."

As she walked through the restaurant, her eyes searched each table…never finding what she was looking for. This only increased her confusion, and her disappointment.

The hostess led Amina to the sliding door that she had always assumed was the kitchen. As the doors opened, Amina saw they led to a large events hall and the only table in the room was occupied by a man in his early thirties. He stood as the doors opened. He was an average sized man and not unattractive. Glasses framed his wide eyes and a freshly ironed suit hung from his shoulders.

"*As salaamu alaikum,* Amina. You're right on time." He shook Amina's hand softly and held her chair out for her to sit down. The hostess placed a menu in front of her and left.

"I hope you don't mind," Mohsen waved his arms indicating the empty room. "I asked them for a table with some privacy and they suggested we use this room. But there are three waiters and a hostess standing in various corners of the room so that you won't feel uncomfortable."

She looked around and noticed for the first time the other people in the room. Their presence alleviated some of the anxiety that had built within her since being brought to the seemingly secluded area of the restaurant.

They ordered their food, then Mohsen began telling Amina about himself. He was polite enough, and after a few minutes, Amina began to warm up to him. She listened with more interest, trying to put aside any preconceptions she had come with about a guy who couldn't meet a decent woman without the help of his mother.

Mohsen worked on Wall Street. His father had passed away many years ago, and he was an only child. Amina agreed with him that leaving his mother alone was more than improper.

"She doesn't work and she doesn't have any hobbies that keep her busy. My living at home gives her something to do."

As if on cue, his phone rang. "*As salaamu alaikum,* mama."

Pause.

"Yes, mama. We're at the restaurant now."

Pause.

"Yes... she's very pretty."

Pause.

"Don't worry. I won't forget."

Pause.

"Okay, see you later, *in sha' Allah* mama."

Pause.

"I love you, too. *As salaamu alaikum.*"

He hung up and looked at Amina, "See, she still thinks I need checking up on. God bless her."

Amina just smiled. Her own reaction to Mohsen's phone call was mixed; part of her felt like it was sweet, the other part knew she was looking at a 'mama's boy', and although that may be his responsibility, she didn't want any part of it.

"I've dominated the whole conversation. Why don't I give you a chance to speak? Tell me about yourself."

Amina didn't like talking about herself, especially not to complete strangers. But the food was taking forever to arrive, and there were no other distractions.

"Well, I've been working as a chemist in a pharmaceutical lab for a few months now. Sometimes the work is repetitive, but when I get bored, I try to remember how important my part is in putting out the meds. That keeps me going."

"Do you think you'll make a career out of it, or is this a first job?" Mohsen wanted to know as much about her as she was willing to divulge.

"I think it may be a little of both. I'd like to do medical research. But for now I'm taking it slow."

"How do you keep yourself busy when you're not at work?"

"I spend time with my family and friends. Read. Watch movies... the usual."

Their meals finally arrived and Amina hoped it would mean a break in the conversation. She was wrong.

Mohsen kept asking about what type of books she liked, what movies she enjoyed, places she had been. As they ate and continued to speak, Amina decided Mohsen was definitely a good guy, but there was no chemistry between them.

As they were finishing up their lunch, Mohsen's phone rang again.

"*As salaamu alaikum*, mama."

Mama? Hadn't his mother just called a little while ago?

"Yes, it's very nice. Next time I promise you'll be my guest of honor," he chuckled.

Pause.

"No, we're almost done."

Pause.

Then Amina noticed Mohsen's cheeks grow rosy.

"Um... I don't know, mama. We can talk about that later."

Pause.

"I understand. God will do what's best."

Pause.

"I love you, too, mama. *As salaamu alaikum*." He hung up.

"Is everything alright?" Amina asked, already knowing the answer.

"Yeah, yeah… everything's fine. Like I said, she just likes to check up on me."

Amina did not approve, but he could take her nod however he wanted. It didn't matter.

After he asked for the check, Mohsen turned to Amina. "I had a nice time with you. It was very nice getting to know you. I hope I can see you again some time soon?" Amina could see that he was anxiously anticipating.

"It was a pleasure meeting you Mohsen. You're kind and sincere and… well, a good guy. But this isn't going to work. Thank you very much for lunch. And *in sha' Allah*, God will help you find what you're looking for."

There was disappointment in Mohsen's eyes, but not surprise. As she walked to the door, she heard his phone ring again. She was unable to contain the laugh that welled up inside her.

Later that night Ruwayda rebuked her daughter for having ended their lunch with such finality. "When he said 'I hope I can see you again,' you should have just said '*in sha' Allah*.'"

"Why, mama? To give him hope for something I know is never going to happen? That's stupid… and mean."

"You hurt his feelings."

"God knows I didn't mean to hurt his feelings. He's a good guy. Truly. There was just no chemistry."

"Amina! Chemistry can come later."

"Mama, do you really want me to marry a man— almost ten years older than me, for your information— who's not only an only child, but is also his mother's ONLY companion? Do you really think that will be pleasant for me?"

Ruwayda calmed a bit. "Why not? His mother will treat you like a daughter."

"A daughter?!" The statement surprised her so much that Amina jumped out of her chair. She stared at her mother for a moment, trying to read her thoughts. Did her mother really believe that, or was it the desperation to have her daughter marry that was speaking? It didn't take her long to figure it out.

"You and I both know that's not true. Did I tell you she called him three times while we were out? Three times in less than one hour! Three!"

"I've heard some pretty scary stories about Arab mothers in law, but she'll be so much worse. You know the stories I mean. Was it your cousin or your aunt? Someone on your side of the family... her mother in law picked out the furniture without even asking her opinion. And some other mother in law used to race her daughter in law to the door when her son came home from work. Or another, who constantly reminds her son's wife to take care of him and make sure he's covered warm at night when he sleeps.

"I can tell you exactly how Mohsen's mom will be. She'll call us everyday. Actually, what am I saying? He'll need to live with her even once he's married. While he's at work she'll call him a million times a day— sometimes to check up on him, make sure his boss isn't yelling at him— and sometimes to complain that I'm not wearing the dress she wanted me to wear. Or I didn't cook whatever she wanted me to. Or I didn't bring her breakfast and feed it to her, too. You know that's how it would be."

Ruwayda knew her daughter was right, but Amina had left room for one last attempt. "Amina, she's his mother. He can't just kick her out on the street. Of course he'll have to live with her once he's married. He's her only support.

"And God tells us in the Qur'an, 'show kindness to your parents.' It would be a sin if he didn't take care of his mother."

Amina sighed at her mother's obvious desperation. "Mama, do you really think that I think he should treat her badly? Put her away in some home, or just ignore her? I commend him for being so patient with her. All I'm saying is that I won't be able to be so patient. I need privacy in my life, and with him there won't be any."

Ruwayda looked up at her daughter with watery eyes, "I just want to die knowing you'll have someone to take care of you."

"Mama..." Amina bent down and hugged her mother. "Please don't say that. God keep you safe and give you a long life. And after your long life, I'll be fine. You know I can take care of myself."

"I know. I just don't want you to be alone for the rest of your life."

They both sighed.

Chapter 16

AMINA SAT READING her book one evening when she realized it'd been some time since she'd spoken with either Layal or Sahar. She picked up the phone and dialed her friend's number.

"Hello?"

"*As salaamu alaikum*, Layal. How are you?"

"Oh, Amina! *Wa alaikum as salaam.* I meant to call you so many times but I always get sidetracked. I've been really busy lately working on this marketing project for work. They're trying to determine if we can expand our clientele internationally, so with all the time differences, it means I've been working all sorts of weird hours.

"But to be honest, I love it! The company is actually kind of doubtful that this move will work, and that challenge gives me a thrill... especially since I think it **will** be successful, after all."

"That's great. It sounds like you're enjoying work even more than usual. And hopefully after all this hard work you'll get that promotion you've been wanting."

"*In sha' Allah*, but I really don't think they're gonna make any decision about the success of the project for at least 18 months. But that's fine. God will do what's best *in sha' Allah*.

"How about you? How's work? Mom and Dad?" Layal asked.

"Good," Amina said. "Everyone's fine. Work is the same. I've gotten to the point where it's very routine... and at times routine can mean boring. But I'm not really ready to make any moves. I'm comfortable with the people I work with, I understand the job, and when it comes down to it I know that what I do makes a difference. All that keeps me going."

"But Amina," Layal demanded. "If you're bored you have to make a move. This is your career. You can't just stay where you are because the people are nice or because you're comfortable there. You should be doing what makes you happy and fulfilled. And you shouldn't settle for less."

"I know. I know you're right. It's just that at this point in my life, I sort of like the lull. I'm getting used to the calm. Maybe I'm just getting lazy, I don't know.

"But you're right," she continued. "and I'm sure I won't let things go on like this for too long."

The girls were quiet for a moment, then Layal cleared her throat. "Um, I actually have some other news to tell you," her voice was a bit nervous. "I'm getting to know this guy and it seems really promising. He's a successful architect in Chicago. He's kind of serious, but very kind. I'm praying God will do what's best.

"It's funny," Layal went on, "I've never thought of myself as the settling down type, but I think I could easily get used to being with this guy. I mean, like I said, God will do what's best, but to be honest, I kind of hope that what's best is that I end up with this guy." She laughed.

Amina was so excited for her friend. "Layal, that's so great!" she almost shouted. "I'm so happy for you. *In sha' Allah* God will do what's best for you and bless you always with health and happiness."

After a few seconds, Amina remembered the conversation she'd had with Layal at Sahar's engagement party.

"So I guess this means you declined Tariq's proposal? How did that go?" Amina hoped his feelings hadn't been hurt too badly.

"You know, Amina, it's so strange. Both things happened at once— Tariq's proposal came the same day I met this guy. I think it was God's way of telling me not to rush into anything.

"Anyway, a couple of days later I called Tariq and I told him that even though it would be an honor to be his wife, I wouldn't be able to see him as a husband because he's been my brother for years."

"How did he respond to that? Do you think he's hurt?" Amina was concerned.

"I think he's fine," Layal let out a soft giggle. "After I said that, he said…" she cleared her throat and tried to sound masculine. "'Yeah… after I proposed I started wondering if maybe it wasn't the right thing to do. I mean, I've seen you after you've pulled an all-nighter… I can't even imaging how much more horrible you look first thing in the morning.'"

Amina laughed. Tariq was obviously trying to conceal his hurt behind a joke, but the fact that he was joking was a good sign that he would be alright.

Layal continued, "Then he went on to tell me about his family and his job. That was a relief for me— he left no time for the awkwardness to begin, so I think my friendship with him is going to be fine, too."

"And you would expect nothing less from a brother," Amina said. "I pray he finds someone to love who will love him back. He deserves that.

"So have you heard from Sahar at all? I tried calling her just now, but no one answered."

"She called me a couple of days ago," Layal replied. "She sounds fine. I mean, not happy nor unhappy. She says her fiancé treats her well. And they're busy planning the wedding."

"So she doesn't sound happy?"

"She sounded stressed out, to be honest. I think the wedding planning is taking a toll on her. It seemed to me she was calling me to help herself relax and get some distance from the whole situation. She kept saying how great it was that I'm so focused on my career. She sounded almost envious; that made me decide against telling her about this new guy… I was worried she'd kill my enthusiasm."

Thinking of her friends' and listening to news in their lives made Amina grow increasingly lonely. Sahar was busy with Yasin, Layal was excited about this new possibility, and Kayla was also seeing someone new. She tried hard to remember that she'd forfeited that experience, that she'd wanted to focus solely on her job, but it wasn't possible. She was only yearning for what humans are born yearning for—companionship. Her friends were great, but at the end of the night, they each had their own life they went home to. She craved that friend who would stay, who would share her life.

Kayla could feel that Amina was going through a lonely period. She tried to invite her out, to ask her to hang out with herself and her new boyfriend, but Amina always refused. She wasn't friends with Kayla's crew, and she always told Kayla that the last thing she wanted was to be the third wheel.

"Well, what about the fourth wheel?" Kayla asked in response to Amina's rejection of her dinner invitation.

"What do you mean? Who'll be there besides you and Damon?" Amina sounded surprised.

"Okay, please don't respond until you hear all I have to say. I didn't actually want to tell you, but I knew there was no way I could trick you into coming either.

"So a while ago I was telling Damon about you and how we've been friends since the beginning of time, and I was so surprise when he said, 'my good friend Mazin is Muslim. His sister has a name like

Amina— Mina, is it? Or Amira? I don't know, something like that.' So I asked him about Mazin. He's 27 or 28, a dentist like Damon (they met in college) living somewhere near Boston. And of course, he's single."

Kayla didn't mean to pause, but Amina wasted no time. "OH, NO! No way, Kayla. No blind dates for me, thank you. And besides, I'm not allowed to date, remember. Oh, so sorry that couldn't work out." She shrugged her shoulders as she made the sarcastic remark.

"It wouldn't be a blind date! I'll be there with you. Let's even tell your parents you're going out with me to meet a nice Muslim guy."

Amina could not hold back her laugh. "Kayla, I don't mean to be mean, or judgmental… but you and I both know my parents won't believe that YOU are introducing me to a 'nice Muslim guy.'"

"How much do you want to bet?" But she didn't wait for Amina's response. Amina had no more than blinked, and already Kayla was downstairs calling for Amina's mother.

"Mrs. A, do you have a minute? I have something I need to ask you."

"Stop Kayla!" Amina said in a hushed yell.

Ruwayda put down her magazine and looked up at the girls. "What's going on with you two?"

"Mrs. A, my boyfriend's good friend is a single Muslim man named Mazin. He's about 27 or 28, and from what Damon tells me, he sounds like a good guy. I would really like Amina to meet him. Damon invited Mazin out to dinner tomorrow, and I would like Amina to come with us. We'll be in a public restaurant and I'll be with her the whole time."

Now that the words were out, Amina had no suitable punishment for her friend. She pinched her as hard as she could, but Kayla ignored her, of course. She was focused on Ruwayda's reaction.

Clearly, Ruwayda was surprised. Kayla was the last person she expected to set her daughter up with an acceptable match. Kayla was too modern, too free, to know any appropriate suitors for Amina. But a nice single Muslim man… when it came down to it, that's what she wanted for her daughter.

"So, have you met Mazin, Kayla?"

"No, I haven't. But he's been friends with Damon for years, and Damon speaks very highly of him. Oh, and just so you know, Damon is a successful dentist. He's very close with his family. Basically, he's not like anyone I've been with before. I think he's someone you would trust."

"I see. Well, as long as the two of you," she pointed to the friends. "will be together all night, then I have no problem with Amina meeting this Mazin. But I will call to make sure you're with her the whole time, Kayla. And I expect you back before 10."

"Of course, Mrs. A. I promise I won't leave her side until we drop her back off here. Thanks."

Kayla had won. But she knew that convincing Amina's mother was only half the battle, so she tried not to be too cocky.

"That wasn't so bad. So what time will you be ready?"

"Nice try. Just because you got my mom to agree doesn't mean that I'm going. I just don't want... I don't want to...."

As Amina struggled for the words, Kayla helped her out. "To be disappointed? So don't let yourself build up any expectations. Think of him as being asexual."

Amina did a double take. "What?!"

"I mean," Kayla explained. "Don't think 'I'm going to meet a new guy.' Think, 'I'm going to meet a new person.' If that person turns out to be a loser, we will not have lost anything. But if he turns out to be a good person, well, we may gain a friend."

"And this is the same convincing speech that Damon is giving to Mazin?" Amina chuckled at her friend's logic.

"No, Mazin's not as anti-social as you are."

"Hey!" Amina slapped her friend's shoulder.

"Well, you are. But he's not. He likes meeting new people."

Kayla sat quietly waiting for her friend to decide. Although Amina wanted to say no, she had no real reason to. She didn't want to be disappointed again, but if she used Kayla's mentality, she would only have something to gain. Her heavy sigh signaled approval despite her hesitation. But Kayla waited to hear her say it.

"Fine. I'll come with you. But if I so much as say I have a headache, you'd better jump up and get us out of there as soon as possible."

"I promise."

The next day Amina got dressed and went over to Kayla's. She had managed to convince her to make it a lunch date instead of dinner.

"You're really going to wear THAT to lunch?" Amina's eyes popped out as Kayla stepped out of the bathroom.

Kayla was wearing a short, low cut, strapless red dress. Her freshly blow dried hair barely touched her bare shoulders.

"What? This makes my butt look too big?"

"No... Kayla you look gorgeous... but a little too overdone for lunch. I mean, I know you're looking forward to being with Damon alone, but that dress makes that statement all too obvious."

Kayla laughed at her friend's innocence. "Oh, Amina. You have so much to learn," she said, mocking superiority. "We meet them for lunch at 1, then he has some important errands to run. We don't get to be alone together until 8 or 9 tonight. This dress is the only thing that's gonna make it impossible for him to focus on anything else but me all day." Kayla smiled.

Amina smiled back, but she was skeptical.

"I know we've been through this before, but I need to ask you again. Do you think you'll end up with Damon, end up marrying him?"

The thought hadn't really crossed Kayla's mind before. Marriage had always seemed too rigorous an institution for her. But she understood what Amina was getting at.

"Sex isn't always something sacred between two people who are committed to each other. Sometimes it's just sex... fun with someone you enjoy."

"It's too intimate to be just 'fun with someone you enjoy.' You want to have fun, go watch a movie or bowl or rollerblade. And if that's all it is, then doesn't it lose its meaning? I mean, it's the ultimate connection with another person. Shouldn't that person be special?"

Kayla sighed. "I think on some level, people are afraid they won't find that special person, so they don't want to make more sacrifices than necessary. Or it's part of the process of getting to know the other person. Have you ever thought of that? What if you wait till you're married, and your husband turns out to be a really bad lover? What then? Then you're stuck."

"Then we learn how to be better, **together**. He'll learn what **I** need— not what other women wanted or what society pressures him to know. And I'll learn what **he** wants— not what movies imply I should know."

Kayla nodded. She understood. On some level she admired Amina for sticking to her beliefs. But on the other hand, she thought waiting for someone who may never show up was more self-sacrificing than she could handle. Kayla didn't want to upset her friend, but she had to ask.

"Amina," she almost whispered. "What if he never shows up? What if you don't find the person you want to spend eternity with?

Don't you want to know what you're missing?"

"Of course I do. But not enough to sleep with just anyone to find out."

Chapter 17

WHEN THEY ENTERED THE restaurant, Kayla spotted Damon and Mazin right away. The two men stood as the girls approached, but Amina noticed that Mazin was much slower in his greeting.

Amina had met Damon only once before, but he was not the type of person you easily forgot. He was tall with dark hair and rich blue eyes. Not the soft blue, but the dark, brilliant blue that seemed to penetrate anything it fell on. His skin was tan, almost golden. He wore a blue button down shirt and dark pants. Amina thought he was, by far, the best looking boyfriend Kayla had ever had.

Damon was also the most polite guy Kayla had ever been with. He pulled Kayla's chair out for her to sit and tried to include Amina in all the conversation, even when it wasn't really necessary.

"You see, Amina, my sister asked Kayla over for dinner a few days ago, but then her son caught a really bad case of bronchitis, so she had to cancel. Kayla thinks she was just using her son's cold to get out of meeting her. She doesn't believe me when I say how badly Liz felt cancelling."

"She could have postponed the dinner. If she really wanted to meet me, she wouldn't have said, 'I'm sorry I have to cancel.' She would have said, 'I'm sorry I can't do it this week but as soon as Billy feels better, I'll give you a call.'" Kayla didn't sound angry, but her words made it clear she was more than just a little hurt.

Damon took her hand gently. "I swear to you that's what she's planning on doing. I swear." He turned towards Mazin. "Mazin, you know Liz. What do you think? Do you think she doesn't want Kayla over her house?"

Mazin had a friendly face. It was the type of face that was always smiling, even when he wasn't.

His eyes were brown, his hair was short, brown and freshly cut. And although she was sure it wasn't possible, she felt like she'd met him before. He was dressed similar to Damon; a button down shirt with beige pants. Amina felt a little sorry for Mazin— he looked very plain in comparison to his friend. When she first heard him speak, his voice had startled Amina a bit. It was very husky, almost harsh. It didn't match his smiling eyes. By this point in the conversation she had somewhat adjusted to it.

"Liz is very kind, Kayla. She was probably just worried about her son and that made her unable to choose her words correctly. I'm sure you'll really like her when you meet her. Don't judge her till then."

"Whatever," Kayla didn't mean to be rude, but she wanted to get the focus back on letting Mazin and Amina get to know each other. "So Mazin, you've told us about your work, and how you spend your leisure time. Why don't you tell us a bit about your family?"

His rough voice let out a laugh.

"I feel like I've been talking non-stop since we sat down. I've bored you with stories about work and my colleagues. I was hoping to hear a little about you, Amina."

She never liked being in the spotlight, but Mazin didn't make her feel self-conscious; actually, she felt very comfortable around him, as though she'd known him for years.

Amina talked a little about work and her family. Mazin was very surprised that she was an only child.

"That's not very common, especially not in our culture."

"After I was born, I think my parents began to understand why some couples prefer not to have kids." The group laughed softly.

"It definitely had its perks: I got my own room, my own toys, no hand-me-downs. On the other hand, of course, you're searching for anyone, or anything to play with. Kayla moved to the neighborhood when I was about 8 or 9, but before that my best friend was the neighbor's cat."

They laughed again. "That's so sad," Damon chuckled.

"Do you think being an only child made you closer with your parents?" Mazin asked.

Amina's eyes crinkled at the edges as she looked into the distance to find the answer.

"I'm not sure. I think it made them spoil me more... not with material things, but with attention. I think they only missed like 2 or 3 of my tennis matches, and I was only an exhibition player.

"The extra attention was sometimes suffocating, though. If I came home upset because of a fight with a friend or anything like that, it was very hard for them to leave me alone, to deal with it on my own.

"But I can't complain. I know God blessed me with parents who love me and want the best for me. Not everyone has that, so I thank God for it."

Amina's words brought sadness to Kayla's eyes. Kayla's mother had abandoned them when she was just a toddler. And after her father recovered from the years of depression that followed, he became more interested in drinking and entertaining women than showing affection to his kids.

Amina hadn't intended on touching the only chord that Kayla was sensitive about. As soon as she realized what she'd done, she felt horrible. She needed to talk with her friend alone, but how was that going to happen?

Mazin's voice broke the short silence and allowed Kayla back to the light-hearted spirit that surrounded the table. "Sometimes I used to think it would be nice to be an only child. My parents used to tell me stories about all the horrible things my siblings used to do to me. Once when I was about 5 or 6 months old, my sister stuck me in the cabinet under the kitchen sink. She gave me a toy to play with so I was quiet. Once they finally realized I was missing, it took my parents forever to find me. And if the toy she'd given me hadn't been playing music, it would have taken them even longer."

Amina appreciated Mazin's distraction even though she couldn't tell for sure if he'd noticed the slight change in Kayla. Maybe he wasn't that perceptive. But the smile he shot toward Kayla made her wonder.

He appears to be a very stable guy, Amina thought. *He has a good job, good relationship with his family, and he seems kind. He definitely has a good sense of humor. And, I need to be honest, I'm enjoying being here. But something's missing.* And she tried for the rest of the lunch to figure it out, but she was unsuccessful.

"Maybe you don't think he's attractive?" Kayla tried helping her out later that afternoon.

"Maybe. But he's not unattractive. I don't know. The weirdest thing is that the whole time I was sure I'd met him before, but I can't figure out where. It's driving me crazy."

"At one of the Egyptian dinners your parents host, maybe?"

"I don't think so." She thought for a minute. "No, definitely not."

A few minutes passed, and Amina decided to give up trying to figure out where she'd seen Mazin. She figured these things tend to uncover themselves if you don't think about them too much. But as she put one thought out of her mind, another crept in.

"Kayla, I'm sorry for upsetting you at lunch earlier. Sometimes I speak without thinking. Please don't be upset."

Kayla smiled. "What are you apologizing for? You didn't say anything wrong. Some people are born into caring families, and some aren't. That's just life."

"Well," Amina said. "I do wish you had gotten a better lot. But I have faith that, *in sha' Allah* God will make it up to you."

"What do you mean 'make it up to me'? If God didn't want this to be my life, then He would've given me a different life. That's if He exists, of course."

"The best way to experience the true pleasure of a reward is when the reward comes after hardship. God is testing you and will reward you for being patient with this family. He'll send you one whose love will compensate for the lack of love you've been enduring."

Kayla was doubtful, but she said nothing. Amina, on the other hand, needed to convince her friend.

"Can we talk about this for a minute? I mean, if you've had enough, I get that."

"No, I'm fine. Go ahead." Kayla could tell her friend had some point to make, and on the off-chance that maybe she was right, Kayla wanted to listen.

"How do you think your family situation affected your life? How would you be different if you'd had someone asking you where you're going and with whom, and when you'll be home?"

Kayla was quiet for a minute. She didn't see what point her friend was trying to make. But after she'd thought for a moment, she answered, "I wouldn't have made some of the mistakes I made when I was younger. Maybe I would've had a better group of friends. Maybe, if I'd found the encouragement, I would have gone to college. Maybe I would've gone out with guys that cared more about my mind than my body. Maybe."

"Maybe. And maybe you're so stubborn that even if you'd had the guidance, you wouldn't have followed it."

"What?" Kayla was offended.

"Are you forgetting that I was there? I was there when you dated— oh, what was his name, Brad or Brian. And I warned you he was bad news. I told you he didn't seem to respect you. And you ignored me. And the same goes for the majority of your past boyfriends.

"And I was there when you graduated high school and I begged you to think about college. 'Even a community college' I said, and you laughed and said, 'I'll learn more in the real world than at school.'"

Kayla was quiet. She remembered.

"Kayla," Amina's voice was softer now, she put her arm around her friend's shoulder. "I'm not saying all this as an 'I told you so.' I'm just trying to explain that the family that loves you and wants what's best for you has always been here. Just because we're not related by blood doesn't mean we're not family.

"And I'm not stupid; I know it's not the same as having your parents there when you need them. But my point is, God has already started to make that up to you. And he'll continue to do so. Just as He blessed me with you in my life to reward me for being an only child."

The friends smiled at each other, then Kayla was pensive again. "But why would God reward me? I'm not even sure I believe in Him."

"He'll reward you for two reasons: First, you could have easily turned out much worse given your situation. Drugs and alcohol are best friends of many people in your situation and you were strong enough to resist. And second, God will put things in your path to make finding him that much easier."

"Good things like you?" Kayla smiled at her friend.

"Of course. Could you ask for anything better?" Amina's chortle framed her joke. The girls hugged, and Kayla thought… *maybe.*

A few minutes later, Kayla said, "So what do you think of Damon. I mean, I know you guys met before, but I think you got to know each other better tonight."

"I think he cares about you a lot. He seems like a very smart, stable guy… very descent."

"Did I tell you he keeps trying to convince me to go to college?"

Amina was pleasantly surprised. "That's great. I hope you like him enough to at least consider."

Kayla shrugged. "I don't know. We'll see."

"You don't know if you'll go to school, or you don't know if you like him enough to consider his suggestions?"

Kayla smiled. "No, I definitely like him enough that his opinions matter to me. It's the first time I've felt such affection from someone. He's so kind and gentle with me. He's definitely one of the good ones."

"I think you're probably right," Amina agreed.

A few days later, Kayla called Amina to tell her that Mazin had asked for her number. "I didn't want to give it to him without checking with you first. So, should I give him your real number or give him a fake one?"

Amina laughed, but she didn't know how she felt about Mazin and she didn't want to lead him on. "I'm not sure, Kayla. I think he's a good guy. I'm comfortable around him and I enjoyed his company. But ya know? He hasn't crossed my mind once in the past three days. I just don't think I see him that way."

The girls were both pensive for a few moments.

"Well," Kayla broke the silence. "Do you want me to tell him that? What you just said?"

"I like being direct, but I think that may be too direct, don't you?"

"I can say that you're willing to get to know him but you don't want to feel pressured by any kind of commitment. If it works out great, if not, no hard feelings."

"That sounds good," Amina agreed. "I'm just worried that he won't believe you. I hope he's not the type of person who hears only what he wants to."

But he wasn't the type of person who heard only what he wanted. Mazin, too, was unsure about his feelings for Amina. He needed to get to know her better to make a sound judgment.

And that's exactly what he said to Amina's father when he picked up the phone. "*As salaamu alaikum,* Uncle Osman. My name is Mazin. I met your daughter at lunch with some friends a few days ago, and I would like to get to know her better… with your permission of course."

Osman was surprised. But he tried not to let his surprise distract him from what he needed to do. "I see. I see. And Mazin, what do you do for a living?"

Mazin answered Osman's question and continued, knowing he would want to know about his family as well. "I'm a dentist, sir. I'm currently working in my mentor's office, hoping to save enough money to buy it once he retires. I have a sister living close by; I'm close with her and her family. And my brother is living in Egypt with my parents. He graduated from business school and he's hoping to open his own business soon.

"My father is retired now but he was a chemistry professor. My mom teaches English to students in middle school."

Osman nodded. *Good social status,* he thought. "And do you consider your family to be religious?"

"*Alhamdu lillah.* My father prays many of the prayers at the mosque. And both my mother and sister have been *muhajabat* for some time now."

Osman expected more, so when Mazin stopped, he prompted him. "And what about you?"

"I do my best to pray the five prayers at their appropriate times. And I fast Ramadan, of course. I try to be charitable. *Alhamdu lillah.*"

"Uh huh. Uh huh. Very good. It sounds like you come from a very respectable family. But aren't you a little old for Amina? You know, she's only 23, and you sound like you could be my age."

Mazin's husky voice laughed, "My voice is much older than I am, sir. I'm only 28."

"I mean no disrespect, son, but... that's hard to believe."

Mazin laughed harder. "I swear, sir. Amina will tell you, I look just about my age. If you'd like to see me in person to be sure, I can come over whenever you wish. I just don't want a visit from me to be perceived incorrectly. I only met Amina once and we really need to get to know each other better, to see if we're comfortable together, before we decide if there should be a next step."

"So do you think you'll be DATING my daughter, then, until you decide? Well-" but Mazin cut Osman off before his anger could intensify.

"God forgive me, Uncle. God forgive me. I swear, that's not what I meant. I'd like to get to know her in whichever manner you feel comfortable. Home visits, phone calls... that is, of course, your decision."

"Of course that's my decision!" Osman declared. "You have permission to call her on the phone only."

"Thank you, sir." Mazin knew from Osman's voice that he had just made the worst possible first impression ever. He felt disappointed, but since there was nothing he could do about it, he just let it go.

"Can I speak to Amina, now, Uncle Osman?" he asked.

"No! She's not here."

"I'll try later then. Thank you again for your consent. *As salaamu alaikum.*"

"*Wa alaikum as salaam.*" Osman slammed the receiver back in its place.

"Amina! Amina!" he yelled.

She came running, out of breath, to the study. Her mother was right behind her. Neither of them had heard any part of the conversation and they were anxious about what had him so worked up.

"Who is this Mazin? How did you meet him?"

But it was Ruwayda who answered. She stepped toward her husband and spoke in a half-worried, half-angered tone. "I told you that Kayla was going to introduce Amina to a Muslim dentist named Mazin. I told you before Amina met him and I told you after she came home that he seemed like a decent man. I told you all this. Why are you acting like you've never heard the name before?"

Osman was quiet for a minute. He hadn't calmed down, he was thinking about what his wife had just said. She was right, of course she had told him. So why hadn't he remembered? When Ruwayda noticed the look of recognition on her husband's face, she continued, "If you would just pay attention when I speak, you'd save yourself the heart attack you almost had. And over what... over a Muslim man asking to get to know your daughter? How did you think she would eventually get married... someone would see her at a party or something, and want to marry her right away? Would you really do that... just trust her to someone who we don't know and who doesn't know us?"

At this, Osman looked up, shook his head, and gave his wife a look that said, 'woman, you don't know anything.' But he never opened his mouth to explain the almost misunderstanding that happened on the phone, so Ruwayda simply shook her head, waved her hand at him, and walked out the door. When Amina was sure her father didn't need to speak to her anymore, she went back to her room.

Mazin called Amina almost everyday for one month. They spoke about their families, their jobs, their friends. Amina tried to find out as much about him as she could. She was looking for something about him, something that could make her decide whether she wanted to continue this journey with him or end it.

She learned that he spent almost all of his free time at home. He didn't like going to the movies: "Their chairs are too uncomfortable. And somehow I always get stuck behind someone with a big head or big hair so I end up leaving the theater with a kink in my neck from leaning my head to the side for two hours."

And he didn't like to eat out: "Home cooked food is so much better than anything I've ever had out."

"But some restaurants have really great chefs. Maybe you just haven't been going to the right places?" Amina argued.

He was definitely polite. "Maybe."

He didn't like walking around the mall: "I only go to the mall if there's something I need to buy. In which case I go in, grab it and leave. I see no point in wasting time 'window-shopping,' as they say."

Nor did he like relaxing at the park: "If I can lie down in my house, on my comfortable clean couch, why go to a park to lie on a blanket on the cold, hard ground?"

They were all things Amina disagreed with. And she let him know it, of course. But some people are just like that, they don't like to go out. And most of the Arab men she knew were exactly like that, so she pretty much expected it. These were all minor points that she couldn't hold against anyone. She definitely couldn't use them to help sway her opinion of him.

Kayla suggested maybe she should see him again. "Maybe if you see who's talking, that will influence you— one way or the other."

"Maybe. But I can't be the one to ask to see him... he'll take that the wrong way for sure. And on top of that, he'll think I don't know how to conduct myself in a proper Islamic manner."

She was quiet for a few seconds, then she continued, "And I'm pretty certain he won't suggest it. Something about how my dad reacted to his first phone call tells me he wouldn't dare ask to see me in person." There was just no way of knowing if Kayla's suggestion would have worked.

Amina was undecided. She knew that eventually she would have to decide, and this not knowing made her tense. She prayed to God for guidance, but she received no answers.

A few days later she and Kayla decided to go out for lunch. Amina sat in the passenger's seat as Kayla pulled out of the parking lot to her apartment building.

"Oh, ya know what? I forgot my wallet. I'll be right back." Kayla ran back into her place and re-appeared a few short minutes later.

Amina noticed there was nothing in her hand. "Where's your wallet?"

"What? Oh, I remembered I have it in my purse after all." She wasn't sure, but she thought that Amina bought it.

After they finally found a song worth listening to, Kayla began to speak. "So, I think things with Damon are getting pretty serious. He keeps dropping hints that he wants us to move in together."

"Wow... that's great." But Amina wasn't getting a happy vibe from Kayla. "Isn't that great?"

"It's fast, is what it is. It's too fast. I mean, maybe after a year of knowing someone, that would seem like the next step... but three months is such a short period of time."

Three months is a short period of time. Amina repeated the sentence, over and over. Was it? Was it an inadequate amount of time to determine if this person would respect you, treat you kindly, and always choose what was in your best interest? Was it?

Kayla's voice snapped Amina back to the conversation, "Amina! Where did you go?"

"Sorry, I was just thinking. Did you say something?"

"I said it's a little strange to me that you feel like you should know how you feel about Mazin over just one month... and a month's worth of **only** phone calls. I've been with Damon for three months, I've seen him, oh, probably 60 days out of the 90, and I don't feel like it's enough."

"But is it that you don't feel like it's enough, or that you're scared to decide?"

Kayla pulled into the parking spot, turned off the engine, and stared at the steering wheel.

"Are you saying that I know what I want, I'm just too scared to face it?"

"I'm saying that's a possibility. Don't you know how you feel about Damon? Don't you know how he feels about you?"

Kayla thought for a moment, but Amina cut her off before she could begin. "Hasn't he always shown you respect? Have you ever witnessed him being disrespectful of anyone?"

"The problem is," Kayla answered. "Just because I haven't seen it so far, doesn't necessarily mean it doesn't exist within him."

"Sure. You're right. But if he were the type of person who is disrespectful or mean or violent, don't you thing you would have seen something to tip you off? Or at least had some kind of feeling about it?"

Kayla was still weary. "He could be purposely hiding it."

Amina knew her friend was right, but she also knew that Kayla's issues with moving forward with Damon had more to do with a fear of commitment than a fear that he had a malicious side.

"But if he is purposely hiding it, then he's not going to let you see it until he wants you to. So whether you move forward now or ten years from now, that's not going to change." She paused for a few seconds.

"I have a good feeling about Damon, Kayla. And, for the most part, I'm pretty good at figuring people out. He's one of the good ones. Don't let your fears of commitment paralyze you from accepting what could very well be one of God's blessings."

Kayla looked up at her friend, sadness and worry in her eyes. "I just wouldn't be able to handle it if someone else I love abandoned me, and I don't want to be the one who hurts someone else like that. I don't want to do to him what my mom did to us."

Amina was quiet for a moment. "There are no guarantees in life. But if you don't take any risks, you miss out on a lot of life's pleasures. You are not your mother. You will not hurt him like she hurt you, because you felt that pain, and you'll protect those you love from it. Your love is stronger than that. Trust it. I do."

They were quiet for a few minutes, then Amina grabbed her purse and got out of the car; Kayla followed suit. Amina was surprised to hear Kayla say to the hostess, "We're supposed to be meeting our friends here; Damon is the name."

As the hostess picked up two menus, Amina whispered, "Kayla, what's going on?"

"I knew you wouldn't go for it and I couldn't think of any other way to get you two together. Please don't be mad." As the girls followed the hostess to their table, Amina looked up and finally understood what Kayla had said. Mazin was even more surprised than she.

"Amina! Kayla! What a coincidence!"

"It's not really a coincidence," Damon confessed. "Kayla called me and asked if we could all meet for lunch. But we knew neither of you would be comfortable coming if you knew, so we kept it a surprise."

"I see," Mazin looked hesitant. "Well, I really appreciate what you guys were trying to do. But I can't disrespect Mr. Abdul Mu'min's wishes. I just asked him a few days ago if it would be okay for me to take Amina to lunch and he refused.

"So, like I said, thank you. But I need to leave. Amina it was very nice to see you again and next time it will be for much longer, *in sha' Allah.*"

Then he left.

Kayla was disappointed by Mazin's reaction. "That was weird. Sorry it didn't work, Amina."

Amina just smiled. But on the inside she felt a small sense of resolution; she had finally encountered her deciding factor.

"Damon, would you mind driving Kayla home— that's if I can borrow your car." She looked at Kayla, then back to Damon. "I have some things at home that I need to do."

"Well, do them after lunch," Damon said.

Amina tried to think of the most polite way to say it. "I appreciate the invitation, Damon. But to be honest, I don't want to be the third wheel."

Then Damon understood, "Oh. Then I'll leave. You were planning on having lunch with Kayla, please don't let me ruin it for you."

He started to get up, but Amina stopped him, "Please, Damon. I think you and Kayla could use the time to talk. And I really should get back."

"Well," Kayla's tone was light and sarcastic. "It's nice to feel so loved, that neither my boyfriend nor my best friend want to stick around to have lunch with me.

"But fight over who gets to leave while I use the bathroom. I'll be right back."

Once Kayla had disappeared into the ladies room, Damon became more serious.

"I'm glad I have a few minutes alone with you. I wanted to tell you something.

"I don't know if Kayla mentioned anything, but I've been giving her hints that I want to move in with her... but that's just a disguise to throw her off. I'm planning on proposing this week." He took a small box from his pocket and opened it. "Do you think she'll like it?"

The ring inside was a gorgeous princess cut diamond laid in platinum.

"Beautiful is an understatement. It's blinding. Put it away before it does any permanent damage." Amina giggled.

Damon placed the box safely in his pocket, and Amina continued, "I love that you love her so much. To answer your question, she will love the ring. But you need to know that Kayla is equally afraid of you abandoning her as she is that she'll leave you. You need to help her resolve those abandonment issues first— a proposal might scare her off. It might be too much for her right now."

"What may be too much for me right now?" Kayla asked as she sat back down.

Damon didn't even miss a beat. "I was telling Amina that I think you did yourself a big disservice by not going to school, and I think you should enroll for next term. She said a full college schedule might be too much right now, but maybe you could take a few courses."

Wow, Amina thought, *he's good.* But neither her words nor her expression betrayed their secret.

"Taking some courses will get you ready to take on a full schedule the following term... or whenever."

"That's a good idea," Kayla said. "I'll give that some thought." As she fidgeted with her menu, she didn't notice the wink Damon gave Amina.

Chapter 18

RUWAYDA WAS CURIOUS about Amina's feelings towards Mazin. As they sat in the kitchen, each reading her own magazine and nibbling on some lunch, Ruwayda tried to be casual.

"So, Amina, you never told me what you think of Mazin. Are the two of you still in touch?"

Amina knew that eventually she would have to answer all these questions, and she did so now with a clear conscience but an ambivalent heart. "He's a very decent man, mama. He talks about his family a lot and how he wishes he could see his parents more often.

"But for the longest time I couldn't decide how I **felt** about him. I think I still don't know, not really. But he did something the other day that really affected me; I got a chance to see a piece of his character that I wouldn't have otherwise gotten to see, except maybe if we were completely alone.

"And it showed me how much he respects me and my family. And it increased my respect for him and my trust in him one hundred percent."

Ruwayda had a hard time extracting what she wanted to know from what her daughter had just said. She couldn't. She had no choice but to be more direct.

"I understand that you respect him, Amina. But we meet many people in our lives that we respect. What I want to know is if he asks to move forward, if he asks for an engagement, will you accept?"

Amina was quiet for a few seconds. Her answer came out just louder than a whisper, "Yes, I'll accept."

She had found in Mazin a man who would respect her and treat her kindly. She could trust him with herself. These were all qualities that, together, outweighed the fact that she didn't love him. *Maybe love will come later.*

Now her decision was out in the open. She had thought that surely with a decision— one way or the other— would come a sense of relief. She waited for the relief. She expected it when her father asked her the same questions her mother had. But it didn't come. She expected it when Mazin, finally obtaining permission from Osman to meet his daughter for lunch, told her that he'd enjoyed getting to know her the past month. He said he recognized in her qualities that would make her a good wife— he noticed her kindness, her honesty, her respect for her parents, her faith. He said he found in her all he was looking for. Then he asked her if she would allow him to pay a visit to her family. And when she said, "yes," relief still didn't come.

After a couple of days, she figured out why she didn't feel relieved; how could she feel relieved when she still carried a heavy burden on her shoulders— a burden of telling a truth, one that happened to her, but which many people may blame her for? Amina knew she would continue to feel its weight until she could release the words. But she wasn't ready to do that, yet.

Mazin had called her father and asked permission to visit the house. Osman's tone this time was jovial. "You're welcome here whenever you wish."

"If we say next Saturday, is that okay?"

"Yes, that's fine," Osman agreed. "I look forward to finally meeting you."

Amina couldn't get over the difference in her father from this phone call to their first. Ruwayda saw her daughter's confusion in the look she gave her father as he spoke on the phone.

"The situation is totally different," Ruwayda answered without waiting for the question. "Because this time he knows Mazin's serious. In their first conversation, Mazin gave your dad the impression that he might be just having fun— playing with our honor and our emotions."

Ruwayda planned all week for Mazin's visit. She planned the menu and prepared whatever could be prepared before hand. There would be stuffed pigeon and stuffed grape leaves, pasta with béchamel sauce and beef piccata with Amina's delicious mushroom sauce.

Amina tried to help her mother as much as she could. She was her mother's sous-chef in the kitchen, helping with the preparations and making the salad. She also cleaned the house and ordered a bouquet of flowers for the centerpiece.

But when Saturday came, Mazin didn't visit the Abdul Mu'min household.

"Amina, I'm very sorry but I won't be able to come today. I know this is extremely unacceptable, but believe me, it's out of my control; my sister became very sick over night and she's in the hospital. I hope you understand." His voice was solemn and apologetic.

Amina wasn't sure how to answer. There was so much going through her mind— how much time, energy and money had been spent on the day, all down the drain. At the same time, he obviously needed to be with his family, she didn't want to be so self-centered that she was unsympathetic to their situation. "I'm sorry to hear that," Amina said sincerely after a few short seconds. "Is there anything we can do for your family?"

"Thank you so much, Amina. I appreciate that. But I really should apologize to your dad. Is he available?"

Amina called her father and a few minutes later, Osman was already off the phone. He was obviously upset; Amina just couldn't tell if it was because Mazin had cancelled or because of the reason that made him cancel. The next day, Amina got her answer.

She walked into the den just as Osman stood from his chair, phone to his ear.

"*As salaamu alaikum*, Mazin. How are you and how is your sister today?"

Pause.

"Good, *alhamdu lillah*. Tell her she needs to take better care of herself."

Pause.

"Don't be silly, Mazin. There's no reason to apologize; your family should always come first."

Pause.

"We can talk about that once your sister's out of the hospital and you're assured that she's one hundred percent back to her normal self."

Pause.

"*In sha' Allah. As salaamu alaikum*, Mazin."

When Osman hung up, Amina waited for a recap. When it didn't come she finally said, "Baba, what did Mazin say? Is his sister still in the hospital?"

"She's getting out tomorrow, *in sha' Allah*."

He just went back to reading the newspaper.

"Well, did he say what was wrong with her?"

Osman answered without removing his eyes from the paper. "He said it was a moderate case of dehydration."

She wanted to ask about everything Mazin had said, but speaking to her dad now was like pulling teeth, so she just gave up.

Later that night Kayla called Amina to see how things had gone.

"Mazin didn't come. He called and canceled this morning because his sister was admitted to the hospital."

"Oh... that's too bad."

They were both quiet for a moment.

"Kayla, do you think this was a sign? I mean, do you think this was God's way of telling me not to move forward with this?"

"Don't read too much into it, Amina. Shit happens all the time and it doesn't stop to ask if there's a special occasion or special circumstances going on. Just leave it at that."

Maybe... but still?

That night Amina had a familiar dream. She was walking along the docks, and someone— a man with no face— called to her and said, "Amina. Look, I've caught so many fish. Look!" But when she looked, his basket was empty. She kept walking until a smiling man— an eyeless, nose-less smiling man— gestured to her to sit beside him. His basket was overflowing with fish. She sat down and looked back up at him. His eyes and nose were beginning to come into view...

BEEP! BEEP! BEEP! BEEP!

The alarm startled her awake. But the dream was still with her. *Did I see his face before the alarm? Did I?* Something inside of her needed to know. But she was left disappointed.

That feeling of disappointment and frustration of not knowing stayed with her through most of her work day.

A couple of hours before she was to leave, the receptionist called to inform her that she had a guest.

A guest? Who could possibly want to visit me at work?

As she changed out of her lab coat and climbed the stairs to the reception area, she went through all the possibilities.

But when she opened the door to the lobby, what she saw in front of her was impossible. There was no way that the person who her eyes were seeing was really standing there.

Chapter 19

HE WAS SMILING AT HER. It wasn't an evil smile, but that's what Amina saw.

"*As salaamu alaikum,* Amina. How are you?"

She knew her mind couldn't possibly be tricking her ears into hearing his voice, too. It really was him.

His voice made her whole body shake. When she noticed everyone's stares, she tried to control herself. His face became most serious. "I know you didn't expect to see me again, but I need to talk to you."

Hearing Rami's voice again sent her body back to shaking.

"Maybe you'll be more comfortable speaking in the cafeteria. Amina, go on and take your guest down there." The receptionist's voice seemed to come from somewhere far away, far beyond this nightmare, but she obeyed.

Without saying anything, she turned and headed for the cafeteria. Rami followed her.

Should I run? But to where? Should I tell security? But what could I say? This isn't real. Wake up! Wake up, Amina! You're dreaming!

She dug her thumbnail into her arm to check, and the sting was a disappointing shock to the reality she was in. Her heart pounded so loudly in her hears that she didn't hear Robert's greeting as she passed him in the hall.

When they got to the cafeteria, Amina looked around, then sat down at the table occupied by the most people.

Rami understood. "Amina, I'm not here to hurt you," he whispered. "I just want to... I just need to ask for your forgiveness. I know that what I did to you was the worst thing a person could do to another. I know I was wrong. I wish I could go back and stop myself... make it not happen. When I think of what I did, I feel like I'm remembering someone else's memories. That wasn't me. I am so very sorry for hurting you... please forgive me."

But Amina didn't hear everything Rami had just said; as he began talking, Amina's mind wandered to the last time she'd seen him. She remembered every detail, as though it were all happening to her again.

She felt his tight grip on her, she felt him tear off her clothes.

"NO!" Her voice had never been louder. The word came out as she jumped from her chair, then ran out the door, dozens of eyes following her.

She ran into the lab, grabbed her jacket and purse and left.

Running to her car she fumbled inside her bag for the keys. Suddenly she felt someone's presence behind her. Turning slowly, she saw her attacker.

"If you take one step closer I will scream so loud that the people in the next state will hear!"

He put his hands up in a defensive pose and took a step back. He was about to speak but she cut him off.

"Do not try to see me again. If you do, I **will** torture you... and God will not punish me for what I do to you!" Her voice was loud, firm and promising.

Finally, the key slid in the lock, the door opened and she sped away.

Her body was still shaking. It was a mixture of fear, sadness, but mostly anger. Anger at what Rami had put her through two years before, anger at having to see him again, and anger that she hadn't taken her revenge right there. She was mostly angry that she hadn't done any of the things that her mind had planned all those months ago in case he returned. She hadn't kneed him in the groin over and over until even the thought of children was impossible for him. She hadn't slid a knife across every inch of his face leaving him as deformed on the outside as he'd made her feel on the inside. She hadn't spit on his face and told him that he was a disgrace to masculinity and to mankind.

After driving a few blocks, she pulled into the parking lot of a drive-thru restaurant, turned off the ignition, and cried. She cried as though she'd just been raped. She cried, pounded on the steering wheel, and screamed. Many moments later, her eyes were finally dry, but, along with her fists and palms, red and throbbing.

She asked God's forgiveness and repeated the last two chapters of the Qur'an a few times. Then she asked Him to give her strength when she needed it, patience, and... she forced herself to say it, though she couldn't really feel it in her heart... forgiveness.

She started the car, pressed play to turn on the Qur'an tape, then drove home slowly.

By the time she arrived home, the redness in her eyes had reduced a bit and only her hands were left shaking. She went straight to her room and climbed into her bed, feeling a small sense of security wrapped in her comforter. She lay there, reciting verses from the Qur'an and talking to God.

Oh, God. I know you do everything for a reason… I want to understand the reason for this. I want to understand.

Is it to tell me I must be stronger? That I shouldn't let anyone infringe on my rights and on my soul and get away with it? Do I need to take my revenge… whether by my own hand or legally?

Or are You just telling me I can't escape my past? No matter how far I think it is, it's never far enough? But I think… I thought I knew that.

Or do You want me to forgive? You are the Most Forgiving. But me… I'm only human. I'm not strong enough.

Oh God. Help me to understand.

The knock at her door startled her. She didn't answer.

"Amina," Ruwayda said softly as she slowly opened the door.

"Yeah, mama?"

Ruwayda walked over to her daughter. "What's wrong? Why are you home from work early? And why are you in bed?"

"I just didn't feel well. I think I need to rest."

Ruwayda put the back of her hand to her daughter's forehead. "You don't have a fever. What are you feeling?"

"I'm just exhausted and kind of shaky. I think it's just a bug that'll pass if I get some sleep."

"Do you want anything? Can I bring your dinner or something warm for you to drink?"

"Mama, I kind of feel like I'm going to throw up, so I'm not going to eat anything. If I start to get hungry later I'll let you know."

Ruwayda smiled at her daughter, kissed her forehead and left. When she got to her room, Ruwayda sat on her bed and put her face in her hands.

She knew her daughter well enough to know she was not ill. Amina didn't know she knew her that well, but she did. It saddened Ruwayda that Amina wasn't sharing with her whatever had upset her so much that she'd come home and gotten straight into bed.

To herself she guessed: *Maybe something happened at work with one of her bosses; maybe Mazin had called her and upset her somehow.* Lots of maybes, but she'd never guess correctly, and she hated seeing her daughter hurt and not giving her the opportunity to help.

She thought about pushing the issue, going back into her room and telling Amina that she could confide in her mother and that if she did, her burden would be split. And Ruwayda made it as far as her own bedroom door, then she turned back around and sat on the bed again. If Amina had wanted to share her problem, she would have done it before. She was obviously upset by something, but Ruwayda would have to respect that she didn't want to share her burden now. *Maybe she'll come to me later,* Ruwayda comforted herself as she got up and went to the kitchen to prepare dinner.

But Amina had no intention of telling anyone what had happened that day. She considered Rami a closed chapter in her life and would refuse to reopen that chapter simply because he tried to contact her. She woke up the next morning determined to forget having seen Rami the day before. She went about her routine as though nothing had shaken it, and all her colleagues who had heard her yell at the strange man were cordial enough to pretend they hadn't noticed.

Ruwayda was the only one still waiting for an explanation. She wanted her daughter to confide in her. Every chance she got, she smiled at her, almost stared, hoping that Amina would tell her what had upset her.

The following day she finally convinced herself that Amina was over whatever had shaken her, and there was no reason to wait for an explanation because the issue was clearly over.

A few days later Amina answered the phone and heard a cheerful Layal on the other side.

"I have some news. I'm engaged!"

"Oh, Layal. That's great! Is it the same guy you told me about?"

"Yeah. He's really great. You'll get to meet him at Sahar's wedding. Did you receive the invitation, yet? Mine came a couple of days ago."

"No actually, I don't think I have. I'll check with my parents—sometimes my mail gets shoved under the couch cushions."

The girls laughed. Amina continued, "But that's awesome. Congratulations! May God always do what's best for you and keep you happy and healthy."

"Thank you, Amina. And may He bless you always, as well."

"So are you guys going to have an engagement party?"

"No... I think it's a lot of money and energy to pre-celebrate...

we're gonna save it for the wedding. He says he's ready to get married now, and although I'm sure he's the one I want, I want a few months to sort of get used to the idea. Plus, it's going to take just about that long to plan a wedding, even a small one."

"You said 'a few months'… does that mean you have a date set?"

"Well, not a date, but a month… I'm trying to book a hall for sometime in August."

"May God do what's best for you, *in sha' Allah.*"

The next day Mazin called Amina and apologized again for having cancelled before.

"If your mom's anything like mine she probably spent days in the kitchen preparing for my visit. I'm very sorry for all the inconvenience."

"Don't apologize, Mazin. You had to be with your family. Is your sister better now?"

"Yes, she's much better, *alhamdu lillah.* She just doesn't take care of herself. She spends so much time and energy caring for the kids and not enough caring for herself. I keep telling her to hire a nanny, even part time, to give her a few free hours a day. After what happened, she's finally beginning to give it some serious consideration."

"That's good."

"So I was hoping I could come over this Saturday to meet with your family. I'm going to speak with your father about it, but I wanted to make sure you wouldn't have any objections, first."

"Objections?" Amina repeated. "No… no objections. Saturday's fine. Should I put my dad on the phone?"

"Yes, please. And Amina… thank you for being so understanding. I appreciate it."

Osman happily agreed to welcome Mazin on Saturday, and once again Ruwayda started preparations.

Amina wanted to feel excited, but she didn't. She kept thinking that Mazin's being unable to visit the week before was some kind of a sign. *Maybe God was telling me not to rush it… that I shouldn't just settle. That maybe the man of my dreams does exist and somehow he will find me. Maybe.*

And again, maybe Kayla's right. Sometimes shit happens and you just can't read too much into it.

She was torn, but her internal confusion was well hidden behind her assisting her mother with the preparations.

On Saturday morning a strange sound woke Amina. When she was finally alert, she noticed that it hadn't been her alarm that had woken her. *Did I make up that sound? Was I dreaming?* But it was much later than she usually slept. She'd felt strange for the past couple of days, but the bug she kept expecting never came. She was clearly more tired than usual, but she assigned it to all the extra work she was doing helping her mom prepare the house for Mazin's visit.

When she finally got out of bed, she heard voices coming from downstairs. Her parents were talking— arguing?— with someone. A man. She couldn't make out what they were saying. She got out of bed, washed up and got dressed.

The conversation that Amina couldn't decipher had begun a few minutes before when the doorbell rang and Osman answered.

"*As salaamu alaikum*, Uncle. I'm a friend of Amina's from college, and I was hoping I could speak with you for a few moments."

The man seemed polite enough, so Osman welcomed him downstairs and asked his wife to prepare tea for them.

"Have a seat, son. What can I do for you? Sorry... did you say your name?"

He didn't want to start by saying his name. This wouldn't work if he did.

"Uncle Osman, I met your daughter at school and we were all part of the same group of friends for three years. And during that time I got to know Amina very well. She's very honest and smart and kind.

"But before I left school, I betrayed her. And I'm here now to fix my mistake. I hope that you can forgive me, and to prove my sincerity, I would like to ask you for Amina's hand in marriage." His voice was shaking, but he got through the whole speech.

Osman's mind was trying to register everything it had heard. *'I would like to ask for Amina's hand in marriage.' That's straight forward enough. But....*

"Who did you say you are?"

This time he had no choice, there was no escaping the name that would hold him prisoner.

"Rami. My name is Rami, Uncle." he muttered.

Rami? Rami? Why is that name familiar? Ram...

And suddenly his mind re-wound almost two years to a scene with him seated at the kitchen table and Amina talking, telling him and Ruwayda that one of the boys she'd considered a brother had raped her.

She had been raped by a boy named...

"Rami!" The anger of that day came back to him ten fold. Now the predator was standing in front of him, within his reach. Osman jumped up and grabbed him by the shirt just as Ruwayda walked in. She dropped the tray, spilling both cups of tea, and ran to put herself between her husband and this stranger that Osman was about to strangle.

"Osman! Osman! What's going on? Stop! He's a guest in your house! Osman!" Ruwayda pushed her husband away, and he let himself be pushed lest he kill the stranger with his bare hands.

"He's no guest, Ruwayda. This is your daughter's rapist!"

The last sentence echoed over and over in Ruwayda's ears. When it finally registered, she searched all around her looking for something she knew wasn't far away. *Where did I drop that knife?*

"Tant, Uncle... I promise you I've come to ask for forgiveness. I know I don't deserve it. I deserve every horrible punishment you could give me." Osman didn't believe them, but Rami's tears were sincere. "And I'm willing to take it. But I need you to know that I did come here with the intention of making things right. I want to give you back the honor I stole."

"What you stole can never be given back! And we are, have always been, and will continue to be honorable despite your filthy presence in our past!" Osman shot the words at him wishing they were real bullets.

Ruwayda was still searching. I *think I left it on the counter.* She walked into the kitchen and picked up the largest knife she could find. *There it is.*

Amina entered the kitchen just in time to see her mother turn around, holding the knife tightly in her fist. Her mother's eyes seemed glazed over.

"Mama. Mama. What's going on?"

"Amina." Ruwayda smiled at her daughter as she whispered her name and stroked her cheek. "I'm about to make everything right."

She intended to walk past her daughter, but Amina grabbed her arm. "Mama. Where are you going with the knife? Put it down, Mama." Amina didn't know what was going on, but her mother's behavior alarmed her. As she managed to free the weapon from her mother's grip she heard a voice coming from the other room. She didn't have time to put the knife down, she ran to see if her ears were deceiving her.

"I'm sorry. I'm so very sorry for what I did to Amina... to your family. But I want to fix my mistake."

Amina entered just then, but the tears in his eyes made it hard for Rami to see the figure in the doorway.

"I know I don't deserve this chance. But I have hope you'll give it to me. I need your forgiveness... Amina's forgiveness."

"Didn't I tell you to leave me alone? Why do you keep trying to torture me?!"

She moved slowly toward him, not conscience that she was waving the knife at him. He didn't move back; he simply hung his head and waited.

Osman, whose entire body felt like it was on fire and whose head was bright red, had been pacing back and forth, wringing his hands to distract them from doing what they wanted to do. When he saw his daughter approach Rami, he wanted to see her take her revenge... he wanted her to destroy the person who had ruined so much of her life. But he was her father... he needed to protect her first. He took the knife from his daughter and held her back. Amina struggled... she tried to get free. God had given her another opportunity to make Rami pay for what he'd done to her, and she wanted to take advantage of it. This was the perfect place, with her parents watching out for her, she could injure him anyway she wanted without once worrying that any stab he took would find it's mark. She fought her father with all her might.

"Rami, I'm going to give you thirty seconds to disappear. After that time, I can not guarantee your safety." Osman's voice was firm but taunting.

Rami lifted his head and looked into Amina's eyes. All he could see was hatred. He was not going to get what he'd gone looking for.

Just as the door closed behind Rami, Osman and Amina heard a loud thud come from the kitchen.

Chapter 20

A FEW HOURS LATER AMINA was on the phone with Mazin. "I'm sorry to do this so last minute, Mazin, but today's not going to work out. My mother fainted suddenly and we had to take her to the hospital. I'm calling you from the lobby."

"Oh, Amina. I'm so sorry to hear that. *Alf salaama* for your mother. Is it very serious? Is there anything I can do?"

Amina chose not to answer the first question; she simply didn't know. "Thank you, but no, there's nothing we need."

"Well, please keep me updated. And let me know if there's anything I can do. Is your father available? I'd like to tell him that my prayers are with your family for your mother's recovery."

"I'll pass on the message, although I'm sure he already knows. He's in with my mom now and I don't think he wants to be disturbed."

"*In sha' Allah* she will be healthier than she was before."

"Ameen. Thank you, Mazin. *As salaamu alaikum.*"

"*Wa alaikum as salaam.*" His confused, concerned, disappointed voice held many of the emotions Amina was feeling about her mother's collapse.

After Rami left, Osman and Amina had run to the kitchen to find Ruwayda sprawled on the floor. She was breathing, but unconscious. When they couldn't revive her after a few minutes, Amina called an ambulance and they rushed her to the hospital. On their way Ruwayda opened her eyes, but when Amina asked her how she was feeling, she didn't answer. Her eyes focused on her daughter, but her lips didn't move. When Amina held her hand, it remained limp.

The admitting doctors did a series of tests to determine the cause of Ruwayda's collapse. When they didn't find anything physically wrong, they asked about what had happened just before she fainted.

"We encountered someone who had hurt my daughter in the past," Osman answered hesitantly. He didn't want to tell them about her grabbing the knife and wanting to destroy the predator. At the same time, he needed to give them enough information to correctly diagnose her. "She became very angry. Then her behavior was strange."

"Strange how?" the doctor asked.

"She became... sort of disoriented. At the same time she showed signs of violent behavior."

The doctor nodded. After a few minutes of deliberating with his colleagues and checking Ruwayda again and again, he came back and explained that Ruwayda seemed to be in a state of mental shock; that her collapse was due to mental distress, not physical illness. She had banged her head slightly when she'd fallen, but that resulted in no more than a small bump that would heal in a few days. They had her transferred to the psychiatric ward.

The doctors there also asked Osman what had happened and tried to get Ruwayda to respond verbally. After their examination, they told Osman and Amina that Ruwayda's recovery would be dependent on her reaction to the medications and therapy. But mostly, it would be dependent on her own will to recover.

Amina and Osman barely left Ruwayda's side. They took turns reading aloud from the Qur'an. They tried to get Ruwayda to recite with them the verses she had memorized, but she refused to speak.

The first night Amina told her father that she wanted to spend the night with her mom, but Osman insisted that Amina sleep in her own bed at home. Amina thought he was doing it for her, that he wanted her to be comfortable and he figured she would only be able to sleep at home. But in truth, Osman didn't want to leave; he needed to be as close to his wife as possible. Maybe he didn't show it, but he loved his wife very much. They had been together about thirty years, and it pained him to think that his wife was in such distress. He wanted to do anything to get Ruwayda healthy again.

After the first 24 hours, Ruwayda seemed to begin to awaken from her stupor. She was confused, not sure where she was or why, but she began to speak. The doctors had warned Osman and Amina not to remind her of the trigger that had sent her to the hospital. They said she wouldn't have a clear memory of it, if she remembered it at all. But even while she was awake, she was withdrawn, not really talking to Osman or Amina except to answer questions about whether or not she was hungry or needed anything.

A couple of days later she began to have nightmares— nightmares that started with the day Amina told her she'd been raped. And the nightmares made it difficult for her to sleep. All those factors worked as a breeding field for anger. Ruwayda snapped at every little thing, from keeping the blinds down in her room, to the awful taste of the hospital food.

The doctors continued to assure them that with enough rest, some short term medications and therapy, she would eventually be able to leave the hospital and go back to her life.

"How long, doctor? I know you can't give me an exact date. I'm just looking for an estimate." Osman was eager to have his wife home and this entire experience behind them.

"Mr. Abdul Mu'min, I can't even give you an estimate... every case is different. Some patients don't appear to make any progress for a week or two, then they have a very sudden, full recovery. And some patients show early signs of recovery, but it's much more gradual so it can take longer. It all depends on-"

Osman cut him off. "But we're talking weeks, right? So far I've only heard you say weeks."

The doctor sighed. "I know you want to be assured that your wife's stay here won't prolong. I can't guarantee that. We're doing everything we can so that her condition doesn't progress into something worse and more long term. We have every reason to believe this will have been a short term condition in your wife's life, but like I said, every patient is different. And no two recoveries follow the same pattern or time frame."

The doctor excused himself, leaving Osman no more comforted about his wife's well-being than he was before their conversation.

Despite the excessive anger her mother had been exhibiting, Amina was beginning to feel hopeful that her mom would soon be back to normal. It wasn't based on anything she saw; in fact, her feeling surprised her when it came. All the evidence— her mother's outbursts, her lack of sleep and constant nightmares— suggested that this would take longer than just a few days or even a few weeks. But something within her felt a small sense of hope that all the prayers she and her father had been making for her mother would soon be answered.

But then, a couple of days after Ruwayda began to speak, something happened to shake that hope. Amina started to notice that her mother seemed to be avoiding her. Ruwayda was speaking more now, and she held short conversations with Osman or the nurses. But whenever Amina started to talk to her, Ruwayda always said she was tired and needed her sleep. The first couple of times it happened, Amina didn't notice the pattern. Then one day, she started to tell her mother something and Ruwayda cut her off, "I'm tired. Not now, Amina." Then she turned onto her side in the bed and pulled the covers as far up as they would go. A few minutes later Amina assumed her mom had fallen asleep, so she got up to get a drink from the vending machine in the hallway. When she returned, her father was talking to her mother, and she seemed wide awake and interested in Osman's story. Amina waited for her father to finish before she began to speak, but Ruwayda stopped her again, claiming she needed some rest.

The same thing happened three days in a row. When Amina confided in Kayla, she couldn't find any words to comfort her friend.

"She's been through a lot these past few days, Amina. Maybe she just needs a rest from everything, even talking and listening."

"But she talks and listens to other people. It's just me that she does this with."

Kayla had nothing. She was quiet for a few minutes, then she asked, "Have you talked to the doctors about it?"

"What would I say? 'My mom's not taking to me?' It sounds ridiculous."

"You can say that she's exhibiting some behavior that is unlike her norm. When they ask 'like what' then you give them detailed examples. You don't just say she's not talking to you, but you describe how, like you just did with me. And about her anger issues, don't just say 'she's much more angry than normal', but 'she freaks out about every little thing from the food being too cold to the shower being too hot.'"

"Do you really think they'll have an explanation?"

"If they don't, they need to know that these things are happening. It might help them make her treatments more effective."

Amina thought about Kayla's suggestions. She figured it couldn't hurt to tell the doctors, but before she did, she went to her father.

"Amina, what's so important that you took me away from your mother? You know she needs us beside her now."

"I know, baba. This will only take a minute. I just wanted to ask you if you've noticed any changes— besides the anger— in mama's behavior. Have you noticed how she keeps avoiding me? She always says she's tired whenever I try to talk to her about anything."

Osman had noticed. Actually, he had noticed more than Amina; Amina still hadn't figured out that Ruwayda hadn't looked at her in three days.

At first it had confused him; Ruwayda valued nothing more in her life than her daughter. She would face any danger for her. But then he began to understand.

"I think she really is tired, Amina. You just catch her at times when she's just taken her medication or she's exhausted from therapy."

"I don't think so, baba. I'm going to ask the doctors about it."

Osman almost jumped out of his seat, "No, no. No, Amina. I'm sure it's nothing. Maybe our being here all day and all night is having a toll on her. We might be keeping her up or busy when she should be resting. Try to cut back some of the hours you spend here. You'll see… it'll make a difference."

Amina wasn't convinced by her father's words, but she would respect the fact that he didn't want her to ask the doctors. *Maybe it's just temporary. I'll leave her alone for a day or two and see what happens then.*

Osman went back to the room and sat beside his sleeping wife. He wasn't sure he'd convinced Amina not to talk to the doctors, and his sadness about the subject grew as he watched his wife sleep. He prayed that Amina would listen to him because he didn't want her to find out what he already knew, and what the doctors would surely tell her if she asked. He didn't want his little girl's heart to break when she learned that her mother was avoiding her because, although indirectly, she was the cause for all this suffering.

Chapter 21

R UWAYDA HAD BEEN in the hospital for just over a week, and almost all of Amina's time during that period had been spent at the hospital. She had explained the situation to her boss right away, and Janice was very sympathetic and agreed to give her two weeks unpaid vacation. This was, of course, anything but vacation, but Amina appreciated that they were being flexible.

When Amina told Kayla that she wasn't going to the hospital for a day or two, at first Kayla wondered why her friend would willingly do something that was obviously very hard on her. But when Amina didn't volunteer a reason, Kayla didn't ask. Instead she took the opportunity to fill her friend in on things that had happened in her life over the past week.

"Remember how I told you Damon was hinting at asking me to move in with him? Well, he's stopped doing that. At first I thought it was a sign that he wanted to break up, but then he kept saying things like, 'when we have kids', or 'when we're old and gray and leaning on each other.' His actions seem contradictory to his words."

"Well, maybe something you said or did made him realize that he was moving too fast for you," Amina offered.

"Maybe," Kayla agreed. "I don't really get it, but to be honest with you, I like it better this way. When he says things like that, it comforts me. I feel like he's really committed to me.

"And I finally got to meet Liz, his sister. Turns out she's not so bad after all. She's a little overprotective when it comes to her kids, but I'm not a mother... who am I to judge?"

She was quiet for a while. When she spoke again, her tone was much sadder, and more serious.

"Do you think I'll be a good mother, one day?"

The question caught Amina off guard. "Sorry?"

"Do you think I'll be a good mother?" she asked, a little louder and more firmly.

"Yes, I do."

"Why?" Kayla demanded.

"Because you're kind-hearted and you look out for the people you love. And because you're honest even when it's hard to be or even when you know it might hurt someone's feelings.

"I mean, you're probably going to have to learn to word your honesty. When your kid asks you why her best friends' grandmother died, you won't be able to say, 'shit happens.'"

Amina's attempt to make Kayla laugh backfired. Her friend became anxious. "But what do I say? When they ask about death and war and poverty and why they happen, how do I answer?"

Amina understood her friend's dilemma, but she remained quiet. Kayla hadn't meant it as a rhetorical question. After a few moments, she asked it again, only she worded it slightly differently, "What will you say to your kids?"

Amina began, "I'll tell them that throughout our lives, God throws us varying situations. Some are good and make us happy— like getting the toy you wanted, or having a safe place to live, or being healthy. And others are bad and make us sad— like being in a car accident, or becoming sick, or having your best friend move away. The good things are blessings and we need to always praise God and thank Him for them. The bad things can be blessings that we can't see or understand. Or they can be tests from God. He tests us to see who is patient and obeys Him, and who follows the wrong path. After we die, those who obey Him will be given a home in a place more beautiful than any imagination could create. In this place, called Heaven, you only have to think of what you want, and you find it in your reach. Heaven has no more death, no more pain, no more poverty... it's the reward for those who obey God, so it only has goodness and happiness."

"What do I say to them if I still don't believe in God?" She said it under her breath, but Amina heard. And her heart ached for the struggle she could see happening inside her friend. She wished her touch could bestow peace, that she could just reach out and hug Kayla, taking away all her confusion and leaving her with a sense of serenity. She reached out and hugged her anyway.

A few minutes later, Kayla asked, "How do I obey God, Amina?"

Amina thought for a few moments before answering. She wanted to make sure she conveyed as much truth as she could without being overwhelming.

"Well, for me, obeying God means that I believe there is only One God, I believe in all His prophets, including Abraham, Moses and Jesus and that the last messenger was Mohamed. It means that I live my life according to the teachings of Prophet Mohamed and the Qur'an. Of course these include worship of God, but equally as important as worship is the treatment of others. Most of these teachings stress maintaining good relationships with your relatives, being kind to your neighbors, being charitable to those in need. Basically, doing good deeds and avoiding evil ones."

Kayla was pensive for a few minutes, then she asked, "Don't you ever feel like your religion lacks... spirituality? Like, it's too focused on dos and don'ts to give you any kind of spiritual experience?"

Amina thought for a minute. "Well, no, not really. A spiritual experience is one in which you connect, through your soul, with God— or something greater than yourself— on another level. I think that the dos and don'ts give you a vehicle to experience that connection. 'Do treat others kindly. Do give charity. Do care for orphans and those in need.' I see those all as opportunities to connect with humanity.

"Then there is, of course, 'do pray.' What better opportunity is there to connect with God?"

"But isn't your prayer very... structured? I mean, how do you have a spiritual connection with God if you're bound to a specific frame?"

"Well, when you're praying to God, you're actually standing before Him. Whether or not you feel that connection goes back to how focused you are and how much faith you have.

"But even when you're not really focused, and you're praying out of a sense of obligation, not of faith, you still have the opportunity to connect with God through supplication. Whether in the frame of the prayer or outside of it, you can always just 'talk' to God— to thank Him for your blessings, to ask Him for whatever you need or want, to express your fears and hopes. To just release everything your heart holds. And when it's all done in sincerity, you'll feel that connection."

"Have you felt it?"

"I've never felt like I could see God or physically feel Him, but often when something troubles me and I turn to Him, I'm overcome by a sense of tranquility, and an assurance that everything will work out. And I know that that's God's touch."

Kayla took in what her friend had said and decided it was important enough to give some real consideration. But not just yet... something inside of her was still doubtful.

Amina sensed that Kayla needed to change the subject. "Did Damon ever manage to convince you to take those college courses you guys had talked about?"

"I didn't tell you? Oh, your mom got sick that day. I signed up to take two summer classes that start in just a couple of months." Her voice was excited.

Almost as excited as Amina's. "That's so great, Kayla! Good for you."

"I'm excited about it, but I'm pretty nervous."

"You're going to do **so** well. I just know it."

Kayla let out a sudden laugh. "That's not what my dad said when I told him. At first he didn't say anything, then his girlfriend heard that I was taking classes, and she thought it was such a great idea that she registered to take a class, too. So my dad calls me up a couple of days later and says, 'I don't know why you're wasting time taking college courses. You've never been smart. And now your stupidity is gonna cost me money because Rebecca wants to copy you.' He blames me for having to pay for his girlfriend's course. Good thing I stopped taking anything he says to heart years ago." She let out another giggle.

Amina, for some reason, was stuck on something Kayla had just said, 'he blames me for having to pay for his girlfriend's course.' It repeated itself over and over in her head. 'He blames me... he blames me... he blames me!' A few minutes later, after her mind had recalled every moment of avoidance she'd experienced from her mother over the past week, she had a brief moment of enlightenment.

"Oh my God." Her voice was softer than a whisper. Kayla wasn't sure if she'd heard something. She looked over at her friend and noticed that she'd become very pale all of a sudden. "Amina, are you okay?"

"Oh my God," she continued to repeat. "Oh my God. She blames me."

The fear that had been building inside of her slammed against the heartbreak that the realization had brought, and she couldn't stop her body from shaking or her tears from gushing.

Kayla didn't understand what was happening, but she dropped to her knees beside her friend and held her as tightly as she could, as though the warmth of her body could ease whatever pain Amina was feeling.

After Amina's outburst had calmed a bit, Kayla tried to get her to talk. "What's going on?" she asked gently.

Amina was still crying, but she managed to utter, "My mother. My mother blames me for what's happened to her."

Kayla had so many questions; how had Amina come to that conclusion? Did she really believe that her mother could blame her? Did she blame herself?

But she forced herself to remain quiet. Amina needed support, not a million questions to answer.

Several minutes later Amina's sobs quieted and the remaining tears flowed silently. She leaned her back against her bed and hung her head between her knees. Kayla sat beside her in silence.

"Now what do I do? Do I face her— apologize?!" Her tears flowed more quickly now and her voice became a bit louder, but it was steady. "And if I do confront her, is that going to make things better? For me? For her? Or will it set her back again? Or do I just wait it out... hope she can get past it?"

Kayla answered softly, "How do you know you've come to the correct conclusion?"

"Because it's the only one that makes sense. I'm the only one she avoids. She talks with her doctors and nurses fine, she's fine with my dad. She's even started having some visits from her friends. The only one she can't speak with, the only one she pretends to be tired around is me."

When she defined it like that, it seemed obvious, but Kayla hated seeing her friend's heart break; she needed to give her some kind of hope.

"You're the one who's always saying we should give people the benefit of the doubt. You never know, there might be a reason you haven't thought of. Maybe you should try talking to her and see where it goes." Kayla didn't feel like her words were strong enough, but it was the best she could offer.

"I need to talk to her," Amina said as she jumped up and grabbed her purse. She was one step from the front door when Kayla said, "Hold on, Amina. You don't have your headscarf on. Go put it on. And I'm driving you."

She had been so focused on what she needed to say to her mother that she hadn't noticed anything around her— not the fact that her hair was bare, nor the fact that she almost left the house in her sweats.

She quickly threw on a pair of jeans and a long sleeved t-shirt and tied her headscarf. Kayla was already waiting for her in the car.

As soon as Amina entered her mother's room, everything she'd been planning to say disappeared from her mind. The doctor was talking to her parents, so she just walked quietly over and stood beside her dad.

"If you can make sure to keep your stress level down and you promise to continue with the medication, at least for the time being, we can have you discharged in a day or two. You'll have to follow up after a couple of weeks, and we'll take it from there."

"Thank you, doctor." Osman said, smiling. Amina's mother also gave the doctor a grateful smile.

As the doctor was about to walk out of the door, he turned to Ruwayda and repeated, "Remember, keep your stress level down."

Amina's face saddened. *He meant that for me.*

Amina's father sat down beside his wife on the bed and Amina sat in the chair. "*Hamdila 'al salaama.* It's going to be good to have you home again. It's been so empty without you." Osman told his wife.

Ruwayda's smile was wider and healthier than Amina had seen since before she was admitted to the hospital. *Maybe she's already over it.*

A few minutes later, Osman left to get some food from the cafeteria. "*Hamdila 'al salaama,* mama. I'm so glad we get to take you home soon."

Ruwayda smiled quietly at her daughter. Her mother's reactions to her seemed pretty much back to normal, so Amina decided it wasn't necessary to confront her about anything. Instead, she tried to start a regular conversation.

"I had a pretty interesting conversation with Kayla today about religion and spirituality."

But Amina felt her heart break again as her mother turned on her side, pulled the covers to her neck and said, "I need to get some sleep, Amina."

Once again, Amina's already puffy eyes began to flow, this time silently. She remembered the doctor's words.

She went over to the head of her mother's bed, kneeled down with her head against her chest and whispered, "Mama, I'm sorry."

Ruwayda didn't understand. She pulled the covers off, held up her daughter's chin and, in the gentlest tone Amina had ever heard, said, "What are you talking about?"

"I'm the reason you're here. This is all my fault. If I had listened to your warnings and acted responsibly, this wouldn't have happened.

I'm sorry."

Ruwayda sat up in her bed and pulled her daughter up to sit beside her. Now they were both crying.

"You think that my being here is your fault?"

The question kind of surprised Amina. "Well, don't you?"

"No... no... no, Amina. Never."

"But... I don't understand. I thought you blamed me for all this. Why else have you been avoiding me?"

Ruwayda could almost hear the sound of her own heart falling apart. "You thought I blamed you? Amina, how could you think that? You're my daughter... my only daughter. I would die for you." She grabbed Amina and held her tight for a few moments. Then the confusion in Amina's eyes made Ruwayda confess.

"I have been avoiding you because you are a reminder that I failed. I failed to protect you. A mother is supposed to protect her children from evil. I failed to protect you. I failed as a mother."

Ruwayda had stopped crying. This is what she'd been coming to terms with all week. This is what had weighed so heavily on her, that had shocked her. But it was her burden to bear. And now that she accepted it, she could carry that burden and move on.

Amina was in shock. "Mama, are you serious?" But a glance at her mother's face revealed only sincerity. "Mama. You are so wrong. You are so wrong. How could you protect me? I wasn't even with you. There is only so much a mother can do for her kids. And you've done so much more than your share. So much more, mama! I am lucky that you are my mother."

"But I failed you," Ruwayda stated, matter-of-factly.

"Who says? Because something bad happened to me? Mama, life is filled with bad things; you can't always be there to stop them from happening to me."

"But that's my job."

"No, mama. That's not your job. Maybe that was your job when I was two and I couldn't always climb down the stairs without falling. Maybe it was your job to not let me run into the street when I was six and to teach me to look both ways first.

"You've protected me as much as you can. And you've taught me right from wrong. You've done your job. And you did it well, mama. All you can do for me now is continue to love me, no matter what mistakes I make. What I need from you most... is your love."

"I will love you for the rest of time," Ruwayda whispered as they embraced.

She appreciated her daughter's reassurance that she had not failed her as a mother, but she was still not completely convinced. It would take a long time for her to believe what Amina had said; that it was no longer her job to protect her daughter.

A moment later, Osman walked through the door with more than just the drinks he held in his hands.

"Mazin called me yesterday and asked permission to come visit you today, Ruwayda. I met him in the lobby."

Osman's voice was normal, but his eyes betrayed the anxiety he felt about what may have just happened between the two most important people in his life. He could tell they had both been crying, but it seemed the tension that had existed between them over the past week was gone. He would not be reassured until he could speak with Amina alone. But for now, everything seemed fine.

"*Hamdila al salaama*, Tant Ruwayda. Uncle Osman tells me you'll be going home in the next couple of days, *in sha' Allah. Alhamdu lillah*," Mazin said.

"Thank you, Mazin. It will be good to be home." She squeezed her daughter's hand and the look in their eyes was filled with love and happiness.

Chapter 22

AMINA AND HER FAMILY spent the next few days getting Ruwayda settled back into her regular routine. She was still on medication and she'd still need to follow up with her doctor, but besides that, her life returned to normal rather quickly.

Less than a week later, Ruwayda told Osman it was time they invite Mazin back to their home to discuss his commitment to Amina.

"Ruwayda, are you sure you're ready for that? You should take things easy for a while," Osman replied.

"Osman, don't baby me. I fell. And I stood back up. I didn't break, so please don't treat me as though I had. And I know my limitations; if this were going to be too stressful for me, I wouldn't have suggested it. But this is going to be exactly the opposite of that. It's going to make my heart happy. Mazin is a good man and he's going to make Amina happy. I want to see them together as soon as possible. So call him today and invite him to come over on Saturday."

Osman hesitated. "Won't that be too forward of us? We should wait for him to ask. That's the proper way."

Ruwayda was getting tired of arguing with her husband. She let out a sigh and said, "Under normal circumstances we would wait for him to ask, but we're the ones who cancelled last time. We cancelled, so we have to re-invite him." *If you would just listen to me, without all the second guessing, you wouldn't waste our time or your breath.*

Osman had no choice but to obey what his wife had said.

The remainder of the week was filled with preparations for Mazin's visit: cleaning the house, taking out the fancy china and special silverware, and preparing the menu. Amina and Ruwayda each planned what they would wear and, of course, Ruwayda chose Osman's outfit as well.

By the time Mazin rang the door bell on Saturday afternoon, Amina and her parents were dressed, the table was set, the meal was warming, and there was a definite feel of tranquility in the house.

Mazin handed the tray he'd brought to Ruwayda. "My sister made this *konafa*. She says she hopes next time dinner will be at her house." Ruwayda graciously accepted the gift and brought it to the kitchen.

Once they'd eaten, had dessert, and drank their tea, Osman led Mazin to the study while the women continued to clear the table. This time Amina was not interested in hearing what Mazin would offer, what he and her father would decide about the apartment or the wedding. She wasn't that curious to know. She knew that her dad loved her and would do what he thought was in her best interest. Even more than that, she knew her father had grown to like Mazin over the last couple of weeks, and there was probably nothing he would do tonight to make Osman change his mind. She had come to terms with her situation, and she'd finally accepted the fact that she would marry a man she did not love. She did so, however, with the knowledge that he was a kind man who would always respect her, and hope that love would grow between them.

When they had finished, Osman opened the door of the study and called for his wife to bring the *sharbat*. Amina noticed her father looked happier, relieved somehow, as though he'd been carrying an invisible load that had suddenly been lifted from his shoulders. It puzzled Amina. She hadn't thought her marriage had been such a stressful issue for her father, but he was obviously lighter now. It made her happy to see her father in such a good mood; she just wished the lightening of his load would have lightened hers as well.

After they had drunk the *sharbat* in celebration of the pending engagement, Mazin announced that he would like to take them out the very next day for Amina to choose her engagement ring. They decided to meet at the mall in front of the jewelry store located on the ground floor.

As soon as Osman spotted Mazin, they all greeted each other, then Ruwayda announced, "Osman, I have some other shopping to get done. Come with me and we'll meet up with the kids in a little while."

Osman was surprised. "Don't you want to help her choose?"

"No. Amina knows what she likes. I trust her judgment," Ruwayda said, smiling proudly to her daughter.

"Okay," Osman said hesitantly. "Should we meet you back here in an hour?" He was looking back and forth between Amina and Mazin, but it was Ruwayda who answered.

"This is not a shirt she's going to pick off the first rack she finds, Osman. This is the ring that will adorn her finger forever; we can't rush them. When they're done, they'll call us on your cell phone." And with that, Ruwayda dragged her husband away, leaving Amina and Mazin to face the task at hand together. Mazin opened the door for her, and Amina walked in.

She was overwhelmed by what she saw. All the jewelry was stunning, and she wasn't sure exactly where to start. But the sales woman noticed her confusion and offered her assistance.

"We're looking for engagement rings," Mazin told her.

"Right over here," the woman said as she walked across the store to the display carrying the appropriate rings.

After Amina had been looking for a few minutes, Mazin asked her, "Is there anything you like?"

Of course there was something she liked... she liked all of them. But she didn't know what Mazin's budget was, and she didn't want to be the obnoxious fiancée who asks for the most expensive ring in existence.

"Umm... I'm not sure. They're all very beautiful. What about you? Is there any one that stands out more than the rest, to you?" She figured that was a polite enough way to let him tell her what his budget was while being discreet.

"No, they're all beautiful. But if nothing stands out for you here, let's check the other stores."

They thanked the sales woman and left.

The escalator was out of order, so they had to take the stairs to the second floor. Amina took the opportunity to be more direct with Mazin.

"Mazin, I appreciate you letting me pick out the ring. But I don't understand anything about diamonds. And at the same time, I really don't know what the budget is. So, I'd really rather you pick out a couple that are possibilities, then I can choose from them."

Mazin just smiled at her. When the sales woman asked if they needed assistance, Amina looked to Mazin, who simply continued to smile and shrugged his shoulders.

Amina sighed. "Yes, please. We'd like to look at your engagement rings."

The woman walked to the display and pointed out some very beautiful rings to the couple. Again, nothing really stood out. They were all beautiful, but Amina didn't know how she was supposed to decide. And Mazin was not being helpful.

"This is our first time looking. Could you maybe explain to me what's different about the rings, besides just their size and shape?" Amina figured the sales woman was her only hope.

And she was very patient, describing as much as she could and answering all of Amina's questions. But they told her they needed to do some more shopping around, and maybe they'd be back later.

"Don't feel pressured to choose just anything, Amina. If we don't find a ring that really stands out, we can go to other places. Don't pick one just to pick one. Pick the one that speaks to you." Mazin said to Amina as they walked up to the last jewelry store in the mall.

This time when the sales man showed them to the engagement rings, Amina's eyes were drawn to one specific ring. She asked the man to try it on, and she absolutely loved how it looked on her hand. This was definitely the ring. But just as she was about to say that, her eyes fell on the price. She'd seen enough rings that day to know how their prices ranged, and this was undoubtedly too expensive.

She quickly hid her disappointment. "It doesn't look that great on," she said as she slipped it off and put it back in its place. Her eyes continued to browse the display, but her heart wasn't into it anymore. It had been a long day, and the one ring that she loved was too expensive for her to even think about.

"Mazin, I think that's enough for today. Let's call my parents and tell them we're done."

"Do you want to try somewhere else today?" he asked.

"No, it's been a long day and I don't want to torture you anymore. We can do it some other time."

"You haven't tortured me at all. I'm enjoying being with you. But if you're done, that's fine."

Before they got into their respective cars, Mazin asked Osman and Ruwayda if the following Saturday would be a good time for them to try again.

"That should be fine." Osman answered.

"There's another jewelry store I know. I can pick you up at your house, then we can drive over together?"

"Perfect!" Ruwayda said.

They said their good-byes, then Amina and her family drove home. Once their car was out of sight, Mazin stopped pretending to fidget with his car radio, stepped out of his car, and went back into the mall.

"So did you find anything?" Kayla asked her on the phone later that day.

"No, not really. There was this one ring... it was absolutely gorgeous. It was also the most expensive ring ever made."

Kayla chuckled. "I'm sure that's not true. Although you do tend to have expensive taste."

"I do, don't I. I blame it on my mother. Anyway, I almost wish he would just pick one out. I mean, I didn't see any ugly rings... they're all beautiful. If he would just pick one, it would make my life a bit easier. Especially since he didn't give me a budget."

"But maybe he didn't give you a budget because he's generous. He's willing to buy whatever you pick out, no matter what the cost."

"I know that's his intention, but come on... let's be real. When a person decides to buy something valuable— whether it's as small as a ring or as large as a house— he needs to give himself a budget. Otherwise he'll end up in serious debt. If he would just pick it out himself, he won't put himself in that position, and he'll really make my life easier."

"But that's no fun," Kayla argued. "Try to enjoy it. It might be a little stressful, but it's a once in a lifetime experience. You have to make the most of it."

"I know, you're right. I had just wished that I would find something right away."

"So once you've picked out the ring, what then?" Kayla asked.

"I tried convincing my mom that we don't need an engagement party, and it's enough to just have a formal dinner with his sister and her family, but she basically laughed in my face. She wants to rent a hall and invite all the Muslims she knows. I'm hoping Mazin and my dad will be on my side and that'll be enough to convince her. We'll see."

"What about your dress? Do you already have something to wear?"

Amina sighed, "No. That's part of the reason I wanted to be done with the ring. The dress is going to be a whole other stressful subject."

Kayla thought her friend would be happier with the steps that were happening in her life, but Amina's reactions now made her doubtful. "Amina, are you sure this is what you want? I would think you'd be happier, but you seem too stressed. Almost annoyed, really."

"I'm not annoyed, Kayla. I'm just stressed because, well, I don't know if all this planning is going to be worth it. I'm worried about Mazin's response when I tell him. He's an Arab man... why should I think that his reaction will be any different than Sherif's was?"

Kayla was quiet for a moment. "Are you sure you want to tell him?" she asked, hesitantly.

"I can't enter a marriage with such a huge lie between us. I need to be honest." She just didn't know when she would be able to face that honesty.

On Saturday morning, Mazin pulled into the driveway and Amina opened the door for him.

"*As salaamu alaikum*, Mazin. Come on in. My mom just needs a few more minutes, then we'll be ready to go."

He sat in the living room with Amina and her father, and when Ruwayda announced she was ready to go, Mazin asked her to join them.

"I went back to the mall a few days after we were all there together, and I thought I would look into the jewelry store to see if maybe there was anything we'd missed. I saw this ring, and it really stood out to me." He took the small box from his pocket and held it out to Amina.

Although this is what she'd wanted— to be saved from the stress of having to pick the ring out herself— she found herself feeling slightly disappointed. She hid the feeling well, but even so, Mazin said, "It's just a suggestion. If you don't like it, we'll leave right away to do more searching. But I'm confident you'll like it." His smile was just slightly cocky.

Amina took the box and opened it slowly. Her mouth dropped when she saw what was inside. She was speechless for more than a few seconds. Then she snapped herself back to reality.

"Mazin... this is... it's... I can't accept this." She closed the box and handed it back to him.

"What, Amina? You don't like it?" her mother asked.

"No, mama. I do like it. I like it very much. But I also know how much it costs, and I can't let him spend that much money on a ring."

Mazin chuckled. He took the box, opened it, and handed it to Amina's mother.

"Tant Ruwayda, I'm not a romantic man. But I am perceptive. I saw how Amina looked at this ring in the store. And usually I would think it is too expensive."

Amina cut him off, "It **is** too expensive."

Mazin pretended not to have heard. "But it was the only ring that made her smile. And her concern with how much it was just made me want to get it for her even more."

Ruwayda and Osman agreed that the ring was beautiful.

"But, son, we can't let you spend more money than you should. There will be a lot of expenses coming up with your marriage. You should be saving as much as you can," Osman said.

Again, Mazin chuckled. "God will provide for us, *in sha' Allah*. I really want Amina to have this ring."

She was about to protest again, but her father interrupted.

"Well, Mazin, if you're sure it's in your budget, then all we can say is, congratulations."

Mazin looked at Amina. "Congratulations, Amina. *In sha' Allah* this is the beginning of a blessed life for us to share."

His sincerity was obvious. He really bought the ring for Amina, not to show off in front of her parents nor to prove how generous he could be. He just wanted to make her happy. The gesture warmed her a bit, and all she could do was smile back to her fiancé.

"Well," Ruwayda said. "Now that that's out of the way, all we have to do is decide when and where we'll have the engagement party. What do you think, Mazin?"

"I'm fine with whatever you decide, Tant."

"Well, we'll need to give our friends plenty of notice. So-"

But Amina interrupted her. "Mama, can we please make this a small family event? Please? Just a small dinner here at the house with us and Mazin's sister and her family."

Mazin heard the desperation in her voice and felt a need to back her. "I had actually hoped it would be a small family event. I don't think our friends will mind. I mean, a lot of people now keep the engagement party intimate."

There was disappointment in Ruwayda's voice when she spoke again. "I was looking forward to renting a hall and mailing out invitations to all our friends. I wanted a nice party in a beautiful place will all the people we love around us."

"If we have it here, it will be in a beautiful place. And all the people we love will be around us," Amina almost begged.

They were all quiet for a moment. Osman knew he would need to make the call. "Ruwayda, let's just have an intimate dinner here with us and Mazin's family. It'll be less stressful that way. We can save the big hall and the invitations for the wedding."

They hadn't convinced Ruwayda, but she was clearly outnumbered. She accepted her defeat gracefully and moved right along to the next order of business. "So, Mazin. You speak with your sister and decide on a day that's good for all of you. Let me know as soon as possible so we can start planning the meal and such."

Mazin nodded. "Of course, Tant." Then he went on, "Since we're all dressed, I'd like to invite you all to lunch."

He wanted to take them to the Italian restaurant at the mall, but Amina had another idea.

They entered the Thai restaurant and sat down. Mazin had clearly never had Thai food before, and he was not comfortable in the restaurant.

"I don't want to take a chance on something and have it come out tasting badly. Will you order for me?" he said, looking at Amina.

She just giggled. "Don't worry Mazin. It won't be that bad."

But even when their meals came, and Amina, Ruwayda and Osman were all clearly enjoying them, Mazin was still hesitant to try.

"What does it taste like?"

Amina laughed out loud. "Try it, and then you'll know."

Her mother kicked her under the table and gave her a very stern look of warning.

He tried to be a good sport, but half an hour later, Amina and her parents had all completely finished their meals, but his plate looked as though it hadn't been touched.

Osman said, "Don't worry, Mazin. Come back to our house and Ruwayda will make up for this horrible lunch. Amina always likes to try new things; most of the time they turn out to be pretty bad ideas."

"No, no, Uncle. Not at all. Plus, it's not about the food, but rather the company."

Amina appreciated that he hadn't agreed with her father.

Later on in the week, Mazin called Amina to inform her that any Saturday would be a good day for his family.

"And my sister wants you and your mom to know she'd like to help out any way she can."

"That's really nice of her; thank her for us. I'll tell my parents and get back to you with a specific date."

They were quiet for a moment. Then Mazin broke the silence, "Amina?"

He paused, waiting for her to respond, needing to be sure he had her full attention.

"Yes?"

"There's something I need to tell you before our engagement party.

I've been meaning to tell you for a while, but it's never been the right moment. Now I know that if I don't make it, the moment will never be right. So here goes…

"Early last year I met a girl— someone my sister had introduced me to— and she and I became very close. We were engaged just a few weeks later and on the morning of our wedding she told me something that made it impossible for me to marry her. It was a huge scandal in the community, how I'd called off my wedding just hours before it was supposed to start. But I wanted to tell you because I don't want there to be any secrets between us. I told your father the first day I met him, so he knows. But I needed you to know, too. I hope this doesn't change how you feel about marrying me."

Amina ignored the question he was obviously asking. She had her own question to ask. "What did she tell you? What made marrying her impossible?" She held her breath, waiting for him to respond.

"She said she'd spent the last couple of years with a guy. With him not just emotionally, but physically, too. Someone who disregards her religion like that and who doesn't respect herself enough to wait for the proper time, is not someone I can trust to be my wife and guard my honor in my absence."

There was a small voice inside her head saying, *This is the perfect time to tell him. He's being honest about his past; now you can, too. And before a date has even been set for the engagement party… it's perfect timing!*

But for reasons she didn't understand, she didn't listen to that voice. All she could do was sit in silence, trying to take in everything Mazin had just said.

His voice interrupted her thoughts. "So?"

She didn't understand. "So?" she repeated.

"Now that you know I was almost married once before, has that caused you to change your mind about our marriage?"

Her answer was honest, yet her voice was slightly shaken. "No."

Mazin sensed the hesitation in her voice. "Are you sure?"

This time her voice was firm. "Yes, I'm sure."

Mazin let out a sigh. "I'm so relieved. I feel so much better having told you. I don't ever want there to be anything we can't share with one another."

She opened her mouth to speak— this was it, she needed to tell him, she didn't want to start her marriage with a huge secret that could end it.

But his voice stopped her. "Well, again, tell your mom if there's anything we can do to help, just let us know. Call me when your parents pick a date."

"Will do."

"Ok. *As salaamu alaikum.*"

" *Wa alaikum as salaam.*" she replied as she hung up.

That was my chance and I just let it slip away. Why? I'm never going to get such a perfect opportunity again. Why am I so stupid?!

A couple of weeks later, a date was set and Ruwayda had all the details taken care of; the caterers were booked, and the flowers ordered. "Now you just need a new dress, and we'll be all set. Do you want me to go shopping with you?"

"No, mama. That's okay. I'll go with Kayla."

And a few days later, as they browsed the racks of the department store, Kayla asked, "So... are you excited or are you dreading it?"

"I'm not sure. Maybe a little of both. Sometimes I feel excited. Then sometimes I get sad. I just wish... I wish I felt something for him."

"You don't feel anything towards him?" Kayla's voice was more shocked than she'd intended.

"He's a good guy."

"That's not what I asked."

Amina sighed. "I know," she whispered. "I mean, I like him. And he's attractive. But," she sighed again. "I just wish I felt more towards him."

"Can I ask you something without upsetting you?"

Amina guessed her question, "You want to know why I agreed when I clearly don't love him, right?" She didn't wait for her friend's response. "I just don't know if I'll be able to love anyone. Mazin's a perfect match for me; he's kind, he's religious, he has good family values, he's respectful of me and my family, and he's successful. He has no real flaws. My problem is I met him after I'd already experienced love. Maybe if I had met him first, I would already be in love with him. And I'm hoping that love will eventually come. But if it doesn't come with him, it won't come with anyone."

Kayla put her arm around her friend. "Well, in that case, we're going to be happy about this. What do think about this? I think it's totally you." She held up a short, low cut, hot pink strapless dress.

Amina pretended to inspect the front and back of the dress with interest, then she replied, "That's not a bad scarf. Now where's the dress to go with it?"

The girls giggled and Kayla hugged her friend tightly. "I want you to be happy. I hope love comes for you soon."

If she had spoken, the tears would have fallen, so she simply squeezed her friend back.

After a couple of hours of looking through racks and trying on dresses, they sat in the coffee shop, defeated.

"We could try the bridal shop up the street. They have evening gowns and prom dresses and stuff. They might have something." Kayla was trying to be positive. Amina just sipped her coffee and shrugged her shoulders.

"I want to forget about this for a while. What's going on with you?"

"Nothing new. My relationship with Damon is getting stronger, more intimate. I finally told him about my fears of getting attached and then being abandoned... or worse, being the one to run away.

"He was very reassuring. He told me he's never run away from anything in his life, and he didn't plan on starting that bad habit any time soon. When problems come up, he said, he likes to discuss them, not pretend they don't exist.

"And he said he didn't think I was the type of person to run away either. He said I could have easily moved far away from my dad and began a new life, somewhere away from all the bad memories. He said, 'your love makes you stay. If you love me, there's nothing to worry about.' Which, of course, had exactly the opposite effect on me than he'd intended. I said, 'there's no guarantee that love will last. What if ten or twenty years from now we fall out of love with each other... then there's no guarantee.' He hugged me tight and said, 'I will do everything in my power to keep you in love with me. And as long as we're always honest with each other and we communicate even when things start to get stressful or hard, then God will keep us together.'"

"Sounds like it was a good conversation. Do you feel better now that you've shared that with him? And was his reaction enough to put your anxieties to rest?"

Kayla nodded as she sipped her coffee. "I don't think he could have said anything more reassuring. And just having it out in the open was like taking a load off my shoulders.

"I didn't expect him to mention God, though. He'd never seemed like a religious or spiritual person. So that began another interesting conversation. And I told him that I'm still searching and I'm beginning to research more on Islam and some other religions. When I said that, he burst out laughing. At first I thought he was laughing at what I'd said, and I was about to smack him, then he went over to his bookcase and took out three brand new books: one on Islam, one about world religions and the last compared the three monotheistic religions. Then we were laughing together."

"That's great. It's another journey you can take together. I hope it works out for the two of you."

"I do, too." Kayla said, smiling.

The next day Amina and her parents were invited to dinner at Mazin's sister's house. It was customary for the families to meet at least a couple of times before an engagement was announced, but due to their time constraints, this would be the only chance they would have to all get together before the engagement.

"*As salaamu alaikum.*" The woman who answered the door was dressed in house clothes and her head scarf didn't even match her dress. But Amina and her family pretended not to notice. She went on, "I've been so looking forward to meeting you, Tant Ruwayda. I'm Amira and this is my husband Seif." She greeted her guests and led them to the living room.

"Please excuse me for just two minutes. The kids didn't give me a chance to get ready. I'll be right back."

Osman, Ruwayda and Amina sat in the living room with Mazin and Seif. The kids, Sarah, Mohamed and Karim, were all between the ages of 7 and 2. They were all wearing their fanciest clothes and they all smelled like baby shampoo. And it seemed they were trying to impress the guests with how loud they could be. When he realized he could barely hear what Osman had said to him, Seif yelled at the kids, "That's enough! If you want to play, go to your rooms. If you're going to stay here, sit quietly!"

He turned to his guests, "Sorry. The rain has kept them in for the past few days so they have no outlet for their energy."

Ruwayda laughed. "Oh, let them play, Seif. We enjoy them letting out their energy on us. *Ma sha' Allah*, they're all very beautiful, may God bless them and keep them safe and healthy."

A few minutes later, Amira came back smelling like soap and fabric softener. She wore a beautiful blue beaded *jalabaya* that was fit for an evening party. Her scarf matched her dress perfectly. The tray in her hands carried glasses full of cool lemonade. After she had served everyone, she placed the tray on the coffee table that sat in the middle of the room and sat down next to Amina.

"I'm so glad I finally get to meet you, Amina. Mazin has only said good things about you. I pray the two of you will be happy together. And I'm excited that I finally get a sister." She squeezed Amina's hand and her smile radiated nothing but love and sincerity.

Amira was only a few years older than Mazin, but her dry hands and slightly wrinkled forehead made her look much older. She was heavier than you would expect from her voice, except of course when she was yelling at her kids.

"We told you kids to sit quietly! Go to your rooms and don't come out until I say so!" At those times her voice was almost masculine.

Once she had led each of the tiny rule-breakers to their rooms, she came back, and in a tone that concealed all traces of anger and with a face soft as serenity, she invited her guests to enter the dining room and begin their meal.

Osman, Ruwayda and Amina were blown away by the quality of the food.

"This is so delicious, Amira. I don't think I've ever tasted these dishes cooked to such perfection!" Osman complimented.

"I'm thinking of cancelling the caterers for the party and just having you do it. I'm sure they can't make meals this good," Ruwayda said.

Amira blushed, but it was Seif, her husband, who replied. "Yes, she is very good," he said proudly. "Food is her passion, as if you couldn't tell." His wife smacked his arm playfully as he laughed. "She worked as a sous-chef in one of the restaurants in New York. Just as she was to be promoted, she had to quit because she became pregnant and we moved here to raise the family."

"Do you miss it?" Amina asked her future sister-in-law.

"Very much. I'm just waiting for the kids to get a bit older, then I'll try to go back to it, *in sha' Allah*. I mean, not in New York, but hopefully one of the prominent restaurants around here."

"Any place would be lucky to have you." He was so focused on his plate that it wasn't clear whether Mazin was talking to his sister, or to her food. Everyone laughed. Mazin looked up confused, shrugged his shoulders, and returned to eating.

"It's actually my dream to open my own restaurant."

Amina caught the exchange of a loving smile between Amira and Seif. It comforted Amina to see them in love. It also brought some questions to her mind; she wondered if they had been in love before they were married. And if not, when that love first started to show.

Amina got the chance to ask her questions after dessert had been served. Ruwayda offered to help Amira with the dishes, and Seif took Osman to show him his latest computer gadgets. The kids were jumping on the furniture and making noise once again, but Amina and Mazin managed to communicate between fits of laughter, screams and lots of "Mama! Mohamed hit me!"

"Your sister's place is beautiful. And her family is, too, *ma sha' Allah*. But how does she do it? I mean, are they always this... energetic?"

Mazin laughed. "I'm tempted to lie to you so you don't run from here screaming. But... for the most part... this is usually how they are."

"God bless them. And give your sister health and sanity." They chuckled together.

"How long have they been married, Amira and Seif?"

Mazin searched the ceiling for the answer. "Let's see... I'm 28 and she got married just as I graduated from high school, so about 10 or 11 years. She had just graduated college. Seif had seen her a few times— he was her friend's brother— and he asked for her hand. A few months later, they were married."

"You said he was her friend's brother, but did they really know each other?"

"I guess not. Not really. He knew she came from a good family and she was well-mannered and religious. And we basically knew the same about him.

"Of course all that didn't really mean too much their first couple of years of marriage. She was very unhappy. They were on the brink of a divorce at least once during that time. But once they got used to each other— to the other person's likes, dislikes, mannerisms— they learned to avoid behavior that bothered the other person, and that brought with it a strong sense of respect. Now they spend more time laughing together than anything. Well, when they're not yelling at the kids." Amina and Mazin laughed as Seif's voice rose from down the hall, "If you don't stop jumping on the couch you will go to your rooms and go right to sleep!"

Chapter 23

IT HAD BEEN A WHILE since Amina had heard from Layal or Sahar. She hadn't yet received the invitation to Sahar's wedding and since Layal had told her more than three weeks ago that she had received hers, Amina knew that something must not be right.

"Hello?"

"*As salaamu alaikum.* May I speak with Sahar please?"

The man's voice didn't reply, but Amina heard a shuffling on the other end.

"Hello?"

"Where have you been, woman?" Amina asked as soon as she heard her friend's voice.

"Oh, Amina! I've been meaning to call you for a few weeks now but everything has been so busy. I never got your RSVP! You are coming, right?"

"I never got the invitation." Amina said.

"What? Yours was sent out with everyone else's, I don't know why you didn't get it. Anyway, the wedding is the first Saturday in June; that's about 3 weeks away."

"You know I wouldn't miss it."

"Oh, thank God. I was so afraid you were going to say it's not enough notice and all that nonsense."

Amina chuckled. "No, no nonsense here. Just send me the time and place and all the details."

"Of course."

"How're you doing? Is the stress any less? Are you excited? Nervous?"

Sahar let out an exhausted sigh. "I'm still stressed. But it's a happy stress, the kind you know only happens once in a lifetime. And I'm both excited and nervous. Most of the details have been taken care of, now I'm just waiting for the day to come and praying it turns out well."

"*In sha'Allah*, it will be perfect."

"*In sha'Allah.* So what's going on with you? Anything new?"

Amina paused for a few seconds. She hadn't told Sahar or Layal about Mazin. Something about telling them would make it more real... more final. But she didn't want them to think she was intentionally keeping her news from them.

"Actually, I've been getting to know this guy recently. He's kind and religious. He comes from a very loving family."

"That's great, Amina! I'm so happy for you! So are there plans for any formal steps, or are you just at the beginning?"

How am I supposed to answer that? Yes on both counts!

"We're having a small family engagement party in a couple of weeks... actually, the last Saturday in May, just before your wedding."

"Oh, congratulations! May God do what's best for you always! I hope he makes you happy."

"Thank you, Sahar. I pray that you're happy, too. Don't forget to send me the details about your wedding."

She was glad that she'd told Sahar about Mazin. It did make it more real for her, but that feeling was surprisingly gratifying, not suffocating, as she had expected. She had found a new sense of relief about her relationship, and she knew that it would only be complete once she had told Mazin everything she needed to. She resolved to stop putting off the unavoidable; she would tell him the next time they met.

But, the next time they met was at their engagement party. Amina didn't think such a topic was appropriate, so she responsibly put it off until their first meeting as an engaged couple.

Amina had found a suitable dress at the bridal shop. The top was fitted, but she chose it anyway. The skirt was long and flowing, and to her delight, it came with a matching scarf. The purple was the perfect shade— not dark enough to make her look pale, nor soft enough to make her skin appear too dark.

"Remember, Amina," Ruwayda called to her daughter from her bed room as they each got ready. "don't wear any rings on your right hand. That's where your engagement ring will go, so no rings. But wear my tennis bracelet; that'll go well."

But Amina was already dressed, jewelry and all. She sat on her bed, make-up just barely noticeable, shoes pinching her toes, and dress forcing her to sit with perfect posture. She was calm, but a little nervous. And slightly angry.

She picked up the phone and dialed.

"Where are you? They're going to be here in less than half an hour... why aren't you here, yet?" She said without returning the greeting.

Kayla was confused. "Amina, you told me it would be a family event."

"That's right!" Amina snapped. "So where in the world are you? Get dressed and be here within ten minutes."

"But, Amina," Kayla was torn. She hesitated.

"What do you mean, 'but'? Don't you want to be here with me?!"

"Of course I do, Amina," Kayla sighed. "It's just that... Damon's here."

"So bring him, too. It's customary to bring your significant other to engagement parties and weddings. And since he's friends with Mazin, it'll be like each of us has a friend there. Now stop wasting time, get ready, and get over here."

Amina's mother knocked on the door and opened it. The action startled Amina slightly and she hung up without saying good-bye.

Ruwayda looked stunning. She wore a formal pants suit of golden material trimmed in satin and lace. Her head scarf, although not of the same material as her suit, complemented it. She wore too much jewelry, of course, but if she hadn't, she wouldn't be Ruwayda.

"Wow! Mama, you look beautiful."

Ruwayda giggled, "Thank you." She walked over and sat next to her daughter on the bed.

Here comes. I'm actually surprised it's taken mom this long to bring up the subject. She's going to try, once again, to convince me to have that surgery... to have my virginity restored so that I don't chase away another perfectly suitable groom.

"Amina, your father and I want you to know how happy we are for you. Mazin is a good man. He's honest and patient... and he's forgiving, or should I say understanding. He will treat you well and he'll make you happy. I know that you sometimes doubt that your feelings for him are strong enough to enter a marriage. But, Amina, have faith and be patient. Sometimes it takes love a while to show up, but when it does, usually that love is strong. I pray it comes sooner rather than later. And until it comes, be happy. This is a happy time for you... enjoy it."

She gave her daughter a tight hug and affectionate kiss on the forehead, then she got up, walked out of the room, and just before she pulled the door closed behind her, she turned to her daughter and said, "When he sees how beautiful you are tonight, he's going to wish this were your wedding and not just an engagement party."

Amina's eyes were welling up, and she didn't really know why. Was it because her mother had exposed Amina's feelings to the universe? Or was it because her mother actually knew how she felt? She wasn't sure. *Both probably.* She stuck her head outside the window to stop the tears before they could begin to fall.

She distracted herself by spending the next fifteen minutes making sure all the flowers were set appropriately and that the furniture was exactly right. They had rearranged the living room so that all the seats faced the loveseat, which would be their make-shift *kosha*. The vases on the two end tables were overflowing with flowers of all types and colors, but the main color, to complement the bride's dress, was purple. The stereo system was programmed to play a couple of CD's; Amina thought a mix of American and Arabic songs would be more appropriate than sticking to just one. The music played softly in the background. Amina sat in the *kosha* to test it out, and just as she did, the doorbell rang. *Must be Kayla.*

But just in case, she got up and went to her room. Her mother had told her not to come down until she called for her. "The bride always has to make an entrance!" she'd said.

She kept her door open marginally as she stood just inside her room. When she heard the kids' laughter, she knew her guests had arrived.

Oh, crap! Kayla, where the hell are you? How dare you make me go through this alone?

But just a few seconds later, the doorbell rang again, and Amina heard her mother usher Damon into the living room and tell Kayla, "Go check on Amina."

"You look…" Kayla searched for the right words. "Breathtaking."

Amina blushed a bit, "Thank you. I'm glad you're finally here. I can't believe you thought I was going to go through this night without you!"

Kayla tried to defend herself. "Amina, you didn't exactly invite me. When you said it was family only, I thought that was your polite way of telling me to stay away."

"Since when am I polite with you? If I wanted you to stay away, I would have said so. You're family, and that means you don't need an invitation."

Kayla smiled at her friend. She knew that Amina was speaking from her heart, and even though that's how they'd always felt about each other, hearing it warmed her. It made her feel like she really did belong.

"I'm a little nervous."

"I can tell. You haven't stopped wringing your hands since I got here. But you shouldn't be. It's just family. And Mazin's sister and brother in-law seem kind enough. I mean, it looked like she was about to throw her middle child across the room, but when we made eye contact, she smiled at me. And not a through-the-teeth smile, but a sincere smile."

"Yeah, they're nice enough. I guess I just…"

But Ruwayda's voice interrupted her.

"Come on, Amina. What's taking you so long? Come down and greet everyone."

"That's our cue. How do I look? Is my make-up okay? And my head scarf, does it look right?"

Kayla gave her friend a quick but serious examination from head to toe. "Everything's perfect. Let's go make an entrance."

After Amina had greeted everyone, and they'd chatted for about half an hour, Osman turned off the background music and began to speak. "*Bism Allah Alrahman Alraheem.* We thank God that we are all here today, two families beginning the journey of becoming one. In the Holy Qur'an, chapter An-Nisaa', verse 21, God refers to marriage as a sacred oath. In chapter Al-Rume, verse 20, God says: 'And of God's signs, He created spouses from among yourselves, that you might live in peace with them, and planted love and kindness in your hearts.' In chapter Al-Baqara verse 187, God speaks of the spouses, saying each is a comfort for the other.

"It is not always easy for two people to unite in marriage, but if they remember that God considers it a sacred oath, they will always treat each other with respect and work to solve their differences. And if they remember to always treat each other with kindness, God will increase the love between them and make their path easier.

"We pray that God increases the love between Amina and Mazin. We pray that He protects them and forbids Satan from coming between them. We pray that each of them will become the comfort which the other always turns to. We pray they will have a successful, happy life together."

"Ameen," the attendees all said in one voice.

After Osman completed his short supplication, Ruwayda turned the music back on to one of the traditional Arabic wedding songs.

Mazin opened the ring box, a different one than the one that held the ring before. This box held three rings; Amina's engagement ring, a gold wedding band for Amina, and a matching silver band for Mazin. He whispered, "I hope you don't mind that I chose the bands myself. I realized at the last minute that we'd forgotten to choose them. I hope you like them."

"I do, they're perfect. I'm sorry we overlooked that— we were supposed to get yours, weren't we?"

Mazin shook his head slightly, "There's no difference between you and me. I had them engraved with our names. We can add a date once we set one for the wedding."

He took Amina's right hand and slipped on first the wedding band, then the engagement ring. Following suit, she placed the silver band on his right finger.

"Congratulations," he whispered to her. She just blushed.

Ruwayda and Amira both let out trills. Kayla and Damon were startled a bit at the sound, but when they realized it was an expression of happiness, they laughed. Everyone got up to congratulate the couple.

The caterers brought out trays of *sharbat* and took back the empty appetizer trays.

As everyone drank their *sharbat* and made conversation, the caterers informed Ruwayda that dinner was ready. Just as she was about to make the announcement, Karim, Amira's youngest, spilled his cup all over the beautiful hand-made carpet.

Amira was fuming and completely embarrassed at the same time.

"Tant, I'm so sorry." She got down on her hands and knees and started wiping it up with some napkins. "If we use some soda, it shouldn't stain."

Ruwayda was disappointed, but she was determined not to let anything ruin her daughter's day.

She pulled Amira up from the floor, "Don't worry about it, Amira. That rug is so old."

"I'm so sorry, Tant. Please just let me clean it up. I'll feel better if I clean it up. If we-"

"You have nothing to feel badly about. Children are children. Don't worry about it, Amira. It's no big deal. Really." She kept one arm around her daughter's future sister-in-law. "Everyone, dinner is ready. Please have a seat at the dining room table."

Before they went in, Amira managed to pull her children aside and warn them about any further misbehavior. She spoke in a hushed yell and whatever she said to them was enough to scare them into behaving for the rest of the evening. Well, that and the look of death she shot them whenever she felt the rules were on the brink of breaking.

Before she sat down at the table, Ruwayda went into the kitchen to make sure everything was under control and to remind the waitress of the order that the courses should be served.

"And if you don't mind, as soon as you get a chance... a cup of *sharbat* spilled on the carpet in the living room. Could you please treat it so it doesn't stain?"

"Sure, Mrs. A. No problem."

The rest of the evening went by perfectly. Mazin and Amina sat beside each other at dinner. Amina felt comfortable. *This is normal calm. Where did I get that from? Did I just make that up?*

As they ate, Mazin nudged Amina. "Look." His fork pointed in the direction of his sister. She was cutting up her kids' meals for them while simultaneously burning holes into their heads with her stare. To her oldest she mouthed "Stop it," referring to the dinging noise she was making with her fork against her glass.

Amina and Mazin laughed. When she heard the giggles, Amira looked up. Her eyes met Mazin's and Amina saw her roll them and heave a silent sigh. Within the next second, Amira grabbed her middle child's arm and told him to stop fidgeting. When Amira looked up this time, it was Amina that she saw. She gave her a crooked smile, shook her head and just shrugged. Then she mouthed to Amina, "Don't laugh. Soon, this may be you." The three laughed out loud, and Ruwayda repeated '*alhamdu lillah*' silently to herself that, at least for now, her daughter was happy.

After dessert had been served and they sat drinking their tea, Amina remembered there was something she had to tell Mazin.

"Next weekend is my friend's wedding. It's in Chicago, so my mom and I are going for the weekend."

"Would you mind if... if... I went with you?"

Amina was caught off guard; she hadn't expected that reaction.

She was really just telling him so he'd know where she was, and so he'd know she wasn't going so far away from home alone.

"Um... no... I don't mind."

Chapter 24

THEY ARRIVED AT THE HOTEL on Friday night. Amina and her mother were tired from the trip, but Mazin was insisting on taking them out to dinner.

"Please, Mazin. I think it's best if we all get some sleep. We'll have all day tomorrow— we'll go out to lunch."

Mazin was disappointed; he had really wanted to spend some time with his fiancée. But he finally conceded.

They all said good night, then Ruwayda locked the door adjoining the two rooms.

"I think he's a little upset, but I really don't have the energy to get dressed and go out. Did you want to go?"

"No. Not at all. I just want to sleep." Amina was clearly too tired to feel disappointed.

The three spent the following day together; they had breakfast at the hotel, did some shopping, and had lunch at an Italian restaurant. Amina noticed Mazin wasn't having as difficult a time as he'd had when they ate together at a restaurant, last.

"Better than Thai food?" she asked, smiling.

Mazin laughed, "Italian is very safe. If in doubt, pasta with plain tomato sauce is satisfying and delicious. Don't you think, Tant?"

Ruwayda was trying to be the invisible chaperon. She wanted her daughter to get to know Mazin as much as possible. She saw in him a great man; she wanted her daughter to see that, too. She knew if she did, Amina would stop feeling like she was settling.

Ruwayda tried very hard to stay out of their conversations. And when she felt like she had to speak, she kept it very brief.

"It's delicious."

They spent the rest of the day hanging out around the hotel and in their rooms. At about four o'clock, Amina said she was worn out, and wanted to take a nap before they had to get ready for the wedding. Mazin politely excused himself and Amina fell asleep while her mother did some reading.

"Amina... Amina, wake up. It's seven o'clock. We have to be at the wedding in an hour. Amina..." Ruwayda tapped her daughter's shoulder and rubbed her back. A few seconds later, Amina woke up.

"What time is it?" she asked, still half asleep.

"It's seven. Come on. If you don't get up now, we'll be late."

Amina yawned and stretched. She got out of bed, adjusted the covers, and sat back down.

"You're already dressed?"

"Well, you had fallen asleep, and I didn't really have anything better to do. Plus, I figured I should finish before you got started so we wouldn't have to fight over the bathroom." Ruwayda sat in the same chair she'd been in before Amina had fallen asleep, reading the same book. But now she was wearing a beautiful silver and black evening dress, adorned, of course, in her best jewelry.

"Should we give Mazin a call to remind him that we plan on leaving at eight?"

"No," Ruwayda answered. "He called a little while ago to make sure we weren't both still asleep. He knows when we're leaving."

An hour later, they were all sitting in the taxi on their way to the wedding. Amina wore the same dress she wore for her engagement party. The day before they'd left, her mother had tried to convince her to take something else.

"Amina," she'd said. "Mazin has already seen you in that. He's going to think you don't own any other formal dresses."

"Mama, he's the only one who's seen me in it... no one else has! And I've only worn it once. Sahar and Layal have seen all of my other dresses."

"So, buy a new one!"

"What? Mama, I'm not going to buy a new one. The ones I own are enough, and this one is perfect for the wedding."

Ruwayda shook her head at her daughter's stubbornness. "If you would just listen..." But she knew it was no use.

The ride to the hall was very short. *If we weren't wearing high heels, we could've probably walked that.*

Mazin, Ruwayda and Amina sat at their table while Amina scanned the hall for Layal.

"I wonder if Layal is up helping Sahar with the finishing touches. I wonder if I should try to find them." She sat on the edge of her seat, looking around, trying in vain to spot any of Sahar's relatives.

"I don't think you should worry about it. It seems the DJ is about ready to begin, so they're probably on their way down." Ruwayda said.

Ruwayda and Mazin admired the beauty of the hall. Amina was also awed by it; it seemed like they were entering a wedding reception fit for royalty. The crystal chandeliers sent the warmest colors on the dressed up tabletops. The center pieces were huge long stem flower arrangements coming up high so that everyone at the table could see everyone else. The table cloths and chair covers seemed to be made of silk. Sahar and Yasin's bridal stage consisted of a love-seat style chair made of the richest green colored satin. It was surrounded by beautiful arrangements of exotic flowers, and framed by curtain-like fabrics draped in strips from ceiling to floor. Fragrant candles of all shapes and sizes circled along the floor of the stage. In her life, Amina had been to two weddings, each very lavish and expensive; Sahar's outdid them both.

"My parents definitely overdid it! I tried to tell them to go simpler... but who listens to the bride?! But everything did turn out beautifully."

Amina admired her friend's extravagant red wedding dress, customary for many Pakistani brides.

"We ordered it online and I was so worried that it would turn out nothing like the picture. I actually think it looks better."

Sahar was more than happy; she was exhilarated. And Amina was no longer in a position to feel saddened that her friend seemed to be settling. She couldn't help but be happy for her and pray that God bless her friend's new union. Amina congratulated Sahar and went back to searching for Layal.

When she finally spotted Layal, she ran over to her. Mazin followed. The girls hugged tightly for a few moments.

"I've missed you so much! You look really great!" Layal said.

"So do you. Actually, you're almost glowing! Can we blame that on your fiancé?" Amina asked.

Layal giggled. "Probably. I'm really happy, *alhamdu lillah*. He's a good guy."

"*Alhamdu lillah*. May God keep you happy and healthy always." Just then Amina felt Mazin's presence at her side.

"And this is my fiancé, Mazin. Mazin, Layal."

"Nice to meet you, Mazin," Layal said, still holding her friend's hand.

"It's my pleasure, Layal."

"So where's your man? He is here, isn't he?" Amina asked.

"Of course. One second."

Layal turned to say something to the man who had his back to them; he'd been speaking with the people from the adjoining table.

Mazin took advantage of the moment they had alone. "I haven't had a chance to tell you, yet. But... you look beautiful. Almost as beautiful as you looked at our engagement party."

Amina smiled and blushed. *Finally. What took you so long?* But what she said was, "Thank you."

He was about to say something more when Layal interrupted.

"Amina, Mazin. This is my fiancé, Sherif. Sherif, this is my best friend, Amina, and her fiancé, Mazin."

And all of a sudden, she felt as though she'd had the wind knocked out of her. The world stopped. There was no more music, no other people in the room— just the four of them.

You've got to be kidding! This isn't possible.

Sherif was equally shocked, and the two of them just stared at each other. *What's the possibility that we'd meet again? Oh! I'm so stupid! Whatever reason he had to show up at the engagement party is still valid. He would have been here even if he wasn't with Layal. Why didn't I expect this?!*

Mazin thought he understood what was happening, but Layal was confused.

"Have you guys met before? Do you know each other?" She tried to keep smiling.

Mazin wanted to end it, but he knew he would have to remain polite. "It's nice to meet you, Sherif." He didn't smile, but he extended a firm hand, and Sherif shook it, mechanically. "Sorry, but we left Tant Ruwayda alone at the table, so please excuse us." He took Amina by the arm, and gently led her back to their table.

Before they were out of earshot, Amina heard Layal ask him, "How do you know Amina?" Amina wanted to hear his response, but the music was too loud.

As soon as she sat down, she stood back up and excused herself. She walked out of the hall to the bathrooms in the lobby. Mazin followed her.

He sat patiently in one of the chairs in the lobby. Alone in the bathroom, Amina cried. She hated herself for not being prepared to see him at the wedding. She hated that she was still unable to respond when she saw him. But one thing she didn't hate, surprisingly, was

Sherif. Remembering what he'd put her through made her sad, but not angry. Finally, all this time later, she realized that she'd somehow forgiven him. All the pain he'd put her through had finally been released.

About 15 minutes later, she appeared, eyes red and puffy and nose pink beneath the tissue. Mazin went right over to her.

He wanted to comfort her, but he didn't know what to say. All he could do was put his hands on her shoulders gently, and kiss her warm forehead. Amina smiled at him. He led her a few feet to the chairs in the lobby, and they sat beside each other.

"We don't have to go back in if you don't want to."

You're a really great guy, Mazin. Really. You're supporting me, and you don't even know why I'm upset. And you're respecting my privacy enough not to ask. You were honest with me and told me about your past relationship. You deserve someone better than me. You really do.

She wanted to say the words out loud, but she couldn't. She just sat there, beside him. Then, a bit surprisingly to herself, she began to speak.

"I met Sherif a few years ago. I was on a plane, on my way home from a trip I'd taken by myself to visit my extended family in Egypt. He was sitting next to me on the plane. A few months later, he called me. We started to get to know each other on the phone, and he visited me a few times at school. We became close. But just as he was about to propose, he found out... something happened, and, well, let's just say, it didn't work out."

Mazin was taken a bit off guard; that's not the story he'd expected to hear. But he was, despite himself, a little hurt.

"But you still love him?" He looked down as he asked.

"No, Mazin. I'm not in love with him. I swear to you, I'm not in love with him. But I wasn't prepared to see him; remembering what he did to me made me sad."

Mazin saw the sincerity in her eyes and just nodded.

"I'm sorry I didn't tell you before."

"What happened in your life before, is the past. You don't have to tell me. But I'm glad you did. I mean, I'm glad you trusted me enough to tell me. Thank you."

Really? You're too good for me, Mazin. You're just too good. So why can't I fall in love with you?

They sat together in silence for a few minutes. Amina was trying to decide what she should say to Layal. Clearly her behavior had been conspicuous enough to make her friend curious. But Amina didn't know what Sherif had told his fiancée.

She didn't have very long to think about it; a few minutes later, Layal walked out of the hall and sat beside her friend. She saw that Amina had been crying, but she was still confused about what had happened inside.

"Amina, are you okay? I don't understand what's happening. Sherif told me that you knew each other a while ago, but he won't explain any more than that. And you were both clearly upset to see each other... I'm not sure how I'm supposed to deal with this."

Her friend was clearly disconcerted, but Amina didn't know what to tell her. Sherif hadn't said anything to Layal, so Amina figured he probably didn't want to tell her. So, was it her place to say something?

"It's true, Layal. We did know each other in the past. But it was for a short while, a lifetime ago. I think we just didn't expect to see each other again. That's what caught us both off guard."

"Is this going to be a problem? I mean, Amina, you're my best friend. I know we don't necessarily talk all the time, but I really do consider you my best friend. Is it going to be a problem for you that he's in my life?"

Amina hugged her friend tightly. "You are such a good friend, Layal. Nothing in this world could make me stop loving you. I wish the two of you only the best."

Layal was still somewhat unclear, but she knew it was no use; no one was going to provide her with any more details. She tried to forget about it. "Let's get back inside, then," she said smiling. "Sahar will think it's strange that we've been gone for so long."

Layal went back to the party, leaving Amina and Mazin alone in the lobby.

"We should probably get back inside."

"We don't have to, Amina. If you want to leave, we can."

"No, I don't want to do that to Sahar. Let's at least have dinner."

Mazin escorted his fiancée back to the wedding. The music was playing and guests were dancing on the dance floor. Ruwayda sat at the table speaking with some women. For more than a few minutes Amina couldn't concentrate on anything; all she could see was Sherif's face in front of her. The man whom she'd considered the love of her life, now the fiancé of one of her closest friends. Yes, she forgave him, but this was still a strange situation. How was she supposed to deal with that?

Then slowly her thoughts turned to something else, something that she didn't expect to find herself thinking about, at least not in this situation. She found herself thinking about Mazin and how he'd stood beside her. She hadn't fully appreciated it at the time, but now, when she thought about how he'd sincerely told her that she shouldn't feel obligated to tell him anything that had happened to her in the past, he grew so much in her eyes. This was a real man.

She looked up to see him speaking with her mother, and her mother laughed at something he'd said. When he made eye contact with Amina, his contained smile grew to cover his entire face. When she smiled back, he winked at her. That spark that had been missing was starting to appear. She made a vow to herself that she would tear down that wall that had been keeping her from getting close to him. She would try harder to get closer to him, to love him.

Over the next few weeks, she made an extra effort to speak with him daily, even if that meant she had to initiate the phone call. She even asked him over to visit with her and her parents a few times. She listened to his stories about his childhood, about his family, about his dreams for the future. And she, keeping to her promise, shared her stories with him. It was happening slowly, but he was definitely becoming one of her best friends.

One day at around the time they usually spoke, the phone rang. When she answered, she was positive it would be Mazin. The woman's voice on the other end took her by surprise.

"*As salaamu alaikum*, Amina. How are you?"

She was caught so off guard that it took her a moment to recognize the voice.

"Hello? Amina, are you still there?"

"Oh, Layal. *Wa alaikum as salaam.* Sorry, I was just expecting it to be Mazin."

"So, how are you? How's everything?"

"Good, *alhamdu lillah.* Everything's good. What about you?"

"*Alhamdu lillah.* But I'm actually calling you because… well, to be honest, I haven't been able to stop replaying what happened at Sahar's wedding over and over in my mind. I asked Sherif about your relationship again and he still doesn't want to make things clear to me. I know I shouldn't care; the past is the past. But still, I was hoping you could lay my anxieties to rest."

Oh, shit. What am I supposed to say? He didn't tell her, so should I? Why does it matter, anyway? What if I tell her everything and she sides with him? What if she, too, thinks that my being raped makes me un-marriageable? Where will that leave our friendship? Oh God, please save me from this.

But there was no way out, no emergency phone calls or parents calling from downstairs. Layal was waiting patiently to hear Amina's side of the story.

"Layal, I'll tell you everything you want to know because you're one of my closest friends and I believe we always have to be honest with each other. But before I do, I just need to ask you... Do you really want to know?"

Layal didn't miss a beat, "Yes, I want to know."

Amina took a deep breath, then she began. She recounted everything about her relationship with Sherif, how they met, how they spent some time together, how he asked for her hand in marriage. She decided not to tell her about his proposal at the restaurant; she figured that might be the kind of information that would hurt her friend for no real reason.

"And I accepted his proposal and we were making plans for the engagement party. But I hadn't yet told him about my rape, and I didn't want to enter a relationship with such a huge secret. So I told him. And he left me. And that's all."

Layal was quiet for a while. When she spoke, she sounded a little confused. "He left you because you'd been raped?"

"That's right," Amina answered.

"That's strange." She paused for a moment. "Senior year, when you got sort of depressed... that was because of him? It was Sherif?"

"Yeah," Amina remembered.

"And you were so hurt because... because you loved him?"

Amina sighed. She'd rather not say, but her friend deserved the truth. "Yes."

"And he loved you?"

"Only he can answer that."

"Come on, Amina. You said you'd tell me the truth."

Amina took another breath. "I thought he loved me."

Layal's silence after that made Amina anxious, but she didn't know what to say. A few minutes later, Layal spoke again.

"Are you still in love with him?"

Amina didn't pause. "No."

"Really?" Layal needed to be sure. Why it mattered, she didn't know. But it did matter.

"He broke my heart when he left. And that was a couple of years ago. And it's taken me all this time, but I've finally forgiven him for that, which makes it possible for me to move on. Be assured that I do not love him. I have a great man in my life now, and I pray things work out for us."

"So… if he and I work this out, and we move forward in our relationship…"

Amina didn't let her finish. "I pray you do, Layal. And I pray you find true happiness together. You deserve someone who will love you that you can love back."

As soon as the girls were off the phone, Amina called Mazin. She recounted the conversation she'd just had. When she finished, he was quiet.

"Well, what do you think? Do you think I did the right thing, telling her everything? Or do you think I shouldn't have?"

"I know Layal is one of your best friends. But I tend to believe that information about past relationships should only be told by the significant other, not by a friend."

"I was just trying to be honest with her."

"I know. But he clearly didn't want her to know, otherwise he would have told her."

"But don't you think this situation might be a little different? I mean, Layal is one of my closest friends, and for a while, her fiancé was part of my life?"

"Maybe."

"What I mean is, she noticed the awkwardness between him and me. I didn't want her to think it was for the wrong reason. And I didn't want her to have to wonder about it at all."

Mazin didn't respond.

Amina was quiet for a second, then she said, "She asked. I couldn't be dishonest with her."

"You're probably right." He was quiet for a minute, then he said, "That's what I like most about you, how honest you are."

His words reminded her that there was something important that she still hadn't told him. So she began, "Mazin, there's actually something I've been meaning to tell you."

"Sorry to cut you off, Amina, but I promised my sister I'd visit with them today. I'm already pretty late. I'll call you tomorrow and we can continue our conversation."

Amina was frustrated… she wanted this load off her shoulders, but every time she started to tell the story, something always got in the way. This time, there was nothing she could do. "That's fine. Have a good night and send my best to your sister and her family."

Chapter 25

KAYLA AND AMINA SAT on Amina's bed, munching pretzels and looking through bridal magazines.

"Have you guys actually set a date, yet?" Kayla asked.

"Not yet. We're still in the research and development stage, as they would say at work. It kind of depends on how long it takes to find an appropriate dress and which venues are available at what times. We're thinking maybe early fall, either late September or early October."

"What about a honeymoon? Have you thought of where you might go?"

The question surprised Amina. "We actually haven't talked about that. I'd totally forgotten about the honeymoon."

They were quiet for a minute, then Kayla asked, "Have you told him, yet?"

"Every time I go to tell him, something gets in the way. I didn't want to wait this long."

"But you know him better now, you have a better sense of how he may respond. Do you think he'll understand?"

"He's a very good guy. And he's very patient and understanding. But I also didn't expect Sherif to respond the way he did, either."

Kayla nodded.

"Anything new with you and Damon?"

Kayla smiled. "No, nothing new. I keep falling more and more in love with him."

Amina's face lit up as well at her friend's comment. "That's awesome, Kayla. I pray God keeps you both happy. Have you talked about the future? Moving in or marriage or anything?"

"I think he still thinks I want to take things slowly. But I'm so ready to commit to him. I've actually been thinking about asking him if we should move in together."

Amina was happy that her friend had found someone who made her so happy. She was relieved that Kayla was in love.

The next few weeks were filled with visits to bridal shops and banquet halls. Ruwayda did most of the work and dragged Osman along with her. She narrowed the search to three different halls that could cater to the number of people expected to attend, then she told Amina and Mazin they should choose their favorite.

The preparations also included refurbishing Mazin's apartment. Before they went shopping, Amina insisted on seeing his apartment first.

"I am very impressed, Mazin. Usually men who live alone take advantage of it and leave their mess all over the place. You're very tidy. Either that or you have a maid come do your cleaning." Ruwayda said as she inspected the apartment.

Mazin laughed. "No, I don't have a maid. I prefer things clean and neat, and I do it myself."

Amina was impressed by something else. "Did you pick this furniture out yourself, or did you have help?"

"I think Amira was with me, but for the most part, I chose everything."

The living room and dining room sat in one open space, and there was only a half wall diving them from the kitchen. The living room held a sofa, loveseat and recliner, all made of black leather. The table in the center was a modern style, made of steel legs and a glass top. It sat on a black and white rug that matched almost too perfectly. Like wise, the kitchen cabinets were black, bordered by white counters, a black fridge and silver stove. The chestnut wood of the dining room added a feel of comfort to the apartment. Amina also approved of the chestnut colored wood which filled the bedroom.

"Well, I think it's all great. And it all looks brand new. I don't really think we'll need anything."

Ruwayda disagreed, of course. "It is all very tasteful, and most of it looks brand new, but we should get you a new bedroom, at least."

Amina fought the urge to roll her eyes. "Mama, the furniture looks brand new. Why waste money?"

"Spending money to furnish your home is not a waste."

"It is if the home is already furnished perfectly well."

"What do you think, Mazin?" Ruwayda asked.

He didn't want to be caught in the middle. Fearing he may give in to her mother, Amina shot him a look that said, 'agree with me, or you will live to regret it.' He decided a shrug was his safest answer.

"Well, since we can't decide, we'll go furniture shopping. If something really great stands out, we can think about it. Otherwise, we'll limit the new apartment things to sheets, towels, china and silverware."

Amina knew Mazin had sheets, towels, china and silverware, but her mother was offering a compromise; disagreeing with her again would only lead to a fight. She had no choice but to give in.

Luckily, Amina managed to find something wrong with every bedroom item her mother picked out. On the other hand, she found herself enjoying shopping for her new place. She picked new pots and pans, china, towels and sheets. But a part of her felt guilty for being so extravagant.

"What are we supposed to do with your old stuff? We shouldn't get all this, we don't need it." She said to Mazin when she knew her mother was out of earshot.

"I like that." He replied.

"Oh, yeah? Which, the towels or the sheets?"

"That you're referring to us as 'we.'" His smile was kind and warm. And contagious; Amina's smile brightened the room.

When Amina showed Kayla the new things they'd purchased, her friend was slightly jealous.

"This is all really great stuff. I love these towels. I think you should put them away, or else I might steal them."

Amina laughed, "If you ask my mom, she'll probably get some for you. She seems to be in the mood to spend money for no apparent reason."

Both girls laughed.

"You seem... different, Amina."

"Oh, yeah? Different good, or different bad?"

"Good. Definitely good. I'm just trying to figure out what's different. Or why?"

Amina smiled slightly and shrugged.

"What is it?" Kayla demanded, sensing her friend was hiding something.

"You're the one who said I was different, I didn't. You tell me what it is!"

Kayla studied her friend for a minute. Then the light bulb went off.

"You're starting to fall in love with him."

"Not in love, yet. But I'm definitely getting closer to him. I think forgiving Sherif helped me break down that wall that was keeping me from getting close."

Kayla said that it was improving her overall attitude as well. "You seem… lighter, if that makes any sense."

Kayla's comments gave Amina's ego a boost. She felt better, and she was glad it showed.

A few days later they had pretty much finished shopping for the apartment and Amina began visiting bridal shops after work and on the weekends. She had hit almost all the stores she knew with no luck. The process was beginning to depress her.

"I've been everywhere. Everything is either off the shoulder, sheer in the chest, strapless, or just plain ugly."

"Have you thought about maybe having it custom made?" Kayla recommended.

"That's what my mom wants me to do. But these dresses are already ridiculously expensive; having one custom made is sure to cost so much more. I just can't justify that."

Kayla thought for a while as she drove. "What about bridal catalogues? Or online?"

"I'm weary of doing that because it's such a huge investment. I mean, what if I order something that looks great online or in a catalogue, but looks like crap in real life? Or doesn't fit right? I feel better choosing it from an actual, physical sample. I want to feel it and try it on before I decide."

"Well, I asked around, and my friends told me about a few more shops that you haven't tried. So don't give up. I'm sure we'll find something soon."

"*In sha' Allah*," Amina whispered.

"*In sha' Allah*," Kayla repeated.

Her broken Arabic made Amina giggle. "That was very good."

"Thank you."

They pulled into the parking lot of the boutique. Amina took a deep breath, and stepped out of the car. A few minutes later, they were back in the car, driving to the next shop.

"Don't get discouraged. We still have two more stores to try."

Kayla pulled into the parking spot, and got out of the car. Amina hesitated.

"Oh God, please let me find a suitable dress, one that covers everything, but that I can feel like a princess in."

They went inside and started looking through the racks. The owner came up to them with a smile.

"Hello, ladies. My name is Maria, and this is my shop. Is there anything I can help you with?"

Kayla knew Amina felt discouraged, so she didn't wait for her to respond.

"Yes, please. My friend is looking for a very conservative wedding dress. She needs something that covers her neck and her arms. Do you have anything like that?"

"Let me see," the woman said, walking over to the rack and quickly looking through the dresses.

She held out one. "This one is actually strapless, but it comes with a bolero that covers the arms. Of course, the neck is bare."

Out of all the dresses she'd seen, this was definitely the best. But it still didn't conform to all her requirements. And it didn't speak to her.

The woman kept looking, and a minute later she held up another.

"Now this one has sheer arms and a sheer chest, but it has that chocker like collar and the rest of the bodice is covered in lace. We should be able to either pad it with satin, or embroider the rest of the top in lace."

Amina was drawn to the dress. She unzipped the plastic garment bag and fingered the lace. But it was Kayla who spoke.

"Is that something you can do easily?"

"The satin underlining would be easiest, but I think, if the dress maker will supply some extra lace of the same kind, that I could probably attach it where it needs to be."

"Are you... I mean, do you do this often? Making dresses, or fixing them?" Kayla inquired while Amina continued to feel the dress and imagine what it might look like with some alterations.

The woman smiled, held up her index finger to indicate she needed a minute, made room for the dress on the nearest rack and hung it so that Amina could continue to examine it. Then she walked across the room, and picked out a completely different dress. This one was off the shoulder, and completely covered in lace.

"This is mine."

Kayla thought it was beautiful, but she didn't get it. "This is your wedding dress?"

"No," the woman said, laughing. "I made this dress. This is mine."

That declaration made Amina's head turn and Kayla's jaw drop.

The shop owner laughed at their reactions. "So to answer your question, yes, I can make the adjustments you need."

Amina could almost picture it, but she didn't want to get her hopes up before she had more details.

"Do you think you could find out for us if they can provide the lace? And how long it'll take for the dress and the material to come in?"

"I'll call the makers now, but I know that it takes two months for an order to come in. If they can provide it, the lace will come with it. I'll call them now. Excuse me for just a minute."

While Maria went to the front desk to make her phone call, Kayla approached her friend.

"So, you like it?" Kayla asked.

"It's perfect. But I'm sure they won't be able to provide the lace."

"Why do you say that?"

"Because I don't have that kind of luck."

A minute later the woman was back. "I have good and bad news. The good news is that they have the dress in stock in your size and it could be here in three weeks. The bad news is that they can't provide anymore of the lace."

Amina couldn't help but laugh.

"But," the woman continued, "I may be able to provide lace that's very similar to the original. Leave your number with me, and I'll call you within the next few days. If I can't find suitable lace, would you like me to underlay the dress with satin, instead?"

Amina ran her fingers against the lace once more. "I guess so. Yes."

"Okay, so I'll order the dress today, that way we won't lose any time."

When they were back in the car, Kayla congratulated Amina. "This is awesome! We should go out and celebrate! Dairy Queen, anyone?"

Amina wasn't as excited. "Sure." Her smile was only slightly forced.

"What's wrong? We found the perfect dress? You should be happy."

"I tried not to get my hopes up when she was describing what she could do with it, but I couldn't help myself. I don't want the satin padding, I want the lace. And I'm sure she won't be able to get it."

"Well, if you don't want the satin padding, why did you tell her to order the dress in either case?"

"Because, even though I know I won't get the lace, I'm not going to find a better second choice."

"It's a beautiful dress, Amina. Either way. And I'm not just saying that. You will look like a princess."

"Thank you," this time her smile was wide and sincere. "So I guess you're right, we should celebrate."

As they ate their ice creams, they went over all that was still undecided for the wedding. Now that the dress was, for the most part, taken care of, they still needed a venue, invitations, a DJ, photographer, and flowers. Suddenly Kayla realized that they hadn't discussed the most important detail.

"Amina, we're doing all this thinking and preparing for the reception. What about the actual marriage ceremony? How's that gonna work?"

"Usually families like to do the 'ceremony' part at the mosque. Only it's not a ceremony at all. In Islam, marriage is a contract between two people. A sacred contract, but a contract, none the less. The clergyman responsible for mediating, shall we say, is called a *ma'zun*. Basically he asks both parties whether they are venturing into the marriage willingly. They both have to be mentally and physically capable of marrying-"

Kayla cut her off. "What do you mean, mentally and physically capable?"

"For example, a man who knows that he's impotent shouldn't be getting married. With the same line of thought, a family that knows their child is mentally unstable or slow— incapable of understanding the responsibilities that come with marriage— should not be marrying off their kid."

"So impotent men or mentally slow people can't get married in Islam? What, they're essentially un-loveable?"

"No, Kayla. That's not it. The point is that both parties need to know the truth about the other. If a man knows he's impotent, and he wants to get married, there's nothing wrong with that as long he doesn't hide his condition. His prospective wife needs to know that before agreeing to marry him. Otherwise, he's tricking her, and the marriage is doomed to fail because one spouse has expectations that the other is incapable of fulfilling. You get it?"

"I think so. As long as you don't hide anything, then everything's cool?"

"Exactly. Once the parties say they're entering into the marriage willingly, then the groom promises to take care of the bride. There are some other things that go into the written contract, like the sum of the bridal gift and any other terms that both parties have agreed to. The couple signs, as do two witnesses. And that's basically it. I mean, the *ma'zun* usually makes a supplication and explains each member's responsibility in a marriage, but after that, they are married in the eyes of God and in the eyes of their community."

"You said this usually takes place at the mosque, I'm assuming some time before the reception. So, do all the guests who are invited to the reception get invited to the... what do you call it? Witnessing the contract?"

Amina laughed. "Something like that. Egyptians call it *katb al kitab*, which literally translated means 'writing of the book.'"

"So is your book gonna be written at the mosque?"

Kayla had been serious when she spoke, but Amina couldn't stop laughing.

Deciding to use the same terminology she'd just heard from her friend, Amina said, "Um... no. My book's gonna be written at the reception itself."

Her conversation with Kayla aroused many anxieties about the wedding. That night she asked Mazin to come over so that they could finally decide on a venue. Osman chose not to get involved, but Ruwayda sat with them as they discussed it.

Mazin was very flexible and didn't really care about how the halls were decorated, what color linens they provided or how huge the chandeliers were. But he did care about the menus. So in the end, they chose the only place that offered both surf and turf, as well as a vegetarian alternative.

As soon as they booked the hall, Ruwayda dragged her daughter and future son in law to pick invitations. Of course she chose the most expensive one, but it was also the most elegant, so Amina didn't argue. And, following his typical easy going personality, Mazin went along with what the women decided.

The hall said they could provide the DJ and the photographer. When Amina and Mazin met with them, however, Mazin didn't like the DJ's style, and they decided to keep looking.

"What about the photographer? Do you think we should keep her or find someone independently of the hall?"

"I think she'll be fine. The photos she showed us were well detailed and captured the happiness of the day. The only problem I had with the DJ is that he was too... 'loud' isn't really the word; I know they'll all be loud. But he was kind of pushy. I think we can get someone better."

They interviewed four more DJ's over the following two weeks, until finally they met one that could keep the party going without being overly loud or pushy.

On their way back from booking the DJ, Ruwayda announced that, except for the flowers and *ma'zun*, everything was taken care of.

"Seif is good friends with the people who run the mosque and when I gave him the date, he called the *ma'zun* immediately and reserved him. So really, all we have left is the flowers."

"I already know what I want, so I'll take care of that after work tomorrow with Kayla. So, basically, we're all done?" Amina was excited that this stressful experience seemed to be coming to a close.

"I guess so. And actually, Amina, I forgot to tell you. Maria from the bridal shop called yesterday morning and told me she found the lace."

Amina was skeptical. "Mama, are you sure that's what she said?"

"Yes, Amina, of course I'm sure. She said she found the appropriate lace and as soon as the dress comes in, she'll call you in for your first fitting. She'll start making the alterations and adding the extra lace right after."

Amina was ecstatic. She had lost all hope that she would be wed in the perfect dress, but now, it looked like it would happen after all. Then she remembered one key detail, and her mood dropped slightly.

"How much is it all going to cost, mama? With the lace and the alterations?"

Ruwayda tried avoiding the question. "She didn't say."

"Mama, of course she said. She had to be sure we'd be able to pay. How much?"

Ruwayda sighed. "Why do you want to know?"

"Mama!" At this point Amina knew it was too much, but now she really needed to know. "I want to know because if it's too much, then we can just have her underlay it with satin. The dress will still be great, and it won't cost as much."

"Amina, stop your foolishness. This is the perfect dress, with the lace, not with the satin. And that's how you're going to wear it, no matter how much it costs."

"I can't let you pay too much for a stupid dress that I'm only going to wear once."

"See, you just said it: you're only going to wear it once. So it has to be perfect! Now stop asking, because I'm not telling you. Your father and I are just glad you finally found something you like."

Amina knew it was too much, but her mother wasn't going to change her mind. She felt guilty that her parents were going to spend so much on a dress that she regretted having even considered the lace. But now it was too late. Her parents knew it was what she really wanted, and they wouldn't be convinced with anything she said to try to dissuade them. All she could do was say, "Thank you, mama."

"Mazin, we're assuming you've got your suit or tux all taken care of?" Ruwayda said to change the subject.

"Yes, Tant. I reserved it a couple of days ago."

Now that the details for the wedding were all taken care of, Amina was free to think of what was even more important: the fact that she still hadn't told Mazin about her rape. It weighed heavily on her and she needed to unload that burden. At the same time, they'd come so far with the preparations, she felt like telling him now might just be an act of cruelty, both to Mazin and to her parents. She hated that she'd put it off this long, but now her reserve to tell him the truth was beginning to falter.

She sat on her bed the next day thinking of how she'd been so dishonest with him. The receiver was in her hands and she'd already begun dialing when her door swung wide open.

"He proposed!" Kayla was beyond happy.

Amina threw the phone down and stood up in equal excitement.

"That's so great!" She went over and hugged her friend. "I'm so happy for you."

"Look! Isn't it beautiful? And he didn't even need my help picking it out." Kayla held out her hand for her friend to admire the new engagement ring.

"It's just as gorgeous as it was the first time I saw it." Amina giggled.

But Kayla was confused. "What do you mean? You saw it in the store, or…"

"No, Damon showed it to me months ago. He's wanted to propose for quite some time."

They sat down on the bed, and Kayla began to give Amina the details. "When he came over last night, I had a candle lit dinner prepared. As we were eating, I started to say, 'I'm really happy with where we are, Damon, but I think it's time we start to plan for the future.' I was gonna say that I was ready to move in with him when he cut me off: 'Please don't say anything more,' he said. 'If you do, you'll ruin my surprise.'

"Of course I was utterly confused. So he comes over to my side of the table, takes my hands and pulls me up. His face is soft, but serious. He stares into my eyes and says, 'For as long as I've known you, I've wanted to spend all my time with you. I resist the urge to call you about 20 times a day, and even then, we end up speaking at least two or three times. Your opinion is the first and only one I want with everything in my life. And I love that you always consider my opinion when it comes to things in your life. There are still many journeys I'd like to embark on in my life, and I would love it if you would be there with me. Will you please marry me?'

"By this time, I'm already crying like a fool. All I could do was nod."

Amina was more than happy for her friend. There were no words that could express how she felt. She hugged her friend again, this time with a knot in her throat that she couldn't quite explain. When Kayla noticed Amina's watery eyes, the emotion became infectious.

"No, no, no more crying. We've both found good men to share our lives with. No tears." Kayla was speaking as much to herself as to her friend.

They sat together for a while, discussing wedding details and plans for the future. Just as Kayla was getting ready to go, Amina said, "I'm going to miss you."

Kayla understood; she felt the same way. In only a few short months, they'd each have commitments that would have to come before friendship. They wouldn't be able to hang out for hours on end without any interruptions. They wouldn't be able to meet and just grab some ice cream or coffee whenever they felt the urge. Their friendship was undoubtedly not ending, but the memories to be made in the future would revolve around at least four people, not just two.

Kayla sniffed back the tears and hugged Amina. "Oh, don't think you can get rid of me that easily. I'm not going anywhere."

When Kayla left, Amina's emotions seemed to be fighting within her. She was elated for Kayla. She loved that Kayla was marrying the man she felt passionate about. She loved that Kayla was overcoming her fear of commitment and abandonment. She loved that Kayla was happy.

But marriage always made Amina a little sad. Even in the best situation, even when it was marriage based on love, it still marked the end of something; the end of a life that a person lived for all those years before the marriage. Part of her hated that their friendship would certainly be changed by it.

She wondered why she hadn't had those same feelings when she became engaged to Mazin. *Didn't it seem real to me? Did I feel like it was too far away? Did I maybe think it would never really happen?* She couldn't find a solid answer for any of her questions.

That confusion made her aware of the slight jealousy she felt. She was thrilled for Kayla, but Amina wished she could be passionate about Mazin, the way Kayla was towards Damon. All she could do was pray that some day that passion would come.

She thought that Sahar could, in her newly married state, provide some extra hope in that department.

"*As salaamu alaikum,* Sahar. How are you? How was your honeymoon?"

Sahar's voice sounded tired, almost bored. "Oh, it was fine. We had a good time."

"Are you back to your routine now, or are you still adjusting to your new place?" What Amina really wanted to know was whether or not Sahar was happy, but she couldn't find a way to ask that.

"Yeah, we're pretty set in a routine. School starts in a few weeks, so I'm still off till then. But I spend my days mostly alone, doing stuff around the house. Yasin comes home at about 5, and basically we eat dinner, then he watches the news until about 10 or 11, by which time I'm already in bed. I feel like we've been married for a lifetime." Sahar chuckled with her last remark, but Amina sensed it was more to cover her feelings than anything.

"I'll probably be less bored when I go back to work. But enough about me. How are things coming along with you and Mazin? Do you have a date set?"

"Yes, actually. It's the second week in October. The invitations haven't gone out yet, but soon."

"That's great! Congratulations, Amina. I pray you find true happiness."

Amina sensed their conversation was coming to a close, but she needed more information. And there was just no way to ask but to simply be direct.

"Sahar, I need to ask you something personal, so if you don't want to answer, feel free to tell me it's none of my business." She paused for her friend to respond.

"Sure. Go ahead."

"When you were first telling us about Yasin, you said you didn't love him, but he was a good guy and you hoped that love would come after marriage. So my question is, has it? Do you love him?"

Sahar sighed. "I understand what you're asking, Amina. But that's a difficult question. I guess my best answer is this: I do love him. I care about his health and his happiness. I wish only good things for him. I get sad when he's sad and I'm happy for him when he's happy. But I'm not in love with him. I want to be, and I still have hope that it'll come, but as of now, I'm still not in love with him. I love him like I love you; like a best friend."

Her answer was honest, and for that Amina was grateful. But it made her sad. It made her sad for Sahar, and for herself.

Chapter 26

WHEN AMINA RECEIVED Layal's wedding invitation, she just held it in her hands for a long moment. This meant Layal and Sherif had worked out their issues; that Layal had accepted Amina's history with Sherif it for what it was— a relationship that had failed and ended a long time ago— and stopped wondering about it. And Amina felt an overwhelming sense of relief. Ever since Mazin had said that 'relationship issues should only be related by the people in the relationship', Amina had a minor doubt about whether she'd done the right thing. But now, this invitation put her mind at ease.

She truly was happy for Layal. She could see how much Layal adored him, and she knew that, although he had hurt her so intensely, he would make a good husband to her friend.

But still, despite her happiness for Layal, despite her forgiveness of Sherif, she couldn't bring herself to attend their wedding. She tried picturing herself there, sitting at a table, watching them hold hands or dance. It made her sad.

Although she knew Layal wouldn't really understand, and that it would hurt her a little, selfishly, Amina filled out the RSVP card, declining the invitation. She wrote a reminder on her calendar to send them a gift a week before their wedding. And she prayed that God would bless them with health and happiness and a successful marriage. And that was all she could do.

Mazin called Amina later that night and sensed something was wrong.

"You sound down. Is everything okay?"

"Yeah, everything's fine. I got Layal's wedding invitation today, and I just... I know she's going to be upset with me that I'm not going."

He didn't know how to respond, so he sat quietly, waiting for her to continue. A few minutes passed in silence, then, realizing Amina was too wrapped up in her thoughts, Mazin spoke.

"Are you sure you don't want to go? Is that why you're sad, that you want to go but you don't think you should?"

Amina giggled. "It's actually the opposite. I know that I shouldn't, but I really want to be there for my friend. I hate that she'll be getting married, and I won't be there to see it."

"So, maybe you should go. We should go."

"I can't. I know me... it'll be too weird, too sad for me. I just want her to understand."

"Maybe you're not giving her enough credit. Maybe she will understand."

"Maybe." But Amina was not convinced.

The only way she could think to relieve herself of the guilt was to call Layal and explain.

"*As salaamu alaikum*, Amina! How are you?"

"*Alhamdu lillah*, Layal. I'm good. How're you? Are you all set with the preparations for the wedding, or are there some things you still need to get done?"

"Basically everything's set. Work is giving me a hard time, though... I want to take a month off, and they don't want me to. I'm tempted to just tell them if they won't give it to me, I'll leave. But who am I kidding? I've come too far in that company to just step away. And I can't see myself anywhere but there, at least not in the near future. So I just have to keep asking nicely, and hope it all works out."

"That's too bad that they're being so tough about it. Do you have honeymoon plans? Is that why you want a month? Or do you just want time to sort of get used to being a newlywed?"

"A little of both," Layal answered. "We're planning on spending some time in Europe, maybe Italy, then I want to meet his family in Egypt. But once we get home, I do want some time to just get settled. What about you? Are your wedding plans coming along?"

"Yeah," Amina said. "Everything's pretty much set. I have a second fitting for my dress in a few days, and besides that, everything's set. We'll be sending the invitations out soon. The only thing Mazin and I haven't discussed is the honeymoon. I'm not sure how much time he's taking off. We'll see."

She heard a rustling on the other end, and sensed that Layal was busy, but she didn't want to hang up without telling her friend why she'd called.

"Layal, I'm just calling to tell you that... I'm sorry-"

Layal cut her off. "Please, no, Amina! Please don't say you're not coming! You're my best friend, I need you there."

Amina felt like crying. "I'm so sorry, Layal. I really want to be there for you, too. But I just think it'll be... I don't know... too awkward."

She heard Layal let out a deep sigh. "I knew this would cause a stress on our friendship and change it. I hate that."

Neither of them spoke for a moment. Then Amina said, "I wish only the best for you, Layal. I pray he treats you well and makes you happy, because you deserve nothing less. And please know that you are always in my prayers. Just because we don't see each other on a regular basis doesn't mean I love you any less. I want only the best for you, for now and forever. I will always listen when you need me."

"I know," Layal sighed again. "I know."

A minute later she asked, "Will I get an invitation to your wedding?"

The seriousness in her voice brought a deeper sorrow to Amina. "What? Of course, Layal. How could you even ask that?"

"I don't know... I thought it might be equally weird to have us at your wedding."

"I fully expect you to come, Layal. You and your husband." And she did; it wouldn't be as strange to see Sherif at her own wedding. She figured she'd be too caught up in the allure of the wedding, too busy being the center of attention, to notice anything that might otherwise have affected her.

It made her sad that she wouldn't be there to see her friend married, but she knew she was doing what was best. To forget her guilt, she turned her attention to helping Kayla with preparations for her wedding.

"Do you guys have a date set, or is it still too early to be making definite plans?"

"We'd like a spring wedding, outdoors. There's this place he knows with beautiful gardens. We're leaning towards that. I'm going to be meeting with the manager in about a week."

"Would you mind if I came with you?"

"What, are you waiting for an invitation? I expect you with me every step!" Kayla said to her friend.

Although they both laughed, Amina was still unsure. "I guess I just... I don't want to get in the way if it's something you want to do with Damon."

"Don't be ridiculous. He's not really into the whole planning thing. I mean, he told me he liked the gardens, then he said 'but do whatever you think is best.' Besides, I'm going to spend the rest of my life with him; I'm going to take advantage of these next couple of months to spend as much time as I can with my best friend."

And they did just that. Kayla was there for Amina's second dress fitting, along with Ruwayda. It was the first time they would see how the dress looked with the lace alterations.

"Do you want me to help you put it on?" Ruwayda called to her daughter through the door to the fitting room.

They heard a wriggling on the other end, then a muffled, "No, I'm just heading toward the light. I think I'll make it."

A few minutes of rustling and shuffling passed, then Amina opened the door. There was no mirror in the stall, so she waited to get her mother's and Kayla's opinions before being able to see for herself.

Ruwayda nodded as she smiled. She placed her hands on Amina's hips and said, "I think it just needs to come in slightly from around the waist, and it'll be perfect."

Kayla didn't speak, but Amina saw approval in her wide smile. She walked over to the wall of mirrors and inspected herself.

"Wow! It's so gorgeous. Even better than I expected."

Maria, the shop owner, smiled, "I'm glad you like it. It looks perfect on you."

Amina continued turning right and left to inspect the dress from all angles. Then she stood still, facing the mirror. The dress was perfect, but something was off.

"Oh my God! My hair! We didn't even think about what we would do to cover my hair!"

Their high spirits started to sink, but only slightly.

"Well," Maria began, searching for something in one of the stalls. "When you came in the first time and I saw you covered, I figured you'd want your headpiece to match the dress. So I took the liberty of making this. It's not all covered in lace because I thought that would be too much and overshadow the dress. But it'll match."

Amina took the headdress from Maria and examined it with her fingers. "Would you help me put it on?" she asked.

"Sure," Maria said. She happily took the headdress and placed it on the bride's head. After a few minutes of adjusting, she pulled away with a smile on her face.

"Oh, Amina! It's perfect. You look like… a princess." Ruwayda's words gave Amina the courage to look in the mirror.

And when she did, her face lit up. "It matches so well. What do you think, Kayla?"

"It looks really great. But I think…."

"What? What's wrong?"

"I think you might be… too white. I'm not saying we change the color of the entire headpiece, but I think it might look better if we maybe incorporate just a soft color into it. What do you think?"

"Like a ribbon of red or blue woven through it?" Maria asked, mostly to herself, as she gently removed it from Amina's head.

"Yeah, something like that." Kayla was relieved that her idea hadn't been struck down.

"What is the color of the flowers you'll be holding?" Maria asked Amina.

"Red. It's a bouquet of red roses."

"Give me a few minutes, I'll see what I can do."

When the shop owner had disappeared from sight, Kayla asked her friend, "What do you think? Do you think maybe some color would add to it?"

"We'll see," Amina replied with a giant smile on her lips.

Her mother, however, was not pleased with the idea. "I don't think we should add color, Amina. A bride is meant to wear white, only white. I think it's better to be traditional. I don't think the color will look good."

"Well, if it doesn't, we'll ask Maria to put it back into its original condition. We have nothing to lose. Plus, remember, mama, most brides don't cover their hair, and that in itself gives them color."

Maria appeared a few minutes later, clearly happy with the adjustments she'd made to the headpiece. She placed it on Amina's head and gave her a bouquet of fake red flowers so she could get a more accurate idea of the final picture.

Before she looked in the mirror, she saw both her mother and her best friend beaming in approval. She, too, was delighted with what she saw.

The only adjustment Maria had to make was to take in the waist about an inch. Amina made her final fitting appointment, and changed out of the wedding dress.

"Do you want to look at the dresses while we're here, Kayla?"

"Oh, I wanted this day to be about you. We can come back a different day."

"Don't be ridiculous, Kayla," Ruwayda said. "We're all here now. Take a look around; we're all done with Amina's fitting and we have nothing important to rush back to."

So Kayla started browsing the racks. Once Amina was back into her regular clothes, she came out and helped her.

"Do you have any ideas? I mean, do you know if you want satin or lace or tulle? Do you want long sleeves or strapless?"

"Um… I don't know. I think I want to get a feel for everything that's available. But the strapless dresses do tend to appeal to me more."

They continued browsing with Amina pulling out any strapless dresses she came across.

"I've been working on this dress, here. I still have some minor touches to add to it, but you'll be able to picture what it'll look like." Maria could tell Kayla wanted something different; something that would make her stand out more than any bride before.

The dress she held up was ivory satin trimmed around the neck and cuffs in lace. It came down a few inches below the collar bone and the chiffon sleeves dipped just under the shoulders.

"I'll take it." Kayla said.

Amina exchanged smiles with her mother, put the stack of dresses she held back on the rack, then went over and put her arm around her friend. Both marveled at the beauty of the dress.

"I have one question. I really liked what you did with Amina's headpiece. Do you think you may be able to weave a blue ribbon through all the lace trim?"

Maria smiled. "I knew you'd want something different. A bride wearing color. No problem."

The girls managed to convince Maria to schedule Amina's final dress fitting on the same day as Kayla's first. The dresses were both perfect, and the brides were radiant. Ruwayda captured the beauty of the day in a full roll of film.

Chapter 27

THE REMAINING FEW WEEKS leading up to Amina's wedding were filled with family dinners, shopping for the mother of the bride, and other last minute preparations. Amina spoke with Mazin at least twice a day, mostly about details for the wedding, but she found that she enjoyed speaking to him about anything. He gave her good advice about work, convincing her to ask for a part time position so she could have time to pursue the master's degree she'd mentioned more than a few times. His views were open, and she loved that he put her best interest first.

"So, when we're married, you won't mind if I'm busy studying?"

"As long as that's what makes you happy, then I'm happy."

"And after that, you won't mind me going back to work full time?"

He laughed. "Amina, all of the women in my life, including my mother and grandmother, were working women. It's your right. I do think you'll have to take some time off when we decide to have kids, but it's far too early to have that discussion."

"I don't think so. I think we both need to know what to expect from each other. But, just so you know, I want to take time off for my children, too."

"And you never know, maybe by that time you will have already found the cure for cancer, made us rich beyond our wildest imaginations, and we can retire somewhere where it doesn't snow into the month of May."

Amina laughed. Being with him was getting easier by the day. But when she tried to imagine that they'd be sharing the same bed very soon, it still made her uneasy.

Despite her feelings, that day arrived very quickly. Before she knew it, she was sitting on the covered toilet, trying to hold still for the hairdresser.

"I mean no disrespect, Amina, but why are you having your hair done if you're just going to be covering it?" the woman asked.

"Because her hair's not gonna be covered all night. Eventually, she's gonna be alone with her husband, and he does get to see her hair, you know!" Kayla rolled her eyes at the woman's ignorance.

But Amina was distracted by something else. *How did I let it get this far? How did I manage to make it all the way to my wedding day without confessing to Mazin?*

I know that if he rejects me I'll have no chance of finding anyone who will accept me. But why does that matter to me? I'm not in love with him, so why has the chance of losing him had such an influence on me?

When her hair was finished and pulled up so that it wouldn't crease under the headpiece, the woman started doing Amina's makeup.

"Please don't overdo anything. I want people to wonder whether or not I'm wearing any makeup."

The woman nodded, but when Ruwayda overheard what had been said, she came running into the room, half dressed. "Don't listen to her! This is her wedding day; she has to look like a bride, so do whatever you need to with that makeup to make her look perfect!"

It was Amina's turn to roll her eyes. Kayla giggled, then she teased, "Mrs. A.... this is a great look for you. The guests are in for a bit of a surprise!"

Ruwayda tried to remain serious, but she couldn't help but let out a laugh. "Oh, Kayla."

While Amina got dressed, the hairdresser worked on Kayla. She was putting the last few pins in Kayla's hair when they heard Amina clear her throat. She was perfect.

"What do you guys think?" The uncertainty in her voice had nothing to do with how she felt about her appearance and everything to do with what she knew was about to happen.

"You look... breathtaking. Simply breathtaking." Kayla's eyes started to water, but she managed to keep back the tears without Amina noticing. She got up and gave her friend a hug. "He's lucky to have you."

Amina smiled nervously. Her mother walked in just then. She examined her daughter's makeup with scrutiny. Then she turned her serious gaze towards the dress.

"Don't you think it'll be more flattering if you darken her eye makeup slightly, and maybe put on some extra lipstick?" Ruwayda was asking the hairdresser, but Amina and Kayla responded in synchrony.

"No... the makeup's perfect."

"Fine. Let me take a picture of the two of you. Amina, tilt your flowers slightly towards me so they show up in the picture. That's good."

Her smile was forced, but no one noticed.

"Kayla," Ruwayda said, "could you give me a few minutes alone with Amina? We're all about ready, and the limousine should be here, so we'll see you downstairs."

"Sure, no problem." Before leaving the room, she hugged her friend and sent her a loving wink.

Amina and her mother sat down on the bed, then Ruwayda began, "Amina, I know you're nervous about this marriage. Everyone is before they get married. But I want you to know that you have nothing to worry about. I have asked God for guidance about this, and one night I had a dream that really set my heart at ease.

"You and Mazin were walking along a path, and suddenly it started to rain. Only you weren't getting wet at all. It was as though he was absorbing the wet for you. And he was happy to do it. And you were smiling. I know it was just a dream, but it comforted me. I felt like I knew you would be happy with him."

Amina nodded as she studied her shoes.

"Now," her mother's mood lightened. "Is there anything you want to ask me about tonight?"

Amina looked at her mother with confusion.

"You know what's expected of you tonight, with Mazin. It'll be a little awkward for you the first few times, but once you get used to each other, sex can be a beautiful thing."

"Oh, mama. Please. I don't want to have the sex talk with you."

"I just want to see if you have any questions I can help you with." There was a slight giggle in Ruwayda's voice, but she did want to make sure her daughter knew she could talk to her if she wanted to.

"Mama, I have a million questions about sex. But I'm not going to ask you!" And with that she stood up.

"Fine," Ruwayda followed her daughters lead. "You look beautiful. He is a good man, but he's blessed to have you." She gave her daughter a hug and kiss, and made her way downstairs.

Amina fidgeted during the entire limo ride. Every so often Kayla would hold down her hands to try to control her friend's nervous movements, but as soon as she let go, the fidgeting began again. Kayla thought Amina was just nervous about taking this next step in her life; she didn't realize that Amina still planned on telling Mazin before they were married.

This was Amina's final chance: her final chance to unload the burden, but some voice inside her said that it was also her last chance to escape settling for a man she did not love. *I'm not that cruel, am I? Is that really why I waited, hoping something else would come along and ruin it so I wouldn't have to do this? Please God... I don't want to be that vicious person.*

As soon as they arrived at the hall, they were escorted into a sort of waiting room while the final preparations for the reception were wrapping up. Mazin and his brother-in-law waited in a separate room so that he wouldn't see her before the time was right. But Amina needed to see him; she asked one of the waiters serving hors d'oeuvres to escort her.

When she walked in, both men stood up, more out of admiration of her beauty than to greet her.

"Wow, Amina. *Ma sha' Allah.* You look beautiful. But I thought it was bad luck or something to see each other before the actual wedding?"

She ignored Mazin's comment and turned to Seif. "Could you give us a few minutes? I really need to speak with Mazin alone."

"Of course," Seif said, and left the room.

She didn't meet Mazin's eyes, and she didn't pause at all. "Mazin, I need to tell you something. And before I do, I need to apologize that it's taken me this long to confide in you. I didn't mean to. At least, I don't think I meant to. Anyway... a few years ago-"

But he cut her off. "Amina, I've already told you, anything that happened in your life before we knew each other is not my business. You do **NOT** have to tell me anything."

His comment made her look up, but she disagreed with him. "I do have to tell you. And when you find out what it is, you'll know why."

"Amina, you don't..."

"Please, Mazin. You're just making this harder for me. Fine, if you think I don't have to tell, then I want to tell you. Okay?"

Mazin wasn't convinced, but he didn't want to stress her out anymore than he obviously had already. He just nodded slowly.

"So a few years ago, when I was at school, I went out with a small group of friends. After the movie, they walked me back to my apartment and I invited them in, but only one of them accepted that invitation. I tried to hurry, so we wouldn't be alone long, but it was long enough. He started to tell me that he had feelings for me, and before I knew it, he was trying to hold me. Then he got more aggressive, and I just wasn't strong enough to keep him away. He raped me."

The words had come out slowly. And although they hurt her, she managed not to cry. After a moment, she looked up to see Mazin, anger filling his eyes, shaking his head. He was looking down.

"I'm sorry," he finally said.

She didn't know what she was supposed to do. She just stood there, defeated... again.

Then she heard his footsteps and looked up to find him walking towards her. He framed her face with his hands and pulled her close to kiss her forehead. When she looked in his eyes, he was smiling.

"I'm so sorry you had to experience something so horrendous. It makes me mad for you. But, just so you know the whole truth, I already knew."

That's not possible. He knew? How could he have known?

"The very first time I visited your house, before we agreed on anything, your father told me. He said you weren't the type of person to keep secrets from people you care about, and he told me you'd eventually tell me yourself. When you didn't, I figured you didn't feel comfortable enough to share something so painful.

"But it didn't matter either way. I knew you. I knew you were an honest, kind, good person, who tries to follow God's path. And that's who I wanted. And anything that happened to you before, was not my business."

They were quiet for a short moment, with Amina trying to grasp the fact that she'd been worried all these months for no reason. She'd been carrying a heavy load, but now, it turns out, that heavy load was actually empty. It almost made her laugh.

"Thank you for trusting me enough to tell me. I pray the trust between us continues to grow. Now go! Get back to your waiting room before the guests start wondering where you disappeared to."

But she couldn't move. The honor and kindness he'd just shown her had her frozen. "You're too good, Mazin. Really, you're too good."

"No, I'm not. I'm just a normal guy who knows what he wants, and sees it in his fiancée. I'm not a romantic man, Amina. I don't understand the flowers, and I don't tend to vocalize my feelings well, but I know that I'm lucky to have you. And I will spend the rest of my life trying to make you happy."

In that second, as she stood there in front of him, she was overcome by an overwhelming sense of calm. Passion or not, this was the right man.

She went back to her room, where apparently she hadn't really been missed at all. Her parents were busy speaking with Amira, and Kayla and Damon were also deep in conversation.

Shortly after, the hall's wedding coordinator announced that the groom and the *ma'zun* were ready to begin and that the guests were standing in the first section of the hall waiting for the marriage contract to be signed. When they heard the rhythmic beating of the drums customary in Egyptian weddings, Amina took her father's arm, and he escorted her into the hall. The rest of her family came in behind them.

Mazin, the *ma'zun*, Seif and the other witness stood beside the only table in sight. When Amina and Osman approached, they all sat down, and the music stopped.

The *ma'zun* began by reciting a few verses from the Qur'an. Then he went on to say that marriage is a sacred bond, and if each party treats the other with that in mind, they will leave no room for Satan to enter and interfere with their lives.

He asked Amina if she was entering this union of her own free will. When she affirmed, he asked her to sign the contract. After Mazin too had signed, the *ma'zun* took Mazin's right hand and put it into Osman's.

"Repeat after me," he said to Osman. "I give you my daughter, Amina, in marriage, by the traditions of Allah and Prophet Mohamed, peace be upon him."

Osman repeated. Then it was Mazin's turn to repeat. "I accept your daughter, Amina, in marriage, by the traditions of Allah and Prophet Mohamed, peace be upon him. I will treat her with kindness and honor this sacred bond that we now create."

When Mazin had finished, the witnesses signed, and the *ma'zun* congratulated them. Osman congratulated Mazin with a firm handshake, then he turned to his daughter and hugged her. Ruwayda, with tears in her eyes, hugged and kissed her daughter, then she took her husband's arm and watched as Mazin came around the table to Amina and placed a loving kiss on her forehead. "Congratulations," he whispered. Many of the women guests let out trills. And the music started up again. Mazin took his bride's arm and led her further into the hall, where now all the guests were standing and cheering.

He led her right to the *kosha*, and as soon as they sat down, many of their guests approached to wish them luck and happiness. Amira and her husband were the first, followed by Kayla and Damon. Amina tried to scan the string of people for Sahar and Layal, but she didn't spot them.

The DJ asked the new couple to step onto the dance floor for their first dance as husband and wife. As Mazin gently placed his hand on Amina's waist, he asked, "Are you happy?"

And she was. It was great being surrounded by all the people who cared about her, who only wanted good things for her. But one of the most important people who cared about her was staring her in the eyes, promising to make her happy for as long as he lived.

Everyone enjoyed the reception. Amina made Mazin stay on the dance floor longer than he liked, but he was having fun. Sahar and her husband finally approached to pass on their good wishes, and after them, Layal and Sherif.

Amina was relieved that her friend had come, and surprisingly to herself, seeing Sherif had no effect on her; she was just pleased to see Layal so happy.

After dinner had been served, the party started to wind down, and soon it was time to leave. Ruwayda and Osman hugged their daughter and new son-in-law and waved to them as they drove away in the limo.

At their apartment, the new couple each took showers, then they stood together to offer a prayer, asking God to bless their marriage, increase the love between them, and help them to always treat each other with kindness.

In bed together for the first time, Mazin tried to be gentle. Amina felt sometimes uncomfortable physically, sometimes uncomfortable emotionally, and just a little bit of pain. But something about being with him also felt very normal.

They lay facing each other, recounting the beauty of the party. A few minutes later, Mazin started to get up.

"Shall I bring some water for you?" he asked.

Amina sat up. "I'm closer. I can go."

But Mazin's laughter stopped her from fumbling with her robe. "Amina, I'm an Arab man. When I offer to get something for you, you should take me up on it without hesitation, because, you'll soon learn, I probably won't offer very often. On the contrary, you're going to feel like I'm a little child, dependent on you for everything. Soon you're going to want to say to me, 'get up and get your own water.'"

They laughed together for a few seconds, then Mazin went to the kitchen. Amina rested her head back on the pillow, and waited for Mazin with her eyes closed. But before she knew it, she had already fallen asleep.

Mazin placed her glass on her nightstand, crawled into bed, and fell asleep with his arm around his new wife.

That night she had a familiar dream. She walked along the pier, and a faceless man approached her, telling her he'd caught a lot of fish.

"But your basket is empty," she said.

"No, it's not here. I'll go get it."

But she kept walking, and soon she met a man whose basket was overflowing with fish. He smiled at her, took her hand, and gently pulled her down to sit beside him. She felt a normal calm, sitting there with him as the ocean spread out before them.

He was the same man who'd appeared in her dream all those times before, but the only difference was, this time when she woke up, she remembered his face perfectly. It was the same peaceful face that rested beside her now.

Glossary of Arabic Terms

Alf salaama literally means 'a thousand wishes for [your] safety.'

Alhamdu lillah literally means 'Praise God.' Muslims say it in times of gratitude for the blessings they have as well as in response to such mundane questions as "how are you."

As salaamu alaikum is the proper Muslim greeting and parting. It means "Peace be upon you."

Bism Allah Alrahman Alraheem means In the name of God, Most Gracious, Most Merciful.

Eid simply means holiday, but is used to refer to either of the two Islamic holidays which occur annually.

Fatha is the first chapter in the Qur'an, the Islamic holy book. It is commonly recited between all parties endeavoring on any sort of venture together, especially between two families who are joining in marriage.

Hamdila al salaama is a term used to greet someone who has arrived from a journey, or who has come out of a bad situation (illness, surgery, etc.). Literally it means "Thank God for your safe arrival."

Hijab is the proper Islamic attire for a woman, requiring her to cover all parts of her body except her hands and face.

In sha' Allah means God willing. Most Arabs, Muslims especially, will always say this term before mentioning any event that is planned to take place in the future.

Jalabaya is often worn by both men and women in Arab countries. It is similar to a long night shirt; some can be very simple, worn just at home or around the neighborhood, while others can be elaborate and worn out, even to formal events.

Katb al kitab literally means 'writing of the book.' It is the contract between a couple which declares them officially married.

Konafa is a traditional Middle Eastern desert made with shredded filo dough.

Kosha is the specially decorated seat of the bride and groom. It is usually slightly raised so that it is comfortably visible from any spot in the room.

Mahr is the wedding gift which the groom presents to his bride. It is an amount of money which should technically be given to the bride for her to do with as she pleases, but is more commonly used by the bride and her family to help furnish her new home.

Ma sha' Allah is an Arabic term that literally means 'what God has willed.' It is said to praise something or express how awe inspiring something is.

Ma'zun is the Muslim clergyman that is responsible for overseeing marriages.

Muhajaba (pl. **muhajabat**) is a Muslim girl or woman who wears the proper Islamic attire, hijab. This requires her to cover not only her hair, but it forbids her from wearing clothes that are revealing or show the lines of her body. The only parts of a muhajaba that show are her face and her hands.

Shabka is the engagement present which the groom gives to his bride. Usually it is in the form of a diamond ring or gold jewelry set.

Sharbat is a very sweet drink served in times of celebration, especially at engagements or weddings.

Wa alaikum as salaam is the proper response to as salaamu alaikum; it means, 'and peace be upon you.'

Printed in Great Britain
by Amazon

81912092R00119